THE GUNS
OF DARKNESS

THE GUNS
OF DARKNESS

Ann Schlee

Atheneum · 1974 · New York

With love to Emily Ann, Catherine,
Duncan and Hannah.

Contents

ABOUT THE BOOK

The ancient state of Ethiopia used to be known in Europe as Abysinnia before the great modernising reforms brought about by the present King of Kings, the Emperor Haile Selassie. It has the longest recorded history of all the African countries. Its rulers adopted Christianity at about the same time as Christianity became the religion of the Roman Empire under Constantine—at a time when many parts of Europe were still pagan. Subsequently in Ethiopia a line of rulers that claimed descent from King Solomon and the Queen of Sheba was established and still continues.

In this long history, Ethiopia has like all countries had its ups and downs. Two hundred years ago the monarchy lost its authority to a number of regional war-lords, and the people suffered nearly a century of civil war and civil chaos. But the hope was never lost that a saviour would appear, and a tradition survived that his name would be Tewodros.

In the middle of the last century, a man named Kasa began to raise an army of ordinary Ethiopians, which began to attack and overthrow the war-lords. With success, many more people joined the movement until Kasa was recognised as the awaited saviour of the nation. When he was crowned King of Kings, the Elect of God, he took the throne name of Tewodros (Theodore).

The new Emperor took full responsibility for all that his chosen name promised his people. When the last of his rivals was subdued, he turned his enormous energies to the task of restoring peace and unity throughout the country. He began to replace feudal landowners with provincial governors paid and appointed by himself. He attempted to reform the Church and to abolish slavery. He welded the many small armed bands that had sprung up throughout the country into a single national army under his personal command, and he made every effort to so discipline and equip this army that it might accomplish his dream of driving the Turks from his borders and eventually of winning back Jerusalem into Christendom.

But although Tewodros brought remarkable abilities to meet this task, it was more than any man could have accomplished in a country fragmented for years by civil war, by tribal and religious differences, and by the very nature of its wild, mountainous terrain. The people were not prepared for the restrictions and the taxation needed to establish a centralised government. Rebellions broke out in the provinces and these kept him constantly in the field. His attempts to wring money from the Church turned that powerful force in the country against him. The army could not be trained out of its old undisciplined style of fighting, and the guns Tewodros had made with such difficulty merely encumbered its movements. It proved impossible to pay so large a force regularly, and in time the great numbers that had followed Tewodros began to desert him. Neither his own countrymen nor the European powers to whom he appealed for friendship shared his fervor for recapturing Jerusalem. His reprisals against his own rebellious subjects became more and more severe. His liking and trust for Europeans turned to *suspicion and hatred. His obsession with guns confused his military judgement. Before the British force landed at Zula to rescue Tewodros' European prisoners, his dreams were in ruins.*

Most of this story is set in the last sad years of Tewodros' career when his great victories and his early promise were already memories, but in spite of the great pressures upon him, his bitter disappointments, his bouts of drunkenness and madness, he never lost those heroic qualities of courage, ingenuity and resolution that make him one of the great figures of African history.

In my father's house

There was a conversation I had often with Herr Waldmeier in the early part of our captivity, which was more in the nature of a game. He would ask me where I had been in the rainy season of the last year, then the year before that. For each year that I remembered he would say, 'Good, Louisa, good,' and make a mark in the dust.

At first I found it difficult but after a little the years formed and separated in my mind so that in the end, piecing together what he knew of my family, we were able to calculate that I must have been eight years old when I first came to live in Herr Waldmeier's house and that now I am fourteen years.

Herr Waldmeier, I know, is thirty-one years for in the small German Bible he has managed to keep there is written, *Theophilus* – his earth name – *Waldmeier. Born 1837 in Canton Argau, Switzerland.* Then there is a line so — and a space where they will write the year of his death.

Under this is written, *Rosa Waldmeier* and the date of her birth five years ago.

And under Rosa's name to please me he has written, *Louisa Bell, daughter of John Bell, Englishman, and the Princess Worknesh Asfa Yilma. Born 1854 at Debra Tabor in Abyssinia,* and then a line and a space in which some day perhaps someone will think to write when I am dead. This book he still carries with him hidden in his clothing.

Once he said, 'Can you remember that time before you heard my name?' I said yes, but in reality I remembered all that time as one time.

'Do you remember the house that you lived in?'

I remembered. My father's house was so large that the roof could not be held up by a single pole. A whole ring of poles was set inside the circle of the walls to hold up the thatch.

I swung in and out between them. The bark dragged at my hands. They were the whole trunks of trees. I counted them. There were ten. Between the poles and the wall my sister and I slept in our place on the same cowhide. My sister's saint name was English, Mary. Her earth name was Jewubdar which in Amharic means 'the limit of beauty'. Then I was born and they gave me for an earth name Belletech, which means 'beyond the limit of beauty'.

I thought: she has stopped at the limit of beauty but I have gone on beyond, therefore I am more beautiful than she. But at that time I had never seen my face, only hers, and wondered and doubted if this were true and dared not ask. I lay and felt my own face in the dark but my fingers told me nothing.

To one side of the place where my sister and I lay slept my mother's aunt, to the other my mother's sister, but our place was separated from theirs by tall jars in which mead was stored. At night my hand could reach out to the jars. Their quiet shapes were about me in the dark. They were the walls of a cave. The roof pole which held a sleeping hen was the trunk of a tree still living in the forest. I, in my cave in the forest, looked up into the branches of the trees where, when the dry season was coming to an end and the roof grown ragged, large unsteady stars were buried.

That house was never quiet and the long nights like a waking dream for we slept and woke and slept again, but whenever we woke it seemed that there were voices and shapes moving and talking by the fire, or heavy breathing and sudden cries from the sleepers, or, when the human sounds were quiet, there were still tiny chewings and journeyings in the straw roof, and outside, from the dark, the bells and hooves of mules.

To Herr Waldmeier, as he sat watching me with his straw hat pushed back on his head, his pale yellow hair falling to meet his beard, his blue eyes narrowed in the sun, I only said, 'It was a large house. Next to the Emperor's it was the largest house in Debra Tabor.'

'And your father?' Herr Waldmeier asked. 'Do you remember him? You cannot often have seen him.'

This was true. My father, John Bell, the Englishman, was a soldier. He was the Emperor Tewodros' commander of horse. In the dry season he fought with the Emperor against the chieftains who rose in rebellion against him. In battle he dressed as the Emperor to draw upon himself the enemy spears, and at night he slept across the opening of the Emperor's tent to protect him.

Only in the rainy season when the army could not travel in the mountain passes did the Emperor Tewodros return to his winter camp at Debra Tabor. Then also my father returned and lived with us.

'Yes,' I told Herr Waldmeier, 'I remember him. He was very tall. He was taller than you. He was taller than any man I have ever seen since.'

'And the last time he came,' says Herr Waldmeier gently. 'Can you remember the last time?'

Most clearly of all I can remember that time. I am again

a child in a child's body standing on a rock waiting to see the army return.

The air has cooled. In the mountains to the north there are thin grey curtains of rain. That means they will come.

All day beggars wait outside our door. My father is a great man and will return with booty from the war. My mother shouts; they must not sit. They must mend the thatch. They must cut grass for the floor. They have dragged out the stale grass that has lain on the floor all the dry season. The last layer was rotten. When they uncovered it, it stank, but when it is dark and I am home again the house will smell of sweet fresh grass.

I want the soldiers to come, the Emperor to come, my father to come. My toes grip on the rock. I look and look. I will be the first to see a horseman enter the parched wide plain below the mountain. I will be the first to cry out.

The light fades. The plain reddens. The sun is behind the mountains. There is no horseman. Then the cry is taken from me. 'He comes! He comes! Tewodros comes!' And still I cannot see.

But now the edges of the bare red land begin to shift and creep. The plain steams with dust. The land heaves like water and I remember now from other years that so great are the numbers of King Tewodros' soldiers that long before the men and mules are distinguishable the wide land itself moves.

Now, coming towards us like a storm, is the rumble of the mules' hooves, the rattling of many thousands of spears and shields. It comes so quickly. It will overwhelm us. We run with our arms above our heads, shrieking like birds. *He comes! He comes! Tewodros comes!*

He rides a white mule. His saddle is gold. Tufts of lion hair toss on his pommel. His rifle lies across it. His white shamma is wound high over his face and the scarlet hem

12

of it flutters behind him. His musketeers run to line the road he will ride upon. The priests dance before him with their bright umbrellas and their silver crosses. *Li! Li! Lil! Li!* The women's shrill voices rise all night.

The Emperor has won great victories over the Wello Gallas. Their warriors he has put to death. Six thousand women and children he has brought back as prisoners. He has brought forty thousand of their sheep and oxen, forty thousand of their horses and mules. The village is full of loud men's voices and the smell of mule dung and the clatter of weapons. My father has fought beside the Emperor, and he is in the house again.

He came with a cold wild smell. My sister and I were afraid of him. We ran and stared at him sitting strangely by the fire. In his hand he held a little bowl of fire and sucked smoke from it down a tube. Smoke blew out of his nostrils and curled up from the corners of his mouth. We ran away. He did not reach out his hands to us or look at our eyes but sat quietly and allowed some change to be worked on him.

One day. Two days. The smell of woodsmoke and cooking was in his hair and clothes. We leant against him. I climbed on his knee. He began to speak to me in his own language, pushing out his lips as he made the words. It was difficult for my father to speak the words clearly. Once he had been wounded in the mouth by a spear and the piece of bone that had broken away inside his mouth he carried in a leather bag hung round his neck. He opened the bag a little way and showed me the white bone. He spoke in his language and I remembered the words. He had spoken them to me before. The more he spoke, the more I remembered. I could say them too.

* * *

13

Already he has been in the house for six days, and now it is the Feast of St John. The soldiers have brought handfuls of flowers and laid them at the door to the house to show their love for him. Flowers piled up to my knees. I jump across them. My laugh is behind me. Cold live flowers under my feet. And back again. A strong sweet smell.

There is a man in the house. His skin is white. His beard is black. He speaks English with my father. I understand the words. He says he will give the Emperor a Bible. My father has a loud lazy laugh. 'Give him a barrel of good English gunpowder. That's what he really wants. He has plenty of Bibles.'

But the bearded man did not laugh. He talked and talked. He was a missionary. My father went away with him to pray in his church and when he came back that was the only time I ever saw him sad.

The feast of St John has passed. Now is the time before Mascal. Mascal is coming: the Feast of the Cross, when the bonfires are lit to pass the news from hill to hill that St Helena has found the True Cross. Honeysuckle smells at night. Grass has a smell in the dark but not so strong. I run after my sister and her friends in the dark places between the huts. When they kneel and scoop up dung I catch hold of the loose end of my sister's shamma. They scoop up dung into a gourd, laughing high and soft. I pant sore in my chest. I cannot laugh. Light shines through chinks in the huts. My sister shakes her shamma out of my hand. I am too small; I hold her back. She wants to run. Now they dare not run. They creep. Boys with whips of nettles are waiting, hiding behind this house. The nettles will hurt. I will feel the hurt now, or now, or now. No. Behind the next house then. Where are they?

And we scream high and long, and shout. Hands are

in my hair and pulling at my clothes. The dung is thrown.
It stinks. I run. My voice and my breath are a pain; my
cheeks and shoulders burn with nettles. Mascal is coming.
They will light the bonfires on the hill. When Mascal
comes the rains are over. When Mascal comes my father
will go away.

On the eve of Mascal there was a feast in my father's house.
They said the Emperor would come. The grass-cutters
came early with more fresh grass for the floor. All day the
grinding stones were worked, and the flat bread baked.
The cow for the feast was tied by its horns to the side of
the house. It held its head low and its eyes were rolled
upwards. The grass-cutters surrounded it when their work
was done, prodding that bit by the leg which was their due
right at the feast.

The Emperor rode to my father's house on his white
mule. On either side ran his soldiers waving torches for
Mascal. They brandished the torches in the people's faces
to make them stand back from the door.

The people shouted and laughed and ran around to the
back of the house where they pressed against the walls
to hear the talk between my father and the Emperor. They
climbed onto the roof and dug holes with their hands
in the new thatch through which to listen. The door was
filled with watching faces. In the chinks of the walls were
eyes, so that the walls seemed alive, watching, breathing,
whispering. For it was well known that the Emperor had
the power to draw from my father the pictures he had
carried in his head from the country where once he lived.

The Emperor is in my house. He stands slight and
powerful by the door. I have seen him many times but
never standing close in my house. I am bowed to the
ground, smelling the sweet grass. My heart beats in my

15

ears. I see his bare brown feet on the grass before me and over my head his sweet low voice. 'Is this your child?'

'My youngest child.'

'Up, up,' he says.

My father lifted me by my arm and the Emperor's thin hand raised my chin so that he might see my face. My eyes saw only his eyes which were large and dark, with an expression of great gentleness. But his eyes saw all there was of me. Though they were gentle, they went deep. It seemed they drew a line about me and said: inside this line is you, which I now know, and outside is something else again. When he looked away that line was gone.

He sat cross-legged on a carpet spread by the fire and motioned my father down beside him. The great men that attended him, Fitawrari Gabrie and Ras Ingada, sat too and then my mother and all her relatives completed the ring around the fire.

My sister, being of marriageable age, sat with them and I was allowed to beg among the guests. I waited, holding with both hands my empty basket, in the dark place away from the fire and watched the Emperor's face in the light of the flames and listened.

The Emperor smiled and said, 'Bell, read to me from your Bible.'

I knew what would happen now. My father reached inside his shamma and drew out a small thick leather book. Often I knew he read from this book to the Emperor. It was no Bible. That was a joke between them. It contained long poems concerning the activities of European kings, and when he was at home my father read from it to my sister and me.

These poems were written in my father's language and were made up in a particular fashion as if the voices of many different people spoke in their turn. But as my

16

father, only, could read the book, he must read all these voices, so that now I could hear him speaking bold and proud: it was a king speaking. Now a courtier, very polite. Now a queen, high and squeaking.

On the evening of that Mascal he read the end of the poem the Emperor most loved, about a soldier who killed the king of his own country while he was a guest, sleeping in his own house, and in his place became king. First he read in the poem's own language so that there was a music in the words and a great mystery and expectation as to what all these people I could not see or easily understand were saying to one another.

Then he told the story in Amharic. The Emperor leant towards him, his eyes sharp, his hand held out, his fingers bent as if they would catch each word, for he himself was a king who had been a soldier and so the story held special importance for him. In that part where the king speaks of his dead queen he covered his face with his hands and wept, his own queen being recently dead. But at the end of the poem he said, 'Although he made himself king, that man was not fit for kingship. He was a fool. His courage failed him. For it might not have been so hopeless a situation as it seemed. Had he waited in his fortress on the mountain the rebels might well have grown hungry and gone away. Was there a good water supply on the mountain?'

My father smiled at him and said he did not know. As there was much rainfall in that country he did not imagine it was a problem.

'Then he should have stayed in the fortress,' said the Emperor. 'If ever my people rise against me in numbers too great for me to fight, I shall not despair but go to my fortress on Meqdela, knowing it to be impregnable, and hide myself there as a plant shrinks into its root and then, when the rains come, bursts forth and covers all the land again.'

Outside, the cow gives a great bellow and everyone is silent, looking towards the door. The wall of faces moves away and through the black gap a man runs with a long strip of dripping meat dangling from the end of his sword.

Ahhh. We can all smell the close raw smell of the flesh as the man kneels before the Emperor. It is a dark and lustrous blue and quivers not knowing yet that it is dead.

I shiver with the smell. The Emperor bites the end of it with his teeth and cuts the meat close to his thin lips with his curved knife. If he drops any of it I will see where it falls. More meat is brought. Everyone eats. My mother's aunt cuts little slices from her piece, wraps them in bread and pops them quickly into her husband's mouth. Tears of pleasure wander over his active cheeks. Everything is quiet. They chew and chew. Nothing is dropped. The Emperor's knife flashes neatly in front of his lips again and again. Now he wipes his bloody hands on a piece of bread. Very quietly I move behind him and the Emperor tosses the bread into the basket.

I do not know whether he has looked at me or not. I bow again holding the basket close to my knees. My forehead is on the drying grass. I smell the fresh blood on the bread.

The servants carry in the jars of mead. First they pour some into their own hands and drink. Then they strain it through cloth into the glass bottles for the guests to drink. I sit out of sight behind them and suck and chew at the Emperor's bread and continue to listen. The talk about the poem rises again.

'Were the rebels that rose against that king disciplined in their methods of fighting?'

'No, king. They fought as your army does, each chief
18

with his followers performing individual acts of bravery.'

There are fine lines in the skin above the Emperor's sharp eyes. He is trying to understand why that king's courage failed him. Then he draws in a quick breath and asks, 'Did the rebels have a cannon?'

'No,' says my father. 'They had no cannon.'

'Then he should not have despaired at their numbers. So long as his water held out, he would have won in the end.'

'But he had no cannon either.'

'Ah,' says the Emperor sadly, 'nor had he. Nor have I.'

'You have muskets.'

'The Turks too have muskets.'

'The Turks are no threat to you.'

'They hem me in. They keep me from Jerusalem. They keep me from my birthright.'

He was silent then. His silence spread uneasily from one face to another while the mead was passed again. When he had drunk he leant back on one elbow and smiled sadly at my father, and when he spoke it was close between them and I must move closer to hear them.

'The only time I have fought against disciplined soldiers, Bell, was at Gedaref. The Turks. Fewer men than I had. And cowards, for when we charged against them they crouched down and hid themselves behind a wall and dared not show themselves but fired over the top of the wall. When one man shouted they all at once hid themselves, and when one man shouted they all at once fired their muskets. We could not come near that wall without being killed. I was wounded, Bell. That was the only defeat I have ever suffered. You know that. But if I had had a cannon then I could have blown down that wall and ridden through and killed the Turks. Is that not so, Bell, that with a cannon I should have defeated them?'

'Very possibly – if they had none themselves.'

'Then it is necessary that I have a cannon if I am to lead an army to Jerusalem.' His voice continued low but so filled with the intensity of his thoughts that it bore down all the voices that murmured in the room. The firelight worked strangely on his face so that its margins seemed to spread and shrink as if affected by an irregular pulse. 'I cannot rest until Jerusalem is free. For it must surely be that God having risen me from the dust intends me for this thing, when the world has waited in confusion through all the centuries and the European kings who have the guns and the armies have used them to fight among themselves, Christian against Christian. If, in all the time given them, they have failed, it remains for this poor man with his undisciplined army, but with God and Saint Michael the Horseman fighting beside him, to drop down out of the mountains and cleanse the earth of infidels from here to the gates of Jerusalem. For is it not written in the psalms that *Ethiopia shall soon stretch out her hands to God*?' And swift as a cat he was on his feet, smiling happily, a spark of light on each eye, his arms outstretched towards Jerusalem.

The room was very quiet then: everyone inside the walls and outside drawn powerfully towards that one goal which it was impossible to believe lay very far beyond his extended arms.

Then into our great desire to follow him where he was going, ran my mother and my mother's aunt and the serving girls, who had heard none of this as they were outside lighting their torches for Mascal. They ran through the room, laughing. My mother thrust her torch into the corners behind the mead jars, under the bamboo tables. And everyone, as is the custom, ran behind her, chanting, '*Ahho Akhoy!* Awake from idleness! Awake from darkness! Mascal is coming!'

20

And so we ran out, the Emperor among us, into the dark. Torchlight stroked the sides of the houses and ringed the dancers with tall bent shadow-dancers. We shouted. We laughed. Tomorrow the soldiers would go away. My father would go.

The bonfires in the town were lit and later, just before dawn a great fire on the top of the mountain blazed and sparked. Far away, scattered across the darkness, were other fires.

The Emperor's voice was still in my head. In a year coming soon his torch would light a line of fires that would stretch unbroken through the dark lands of the Wello Gallas, down to the coast where the Moslems trade, across the sea and over the land to Jerusalem itself. But the Emperor could not lead that army to Jerusalem while wicked men still rose against him in his own country. First he must fight these rebels, and my father must fight with him.

With first light lines of horsemen and men carrying spears moved against the hillside, climbing up to Debra Tabor to join the Emperor for a new campaign. The following day they left, horses, mules, soldiers, camp-followers, beggars. The rains of that year, 1860, were the last my father spent with us. He died a few weeks later.

This is how he died.

Gared, the rebel of Tigre, waylaid and killed the English consul, Plowden, who was my father's friend and friend also to the Emperor. Then Tewodros and my father rode against Gared and came upon him suddenly in a little wood in Waldabba, the Emperor riding ahead and my father just behind. My father, understanding who these strange horsemen were, rode swiftly in front of Tewodros and at the same time fired his gun and killed Gared. But in that same second Gared's brother, who had recognised the Emperor and taken aim, fired, and the bullet intended for Tewodros passed through my father's skull and killed him instantly.

Then Tewodros shot Gared's brother and when he lay dead the Emperor drove his spear through his skull at the point where his bullet had entered my father's brain, and afterwards, as is the custom with traitors, seventeen hundred of Gared's followers had their hands and feet severed and were left without water to die, although many of them were the Emperor's kinsmen. That was a measure of how Tewodros loved my father.

I go to Gafat

When my father was killed, the Emperor took my sister and myself under his protection. For a time we continued to live in the house in Debra Tabor with our mother, but later in that year Ras Ingada came to the house to say that the Emperor had arranged a marriage between my sister and one of the European missionaries whom the Emperor had settled four miles away in the village of Gafat. The name of the missionary to whom she was to be given was then told us for the first time: Theophilus Waldmeier.

My sister covered her face with her shamma and hid behind the house. But she was not needed in the negotiations that followed. Nor was Herr Waldmeier required to see her. My mother's sister's husband and Ras Ingada completed the arrangements between them and exchanged the promises.

The Emperor sent eighty oxen and five hundred sheep for the wedding feast which lasted a whole week, but this also Herr Waldmeier did not attend, it being contrary to the custom of his church.

At the end of that week Ras Ingada came with a large escort of musketeers to accompany my sister to her church wedding at Gafat. He brought from the Emperor a gift of two blue velvet cloaks richly embroidered in silver. For it had been decided that I, being too young for marriage, should be sent to live in my sister's new household and receive from Herr Waldmeier a European education. My mother and my mother's relatives were returned to their own village.

The cloak was very hot. It dragged at my shoulders and pinned in my arms so that I could not freely brush away the flies or wipe the sweat from my face. Besides, it began to smell of the person who had worn it before and I wondered who she might have been, so small as I, and why it was no longer hers.

So we rode down from the mountain and through the foothills to within half a mile of Gafat where Herr Wald-meier had ridden out to meet us.

He was a young man with a broad face, red as if it pained him; hair and beard the colour of fresh thatch and thick and straight as monkey's hair. For his wedding he wore a bright red silk shirt and a shamma. On his feet I remember were high leather boots.

Behind him rode a little group of Europeans: two men that later I would know as Herr Saalmuller and Herr Flad, but at that time their names made no sound that I could keep on my tongue. Their raw naked faces were all twisted into smiles that, coming so from strangers, carried no meaning for me.

Only Herr Waldmeier did not smile. He took my sister's hand in the European manner and stared at her quickly. Then Ras Ingada led him to me and he stood for a moment looking at me in confusion. His thick red hand lay against the neck of the mule, trembling so that it disturbed the little bells on the harness. He picked my hot hand from the pommel and surrounded it with his hard cold shaking one. Then he turned away and taking the bridle of my sister's mule he walked beside it in his fine leather boots up the hill to Gafat.

Gafat was still a little village then. At the top of the hill

24

the wide round roof of the church showed above its grove of trees and near it were a cluster of huts with bright yellow thatch where the Europeans had recently built their new homes.

Herr Waldmeier's home consisted of a number of huts built around a large kosso tree. There was a kitchen hut, a larger hut where he and my sister would live and smaller huts for myself and a servant. He led my sister from one to another of these gravely and proudly, showing her how he had made wooden doors and shutters and how he had covered the earth floor with strips of wood. He knelt down and smoothed these with his hand to show her that there were no splinters for her feet. Each thing he showed to her he named in a loud voice, first in Amharic and then in his own German tongue which we had not heard before.

The other Europeans followed, and I, not knowing what was expected of me, followed with them. They were joined now by a lady whose dress covered her feet, and two children: a girl younger than I, and a little boy. From behind their mother's wide skirt they stared at me and I at them for such small Europeans I had not seen. The lady, too, spoke loudly, and they all continued in the same strange way to smile at nothing.

Now the lady knelt on the wooden floor in front of me. Why did she kneel to me? She did not bow her head. Her face stared boldly at my face. Her face was not red like Herr Waldmeier's. It was pale with small brown marks scattered over her nose and cheeks like spattered mud, but being so close I could see they were not dirt but a part of her skin. Why were they there?

'Frau Flad,' she said very loud, and smiled. Her eyes were as pale as sheep's eyes and bulged from her head as a sheep's do. 'Frau Flad,' she said again and turning her hand she laid her own finger against her own breast. Then

25

she reached out and touched me with the finger.

I took a step away, still staring at the marks. I did not want the finger to touch me. And at that the smile fell off her face very suddenly and she rose to her feet and went away, and pulled her children after her.

My sister and Herr Waldmeier were to be married in the afternoon, and when it was discovered that neither of us had been baptised in the European church there was a great argument. But as the wedding could not be delayed for fear of offending the Emperor, we were baptised in the house of Herr Waldmeier in the morning, and in the afternoon taken by mules to the Abyssinian church at Gafat, still wearing the heavy velvet cloaks that the Emperor had given us. There Herr Waldmeier and my sister took Communion together, thereby binding themselves in marriage until death.

My sister is become a stranger to me.

'Why do you not eat?' she says, in a whisper for he is leaning in at the window watching her grind corn. 'The food is the same. He does not punish you. You will be ill.'

His big red hands pray over the food. I cannot eat. All day he is away from the house. He teaches the boys of the village to read and write. He teaches them to use his saw and hammer.

Then in the evening he comes back. His voice is loud in the huts. His boots are loud on the wooden floors. He calls to me, 'Louisa', and puts his hands on my shoulders, but his hands are stiff. He has no pleasure in me. He points to the tree and the fire and the mule and says their name in German. His voice is loud and harsh and my mind closes against the words.

'Why are you stupid?' says my sister. 'Why cannot you learn? I can say many things.' And she repeats the names for all the things I cannot say. Herr Waldmeier smiles at her shyly and proudly. He has given her a gold bracelet. She plays with it on her arm and looks away from him and laughs at nothing.

I knew that my sister must now sleep with Herr Waldmeier but I had not understood that I must sleep alone. Each night I must lie down on a straw mattress in an empty hut near to theirs. I did not like the mattress. It rustled strangely and shifted under me. I did not feel safe on it. I spread the hide I had brought with me on the floor and lay on that. I had never slept in a place by myself before.

Herr Waldmeier seeing that I did not want to go into the hut said that he would shut the shutters and the door so that I need not be afraid. Every night he made it his duty to go before me into the hut and fix the shutters, and close the door behind me.

I cried at night and unless I cried I heard no human sound.

One night there was a wind and Herr Waldmeier came to my hut to make sure the shutters were securely fastened. He heard me cry. I thought he would be angry because I slept on the floor. I lay as still as I could make myself, hoping he would go away, but I shook with crying and some sound escaped. He came and knelt beside me and turned me over as one would something lying stiff in the road, to see what was the matter with it.

I lay very stiff and kept my eyes shut. 'Why do you cry?' he said in Amharic, without pity although truly interested to know. I did not answer. I did not know an answer.

'Does the wind frighten you?' He lifted me up by the shoulders and shook me slightly so that I answered out of fear, without thinking, 'I want to see the stars.'

'You want to see the stars,' he repeated. He took the

blanket from the bed and wrapped it around me. He lifted me in his arms and without a word carried me outside into the windy night. He set me on his shoulder and carried me down the dark road that led from the village.

I did not know what he meant to do with me. I thought he wished to be rid of me, that he might leave me somewhere and go away.

He began to lope and jog down the hill shouting, no words but pitching his voice against the wind and laughing harshly but not unhappily.

I clutched his head and dug my hand into his hair. I feared I would fall. He had me by the legs and ran and ran.

'Stars,' he shouted in my language. 'Stars.'

The sky was flung along the black hills in the wind like the hem of a robe weighted with gold. My cheeks dried and stiffened in the wind. 'Stars,' I sobbed, and shouted and clung to his stiff thick hair. 'Stars.'

I had not wanted the stars, nor known what my wanting was for, but I understood that he had thought I wanted them and had tried to give them to me. In time I grew quiet and Herr Waldmeier slowed to a walk and turning climbed the hill again. He carried me back to the hut and laid me on the mattress and went away. When he had gone I stayed on the mattress and from that time learned to live in his house. As well as his studies in Amharic he taught my sister and me German and he made us teach him all we knew of English and soon there were three languages in which we might speak.

In a year from my arrival at Gafat the missionaries had built a school where they intended to teach the reading and writing of the Amharic language so that people might read a translation of the Bible, for until now the Bible

28

could only be read in an ancient language known to very few besides the priests.

The Emperor would admit to no purpose in their teaching people who were already Christians, yet knowing that they had skills which were necessary to him – Herr Waldmeier is a carpenter, Herr Saalmuller a blacksmith – he sent to them captive Galla children who are infidels, saying better any kind of Christian than no Christian at all, and provided these children with food as he had provided all the materials necessary for the building of the school.

So in the mornings these boys squatted on the floor of the school room chanting the alphabet, *'ha, hoo, hay, ah, hee, hö, ho,'* and in the afternoons Herr Waldmeier, Herr Flad and Herr Saalmuller taught them the mechanical arts they had brought with them from their own country.

I am standing at the corner of the school yard. Herr Waldmeier shows the boys his shining saw and heavy hammer and the boys stand on either side of him in rows, leaning their brown stick arms on each other's shoulders, holding their shaved heads attentively over the strange tools. The smell of the sawn wood is sweet. Herr Waldmeier blows along the plank he is cutting and the sawdust rises and falls in a quick bright cloud. The Emperor has ordered him to make a chariot like the one on which King David rode into battle.

I hate Rita Flad. She is horrid. Her white hair is scraped back from her thin small face in two skinny plaits and where her hair parts on her bent head you can see that the skin of her head is pink. She plays at my feet with her little brother, Martin. Although I am older than they, I am standing waiting for them to ask me to play with them.

But Rita Flad, knowing that I am there, will not look at me. They play with the sawdust and the shavings. They

29

shape the sawdust into huts with their hands. Beside each
hut they put a curled shaving. That is the fire. They make
their fingers walk among the huts.

Martin cannot keep his eyes away. He looks up at me
and at once his sister sees this and pokes out her elbow into
his side. I smile at Martin quickly. I know that you smile
to make the other person smile back at you. That is the
signal that you wish to speak with them, and if they smile
it is the signal that you are permitted to do so. Martin
opens up his face and smiles back at me.

'Why do you smile at her,' says Rita crossly. 'You know
you are not to.' His eyes wander quickly towards the
sawing. I go on standing.

After a while Rita Flad squats back on her heels and
says in a small clear voice that only Martin and I can hear,
'Your mother is a savage.'

My voice without my thinking says, 'My mother is a
princess. Your mother is a sheep.'

Rita Flad looks quickly round. Seeing her father continue his work unmoved she raises her elbows and digs
her fists into her eyes, twisting them this way and that to
hide that she is not yet crying. Then she begins to
whimper and runs across the yard to Herr Flad. He goes
down on one knee and she leans against his shoulder,
rolling back her head and points at me. Then she says
loud and clear, 'She called Mama a sheep.'

Martin quietly walks away and sits behind the woodpile. Herr Waldmeier stops sawing. The pleasure in what
he is doing fades from his face. He looks from one to
another, slowly deciding what he is to do.

'Sheep is not a bad word,' says one of the boys. 'To have
called Frau Flad a donkey would have been very bad but
to call her a sheep means nothing.' The others hang their
heads and titter. Almost he has managed to call Frau Flad

a donkey and the two teachers can do nothing about it. Now they repeat among themselves, 'To say "donkey" is very bad,' tasting the forbidden word on their tongues in safety.

'Be silent,' says Herr Waldmeier. At once their bodies and faces stiffen. They make no sound. Herr Waldmeier walks angrily towards me.

And I cry out, still in some fear of him, 'I did not call her a sheep because it was bad but because she looks like a sheep.'

Now he is running towards me. His face is very red and drawn together in anger. I, too, want to run but cannot. He raises his hand. His hand and his face are between me and the sky.

Then his face changes and he no longer wants to hit me. He brings down his hand and looks at it in perplexity as if it had tried to act without him. He is sorry that he wanted to hit me. But he is sorry to himself. He is not sorry to me. He is still angry at me. He lifts me up under his arm and strides up the hill to his house. Perhaps he will beat me there.

His ribs and his arm are hard. He carries me under his arm, gripped around the waist, facing downwards so that the dust and the stones on the road flow past like water. I feel sick. I am nothing to him.

My sister runs to meet us, all concerned, thinking that I have hurt myself.

'She has been wicked,' says Herr Waldmeier. 'She has said an unkind thing about Frau Flad.' He tips me onto my feet and goes away.

My sister begins at once, loudly so that before he is out of earshot he will hear how well she does her duty, 'You are ungrateful. Herr Waldmeier gives you a home and you give him trouble. You are bad. Frau Flad is a learned lady and good and you find bad words to call her.' She leans back, arching her spine and placing her hands on either side of her stomach which is swollen with child. And now that Herr Waldmeier can no longer hear she makes an angry face at me and goes swaying into her kitchen with her hands in her hollow back.

I will stay in my hut. I will not eat. I will not come out until they ask me to. In the end they will have to come to the door and ask me to come out.

No one comes. The sounds of the household are unaffected by my not being there. The chickens complain in the yard. My sister shouts to her servant girl. Herr Waldmeier's voice returns loud among the huts. My throat and eyes are sore with crying. I do not want to go on crying. I can smell meat cooking in the kitchen.

When I opened my door and came outside, Herr Waldmeier was sitting alone outside the hut in which he slept with my sister. There was a lantern on the ground beside him and he worked, bent over, at a lump of wood in his hand. I lowered my shamma humbly from my head and stood a little way from him.

At first I thought that he did not look up because he was still angry. Then I saw that his mind had caught on the thing in his hand and was busy there. He had forgotten.

Then I hoped that he would remember and be angry again. I went closer to him and said, 'What are you making?'

'Good evening, Louisa,' said Herr Waldmeier without looking up.

'What are you making?' I said again.

'The stock of a musket. Feel it, Louisa. Is it smooth?'

It felt like skin. It was warm from his hand. 'What use is it,' I said, 'without the metal part?'

'Ah,' he said and laughed a little. 'You see the Emperor

has asked me to make a musket and I do not know how to. So with this gift I shall say: this is the only part of the musket I know how to make because I am only a carpenter, but I shall make it as well as I am able. More than that I cannot do.'

He turned me round with his hands and fitted the wood against my shoulder. 'There, how is that?' he said. He was very pleased with the stock as he always is with the things he has made. I went to the kitchen and asked the servant for some meat.

At this time, when the chariot was nearly finished, the Emperor rode daily from Debra Tabor and stood in the schoolyard leaning on his spear, watching the Europeans at work.

Herr Saalmuller explained to him that although they could build the body of the chariot, they could not provide it with wheels. The Emperor said that was of no consequence. His soldiers could carry it like a litter. The chariot was fitted with two long poles. Every day for a week after its completion the army met and charged in mock battles on the plain below Debra Tabor with the Emperor swaying in the dust clouds over their heads, trying to adjust the aim of his spear to the motion of the chariot.

At the end of that week the Emperor rode again to Gafat and told Herr Waldmeier and the others that after the coming Sabbath they must make him a mortar and some bomb-shells.

The first gun is cast

In the evening Herr Saalmuller and the Flads came to Herr Waldmeier's house to discuss what they should do about the Emperor's demand. They brought with them Herr Moritz, a tall thin man who had recently come to Gafat – why, no one knew. Certainly he was no missionary. The country he came from was called Poland and he had for a time, he told Herr Waldmeier, served with the Russian army. There was little for him to do in Gafat yet the Emperor paid for him to stay. Behind his hut he made a distillery and, asking advice of all the servants as to how to distil spirits from mead, he soon became more expert than they and his arrack was in great demand. Frau Flad said that he was not a Godly man, but pleasing, and a new face was always welcome.

My sister was near her time and lay down in the evenings. Because she did not like to lie down in the room where there were visitors, she lay on my bed and I was allowed to stay up. I stood outside, watching the lanterns coming through the dark from the separate houses, joining together and moving closer.

When they had entered the hut it was realised that Frau Flad could not be asked to sit on the floor, there being no chair. Accordingly a mule-saddle was brought for her and when she had hit the dust from it with the piece of cloth she uses to dry her face, she settled herself sideways upon it. Shaking out her skirts over her ankles and folding her hands over a pouch she carried, she waited to pray.

The men knelt on the floor, and because it was Herr Waldmeier's house it was he who spoke first to God. 'Oh Lord, help us in our perplexities. Let us not trust in our own counsels, but always in Thy holy word.' I knelt too, folding my hands as Herr Waldmeier had taught me. 'Speak to us, Lord. We are weak. Give us Thy strength to labour discreetly in Thy harvest field. Guide us, Oh Lord. Speak to us.'

Did he hope that God would speak out? The room was silent and listening but no voice came. Then there was a clearing of throats and the men shifted and sat cross-legged on the floor and began to speak to one another and Frau Flad took from her pouch her spectacles. Then she took out a needle and wool and a pair of socks.

'I am mending your socks, Herr Moritz,' she said, smiling brightly upon that tall man. 'See, I picked these scraps of wool from Martin's old jacket and they will do very well.'

'You are too kind, Frau Flad,' said Herr Moritz with a stiff little bow.

'Ah,' she said, 'you single men need someone to care for you. Please, please,' she waved her sock at the rest of them. 'I am keeping you.'

'Louisa,' said Herr Waldmeier, 'hold the lantern so that Frau Flad can see to work.' So I must hold the lantern and stand beside her.

'The problem before us is this,' said Herr Moritz. 'Today the Emperor has asked Herr Waldmeier and my-self, nay, has ordered us, to build him a mortar and to make the shells to fire from it.'

'This is of course impossible,' said Herr Saalmuller anxiously.

35

'So I have said to him but this he cannot understand. He himself has constructed a cannon out of a tree-trunk, which of course exploded when he lit the first charge, but this has convinced him that all that is needed is a knowledge of metal to build a successful cannon. And this art he believes us to have in every detail. There is no way of explaining to him this is not so. He is determined that we build him this gun.'

'Have any of us the knowledge to do this thing?' asked Herr Waldmeier looking around him. 'Can we obtain the materials?'

When no one spoke, Herr Moritz said in a low voice, 'I have a little experience of such things owing to my brief association with the Russian artillery.'

Frau Flad coughed in her throat and stabbed at the sock without raising her face from it. She said mildly, 'Herr Waldmeier does not seriously suggest that you should undertake such a task. He is merely establishing that it is out of the question for any of us to agree to it.'

Herr Waldmeier frowned and said politely, 'Have we the benefit of this choice?'

Frau Flad continued bent over her sewing, only signalling me to hold the lantern closer. 'I need not remind you, Theo,' – for this is how they call him – 'that our purpose in coming to this country was not to make guns.'

'The condition on which we stay here at all,' said Herr Waldmeier, 'is that our labours continue to please the Emperor. If we go against him in this thing, if we refuse to try – I agree we can give no promise of success – but if we refuse even to try, we risk not only all that we have achieved so far in the school, in the example our lives have set, but we risk the future of all missionary work in this country.'

'But is it not more dangerous,' said Herr Saalmuller,

36

'to try this thing, which we agree to be impossible, and then fail? Will not the wrath of the Emperor be all the more terrible against us if his hopes are raised and then dashed?'

Herr Waldmeier who had sat staring at the floor looked up at him quickly and said, 'It is only you, Carl, who have used the word impossible.' He shifted his glance to Herr Moritz who rested his chin on his hand and stroked his cheek thoughtfully with one long thin finger. 'The clay is suitable in this vicinity for the making of the mould. I have asked about metal and it appears that the Emperor has large quantities of vessels, brass dishes and so forth, that he would willingly have melted down. The problem is not materials. It is, as Herr Saalmuller says, whether between us we have sufficient skills to succeed.'

'The whole process is one of great danger,' began Herr Moritz.

Herr Waldmeier interrupted, 'But is it possible?'

'Yes,' he said reluctantly, 'it is possible.''

Frau Flad's sewing had gone still in her lap and now she turned up her face so that her quick eyes were hidden behind two flat expressionless circles of light. These she turned fixedly upon Herr Flad who, as if touched by a match, began at once to speak in a rapid sonorous voice.

'It is not the will of God that we should do this thing. We came to this land to spread the word of God among a deluded and corrupt people, to show them the true beauty their faith could assume if purged of ignorance and vile practices by daily contact with the Gospels. It is not His will that we should manufacture engines of destruction for a despot. Our lives are wholly given to following in the footsteps of our Master, who would never Himself have consented to follow such a course. Put not thy trust in Princes, Waldmeier. Put not thy trust in thine own abilities. To do the will of God is our sole concern and it is not God's will that we should do this thing.'

He knew so positively that God had perhaps whispered to him in the silence of the room. Frau Flad wove intently the strands of grey wool in and out of the barred hole across her hand. I watched over the lantern Herr Waldmeier's hands, restless and wanting to do the work. He said stubbornly, as if Herr Flad had never spoken, 'We have made other things at the Emperor's request. It is only the gun to which there is an objection.'

'That is true. That is true,' said Herr Flad.

'We do not know against whom the gun is to be fired,' prompted Frau Flad gently.

Herr Moritz gave a snort. 'It is we, who would have to fire it for the first time, that are more likely to be killed than any enemy of Tewodros'. My dear lady, it is so unlikely that we shall achieve this thing that you can wipe all such considerations from your tender conscience.'

'Our work is as the teachers of the Gospels and not as hired labourers—' Herr Flad began, but Herr Waldmeier interrupted again.

'There is no shame in working with the hands. Christ used His hands. The disciples were fishermen and makers of tents. This is how we live.' And he shook his square red hands before Herr Flad's mild perplexed eyes. 'This is our power over the people we would reform. Think,' he said, turning to them all. 'If we say that we shall do this thing Tewodros will deny us nothing. To help us with the work, he will send us the best men he can find from throughout the country. What an opportunity is that to spread our teachings. When the work is complete,' ('If it is ever complete,' muttered Herr Moritz) 'they will return to their villages with the uncorrupted word of God and spread it there. So we will achieve more than by years of
38

devoted teaching in this one spot. When shall we find—'

But Frau Flad, whose sharp eyes had fixed themselves upon Herr Waldmeier, now broke in in a low reproachful voice. 'Theo,' she said, 'you have hurt your wrist. Why did you not bring it to me to dress?'

He looked blankly down at his wrist which was tied with a dirty rag, his mind still moving rapidly ahead with what he had been saying. 'It is nothing. The saw. But nothing. It heals by itself.' He put the wrist protectively behind him but Frau Flad went on in the same melancholy gentle tone, 'How careless you are of yourself when we all depend so much on your youth and strength. Come, come bring it to me. Let me see it.'

He did not want to come. But Frau Flad had very quickly folded the sewing away into her pouch and smiling held out her hands to him. What could he do but submit and stand there stooping awkwardly while I held the lantern and Frau Flad picked at the rag and gently pressed the flesh around the cut and clicked her tongue against the roof of her mouth?

The other men shifted restlessly. Their thoughts left Herr Waldmeier and became scattered and confused. 'Leave it uncovered tonight and come to me in the morning when I shall dress it properly,' said Frau Flad. She dropped his hand and sank onto her knees on the floor. 'Dear Master forgive our foolish ways.' She paused. The others caught unawares, were noisily attempting to kneel. 'Re-guide our footsteps into the paths of righteousness. Guard us from the sin of pride. Save us from temptation to self-aggrandisement. Let us turn more truly to Thee. Amen.' And she was briskly upon her feet, smiling at Herr Waldmeier, 'Tomorrow morning,' and left the room.

Herr Flad and Herr Saalmuller hurried after her, nodding over their shoulders. Herr Moritz followed with a shrug of his. When they had gone Herr Waldmeier turned from the door and made an angry sound in his throat. A moment later he said, 'She is a good and Christian woman,' and went to help my sister into her own bed.

But as it happened Frau Flad's victory on that evening was lost her, for the Emperor imprisoned the Flads' and Herr Saalmuller's and our own servants and would not hear of their release until work on the mortar was begun. Fearing what these innocent people might suffer, they agreed to make the gun to the best of their ability.

So they began to work, not because God had permitted them, nor Herr Waldmeier persuaded, but out of their very first fear of the Emperor.

Rosa was born. My sister suckled her and carried her on her back like a paler portion of her own body, but Herr Waldmeier carried her about in the crook of his arm, looking at her with wonder and great caution as if his arms which are unusually strong would suddenly fail him and that small creature that I could easily lift prove too much for him to hold.

'Is she not beautiful, Louisa? Is it not a wonder that she has perfect fingernails? Look, are her hands not beautiful?'

The work on the gun was greatly helped when Monsieur Bourgaud arrived from France. Monsieur Bourgaud is a gunsmith, a big man with a ruddy well-favoured face and bright blue eyes that seek about him in a speculative way.

Madame Bourgaud will say sometimes twice in the day, 'What can one do with such a man as Monsieur Bourgaud?' Almost any event prompts her to say this. When she came to Gafat she had two children. Now she has five. Her arms are big and red with only a dimple to mark the elbow and when she laughs it affects all her body. Frau Flad said that she was a good sensible woman who bore her burdens with resignation. She paid Madame to do her washing.

Monsieur Bourgaud and Herr Saalmuller working together could melt metal until it ran at their bidding and grew hard again in whatever shape they wished. The old people in the village were fearful. They said that men who tortured water and metal so with fire must have learnt their arts in hell.

No one heeded them. The Emperor sent more and more people to work at Gafat until the huts spread down to the base of the hill and men worked all day. They gathered stones and built a furnace like a tower in which to melt the metal for the gun. They dug a pit and lined it with stones.

Then Herr Waldmeier shaped a piece of wood and wound it round with plaited straw. The end of the plait of straw that was not needed Herr Waldmeier gave to me for a skipping rope. For several days I went and skipped on our threshing floor, the first excitement of watching the gunmaking having by that time somewhat lessened. When I went to watch again, the wood and straw were covered with clay and the whole cooking over a charcoal fire.

This was the mould. When it was dry the straw was removed and in the place where it had been the metal was to go. Now the mould was lowered into the pit and the metal vessels that the Emperor had given were crushed with stones and put into the furnace. Then great quantities of wood were collected and a fire was built inside the furnace and fed continually night and day. But on the second day there was a cry and the men began to run shouting away from the furnace. Before our eyes the tower began to heave and sag and finally with a great noise crumbled away in a cloud of smoke and dust. The metal spread in a mass amid the ruins, as shapeless as mud.

Herr Waldmeier said that the intensity of the heat had melted portions of the stone and these had flowed into the metal ruining both stone and metal at once. But in the village it was said that the hand of God had struck the furnace.

Now all the work must be begun again, but the Emperor was not angry. He sent letters to Herr Waldmeier from Gojam, far to the south where he was campaigning against the rebel Tedla Gwalu, saying, 'Be patient, my son. Try again. In the end you will succeed.' With the letters were gifts of money.

In the weeks that followed came a gift of more significance. One day Ras Ingada came to our home and folding back his shamma showed in the bend of his arm a lion cub no bigger than a little dog, watching us with round yellow eyes. Until that day no man other than the Emperor had been permitted to keep lions. Now he had sent this lion to Herr Waldmeier.

Herr Waldmeier fed the lion by dipping his finger in a dish of milk and the lion lay on its back and in Herr Waldmeier's lap and placed its large paws around his wrist and closed its eyes with pleasure and sucked.

'What does it feel like?' I said. Leaning against his shoulder I smelt the lion's smell.

'You may try,' said Herr Waldmeier, so I dipped my finger in the milk and gave it to the lion. The fierceness of its sucking was terrible, the tongue like a supple rasp, the little throat warm and muscular, drawing in my finger then my hand.

I cried out and pulled my hand away.

'Gently, gently,' said Herr Waldmeier and gave back to

42

the lion the thick milky finger to which it was accustomed. 'See how tame he is.' Although he spoke to me, it was in a soft rocking voice to please the lion. 'Is it not a joy to handle such a creature? It is a lion, all that is awesome and terrible in God's creation, and yet if I treat it so, with kindness, even Rosa, even so little a child, may lie in safety beside it.' He called the lion, Hagos, which in my language means joy.

More lasting stone was fetched and the furnace built again. The layers of wood and straw and clay were placed one upon the other, and again the mould for the gun was lowered into the pit.

The fire was lit but this time the furnace stood firm and when Herr Saalmuller took away the door of the furnace, the metal sprang down the channel prepared for it and ran into the pit in a thick golden curve. Herr Waldmeier lifted me off the ground to see it, crying, 'Look, Louisa, look! It is the brazen serpent. Is it not a miracle that in this remote place God has inspired us to make this thing – has given us a means to increase and preserve the mission?'

When the Emperor returned from Gojam he rode to Gafat with Fitawrari Gabrie and the other chieftains who had been fighting with him, to see the mortar tested.

It was a little thing out of its mould, scarcely bigger than a cooking pot. They carried it onto the open ground behind the furnace. The Emperor sat on a carpet, waiting while the gun was put in position. The Europeans and their wives and children were seated on either side of him in a semi-circle and a great crowd of people gathered on the slopes of the hill behind. Herr Waldmeier had brought Rosa to him, for although she was now a year old, the Emperor had never seen her.

He smiled at Rosa and held out his arm to her and Rosa

43

went to him with no fear at all, sitting on his knee and snatching at a string of silver prayer-beads he dangled for her with the other hand. All the time that he played with her he questioned Herr Waldmeier gravely and intently about the mortar. What weight of metal had been used? Why was one stone suitable for the furnace and another not? Of what weight was the stone ball they intended to fire this afternoon?

When Rosa caught the beads he laughed and held her up above his head as high as his arms would reach. 'She is strong,' he said to Herr Waldmeier. Then he asked what weight of powder might be used.

'We are ready,' called Herr Moritz.

The Emperor rose to his feet, everyone rising with him. Herr Waldmeier reached out for Rosa but the Emperor seemed not to see him, so fixedly was he staring at the little gun. He held Rosa carefully with his hand covering one ear and her other pressed against the folds of his clothing. Rita Flad and Martin stood with their fingers plugged into their ears and their faces puckered up in dreadful expectation.

Herr Waldmeier ran forward and placed the charge of gunpowder, everyone being very quiet so as not to awaken the life in the powder until it was safely settled. Then he held the rounded stone high in the air and a great cheer went up from all the crowd. Then he stooped and fitted it into the mouth of the mortar. Then he ran back to Herr Moritz who touched the other end with a burning stick.

The gun roared unspeakably, and leapt back, alive and having great power. The world shook and white birds were flung up against the green hillside. I screamed and clutched my sister, her eyes buried in my shoulder, mine in the folds of cloth at her neck. The voice of the gun

44

flung about the hills, growing all the time fainter, and when we looked again the world was unaltered.

A small foolish ball of smoke hung in the sky. Fitawrari Gabrie and the chiefs spurred their mules and galloped, shouting and whooping across the plain to measure out the flight of the ball. People in the crowd ran to and fro clutching their heads and shouting distractedly. Only the Emperor remained standing where he was, carefully holding Rosa with an expression of great joy and triumph on his face.

Some said the birds were the souls of people that the gun's breath had destroyed although no bodies were apparent. Some pointed up to the puff of smoke and said it was the evil spirit emanating from the gun that would stay over Gafat for ever. But very quickly the cloud dissolved.

Tewodros in a low sweet voice called for them to be quiet and instantly they were quiet. He said the gun was their friend and protector as he was, and the destroyer of their enemies, and they believed him.

The following day he came again to Gafat asking to see plans for the next gun which he suggested might be a howitzer.

I see the captives

When the first gun was cast and successfully fired, the Emperor gave fresh gifts to the Gafat people. He gave each man that had worked on the mortar one hundred dollars and to their wives he sent rich dresses, so that now my sister changed her clothes in the afternoons and sat waiting for Frau Saalmuller and Frau Moritz, for those gentlemen had by now taken Abyssinian wives, to call on her in their finery.

Herr Waldmeier was singled out for especial favour. As well as Hagos the lion he was given a white horse with a fine wooden saddle mounted in gold. On the morning after the horse was brought to his house he decided to ride in the direction of Debra Tabor, hoping that he might meet the Emperor and express his thanks.

As I had not then done my full growing he leant over the horse's flank and told me to hold on to his arm. Then he swung me easily up into the saddle in front of him. He reached his arms around me and fitted my hands one on top of the other on the high pommel. 'Hold tightly, Louisa,' he said. I had never ridden so high but I gripped the pommel and his thick arms holding the reins stretched on either side of me so I did not fear that I would fall.

Seeing Rita Flad emptying refuse in the lane outside her house I did not trouble to smile at her but stared ahead over the horse's ears. 'Good morning, Rita,' said Herr

Waldmeier freeing his hand and tipping up the brim of his straw hat to her.

'Good morning, Herr Waldmeier,' and she turned up her pinched little face, shutting one eye against the sun. 'My father is going to buy a horse.' She had to call after us for the white horse had moved steadily on. In any case it was not true.

At the bottom of the hill we turned towards Debra Tabor. The dried bed of the river was on our right. The road wound beside it into the mouths of watercourses and out around the spurs of little hills. Because it was a Saturday the horse had to move slowly through a flow of people and flocks coming into Gafat. We scattered the shining goats so that they spilled over the edge of the road and the children ran shouting after them, waving their sticks.

'I never thought that I would own such a horse as this,' said Herr Waldmeier. 'I know what I am : a poor man. If one is born so, one must accept that one always is. But now I own a horse.' He spoke simply and happily, not particularly to me yet I felt included in his happiness.

The men that passed us with their long springing stride turned up their dark faces and reached up their arms. Many of them greeted Herr Waldmeier by name. Everyone could see that he was a great man. They carried sticks over their shoulders. Over every stick was laid a stiff goatskin folded in half along the back so that it looked like a flattened animal and its four legs continued to dance on air. Troops of bowed and patient donkeys parted to let us through, loaded with sacks and baskets and sewn goatskins bloated out with grain. There was such plenty in those days. Hens rode on top of the bundles, settled down between their wings. Once I thought they rode there of their own free will, but one day I looked in

47

the market and saw that their bent claws were tied to the thongs that bound the bundles.

As we rode further out of Gafat the crowds thinned and the road grew silent except for the sounds we brought with us. I rode high and light on the horse, leaning back against Herr Waldmeier with the sun on my face. He laughed quietly and comfortably like someone who is alone. Then he began to sing a song in his own language that took him far away to a place I had not been. I could not go there too. Yet it was a childish song. Partly he sang it to me. I heard his deep voice over my head. Between my shoulders I felt it vibrate in his chest. I heard it echo in the hills. The song surrounded me. I was entirely happy.

He stopped singing but the silence that followed seemed a continuation of the song. The chinking and creaking of the harness were lost in it, as were the sounds of the horse's hooves picking over the loose stones of a watercourse. Ahead the road wound out past a great pile of boulders. And from that part of the road hidden by the rocks came another sound.

It was as if a boy should take a stick and rattle it carelessly over flawed or broken bells. The silence now seemed after all to have been nothing but a tensing and lying-in-wait for the thing approaching with its sad and heartless sound.

Herr Waldmeier had heard it too. He turned the horse's head sharply and urged it off the road, up the watercourse. There we turned again and stood looking down on the road while the horse moved its hooves unsteadily on the slippery broken stone.

There were sounds of other hooves and shouting. Around the bend in the road came two mounted soldiers with their shammas pulled up to their eyes to keep out the dust and their muskets laid across the necks of their mules.

Following them came a group of near to twenty ragged men walking two by two. They were chained together at the wrist. The sound we had heard was made by the clanking of the metal chains as they moved.

Next, riding on a mule, came a woman. She was dressed like an Abyssinian, but her face which she held very high was pale-skinned. She held onto a little sickly child who slumped against her with his eyes fluttering open and shut, not looking about him at all. She was a white woman. And at once I felt confused and could not think who she was or how she came to be there.

A sad anxious man rode beside her and behind him came two more men. They rode as the other prisoners had walked, each with one arm extended towards the other and chained together at the wrist. They were also pale-skinned and though dirty and unkempt, undoubtedly Europeans.

The one nearest us rode with his head sunk forward and his big black beard low on his chest. The other rode with his head thrown back, staring fixedly with pale eyes at something just out of sight above the road at which from time to time he nodded amiably. He wore a long black cloak and long lank hair of no particular colour fell to his collar from under a cap.

In spite of the strangeness of seeing white men chained, all the time I looked and looked at the woman and the sick child riding slowly past. They did not wear chains. Still I felt as clearly as I saw them that they were in great trouble of a kind beyond my understanding.

I watched them almost detachedly, high on the horse in the shadow of the hill, so sure was I that Herr Waldmeier would intervene, that everyone would do as he said, that the wrong would be set immediately right.

49

The minutes stretched. I would not let them pass, in my certainty that Herr Waldmeier's voice would call out above my head. The man and woman and child had ridden past. The two chained riders had come up to us. Still Herr Waldmeier had not said a word.

Now I twisted around in the saddle to look at him, wanting to know from his face what I should be feeling. But his face was turned away. He was coaxing the horse gently with his hand further up the watercourse. He did not want these people to see him. How could that be? It came to me cold and unpleasant that there might be some connection between ourselves and these people and at that moment I recognised the bearded man as the man who had come to my father's house and taken him away to his church and sent him back unhappy. He was a missionary as the Gafat people were missionaries. Still they went slowly past. I thought *he is afraid*. I could not speak.

The man in the black cloak held the reins of his mule loosely in his free hand but now he absently let them fall and raised his hand to scrabble at the collar of his cloak as if it chafed his neck.

Then I managed to whisper, 'Who is that man?'

Herr Waldmeier answered equally low, 'He is the British consul in Abyssinia.' But this could not be. Englishmen were not like that. Yet I remembered the missionary had spoken English to my father. Such things as this did not happen to English people. In this confusion I continued to stare stupidly down onto the road.

The consul's mule feeling the rein drop onto its shoulder suddenly leapt forward across the road. The consul grabbed the mane and kept his seat but the bearded man being chained to him and taken unawares was dragged half off his saddle. First he cried out in pain; there was fresh blood under the manacle on his wrist. Then he began to shout at his companion, abusing him in English I could not follow.

The two musketeers that led the troop wheeled back and called a halt. Immediately the band of native prisoners squatted down in the dust, with their brown knees poking stiffly out of their rags. They eased the shining manacles up their arms and with their free hands began quickly and busily to pull the twigs and thorns out of each other's bushy hair. Some fell asleep instantly where they sat, with their heads balanced against each other. An old man worked intently at a thorn in his foot while the man that was chained to him steadied the foot on his knee and patted it with his hand as if it were a part of himself. The child began to wail and the woman rocked him fiercely to her.

The consul sat all this time patiently and unsteadily on his mule, plucking at his neck and looking up the road in bewilderment while the soldiers slapped at the flanks of his mount until it was back in place and they could haul the missionary upright.

Now our white horse, disturbed by the shouting and the turning flicking rumps below him, began to sidle, sending little stones running down the watercourse. One of the musketeers looked up and recognising Herr Waldmeier swept his shamma off his head and bowed low over the pommel of his saddle.

'Are you well, Waldmeier?'

'Thanks be to God,' muttered Herr Waldmeier, 'I am well.'

The bearded man had heard the soldier and now he raised himself in the saddle, staring at where we were. 'Waldmeier!' he shouted in German. 'For God's sake, Waldmeier!' When Herr Waldmeier did not answer he began again in a different tone, 'Is that you, Waldmeier?

51

Sitting on your fine white horse watching our misery?' His voice continued to grow in strength and hatred until there was a kind of music in it, as if he repeated a chant or curse. 'Why don't you climb down off your horse, Waldmeier, and extend the hand of charity to suffering Christians? Do you pass by on the other side of the road in your finery with the fruits of your misalliance while this sainted child languishes in captivity?'

Dirty, bleeding, chained in the road, the conviction and dominance in his voice kept the soldiers from moving forward. Herr Waldmeier did not say a word. The tired prisoners squatted in the road and stared dully from one to the other. 'Do you go about your tyrant master's business while we go about God's? Are you a slave to Moloch?'

There was a clattering on the road out of sight behind the rocks. The guards came to life, shouting orders and driving the prisoners off the road as another troop of mules appeared jogging towards us held together in a cloud of yellow dust. Their leader in a white shamma swathed to the eyes was the Emperor, on his way to Gafat.

Herr Waldmeier's big cold hand gripped my head and pushed it down. The native prisoners stumbled from the road tossing the folds of their dirty shammas from their heads. The bearded man instantly shook his head bare and quickly with his free hand snatched the cap off his companion. By the time the Emperor had trotted up to him he seemed to cringe on the saddle, nevertheless his voice had a loud demanding tone. 'Have mercy upon us!' he shouted. 'In God's name, release us!'

Tewodros reined in his mule. He stared narrowly at the bearded man, then lowering the folds of his shamma clear of his mouth he said abruptly, 'Can you make guns?'

'I am a man of God, King, and have no need of guns.'

'Then you are nothing to me,' and digging his heels into

the mule's flank the Emperor rode on at great speed with his soldiers hurrying after him.

Herr Waldmeier turned the horse and kicked it so that we jolted forward and came scrambling down onto the road ahead of all the prisoners.

We followed in the Emperor's dust and the prisoners were shouted forward again in ours until the three groups were strung out along the road and we were alone, the joy of that day being entirely spoiled.

After some minutes Herr Waldmeier's hand left the rein and patted my shoulder heavily and awkwardly. 'You are to forget this thing, Louisa. It is no concern of ours.'

I was silent, feeling that a great wrong had been done and that he had been shamed. I twisted my shoulder out from under his hand and leant forward so that I touched him nowhere. I wanted to be separated from his shame, to quarrel with him and damage the thing that held me to him.

'What is the matter with you?' he said irritably.

I began to cry painfully inside my chest and my nose, just loud enough for him to hear.

Now he was pinching my shoulder in his hand, shaking me, saying in a loud and angry voice, 'What would you have had me do, then?'

Confused and shapeless in my head were the many things he could have done. I twisted to get my shoulder away from him again.

'They were your people. That man knew you.'

He made a noise in his throat as if he might spit. 'Do you think I do not want to help them? Stern is no friend to me but I would not wish that fate on anyone. Do you know where they are to be taken? To the prison on Meqdela, and for how long? Good God. But what can I do?'

Then I was confused, for remembering the Emperor's indifference to these people I thought they must be wrong-doers. I said more quietly, 'What have they done?'

It seemed that he would not answer me but then he sighed and said, 'They have been disrespectful to the Emperor.'

This had no meaning for me. I said with scorn, 'And the child?'

'So there was a child,' he said harshly. 'And all the more reason for that child's father to be careful. No one asked them to come here. No one asked me to come. Nor Flad. Nor Saalmuller. But we at least have earned our bread and taught our trades. Who are they that, in the name of Christ or England, must come and meddle and pass judgement and sneer at what they do not trouble to understand? So that little child will suffer because its father did not take care, as I take care of you and Rosa, and if I did not, our lives would not be worth a straw. Do you understand that? If I were not loyal and useful, our lives would not be worth a straw.'

These words I was unwilling to understand. The near-ness of the quarrel bred a kind of excitement in me that would be lost if I returned to sympathy with him, and knowing by instinct where to wound him, I said, 'You wanted the horse. You said you wanted the horse.'

That made him angry. He shouted, 'What has the horse to do with it? I want to stay alive and keep Rosa alive, you and your sister, all of us, alive.'

'But who is trying to kill us?' I shouted back at him. 'Who would dare to kill us?'

It seemed to me, so little did I understand, that there must be some threat from that chained and helpless missionary. That he could mean the other person we had met with on the road never once occurred to me.

54

The arrival of the British ambassadors

Two years passed before I was to see the European prisoners again. In that time Herr Waldmeier continued to manufacture guns, making howitzers and cannon and larger mortars as well as supervising the making of cannon balls and gunpowder. The school continued to grow and the boys attending learnt zealously to read the Bible. They were now instructed by Debtera Sahaloo, Herr Waldmeier's time being so taken up with the gunmaking that he was now only free to teach the Gospels on Sundays.

Then, with his great Amharic Bible slung across his back like a slab of wood and taking Hagos by his chain, he walked to the villages near Gafat to preach and read in the groves outside their churches. He walked barefoot now because the boots he had brought with him from Switzerland had worn out and no one could make him new ones.

Now there was a foundry built at the foot of the hill at Gafat and a waterwheel set in the stream to turn the machinery. When this was complete, Herr Waldmeier, with the money given him by the Emperor, paid the workmen to build him a new house. It was built of stone like the foundry, with two separated rooms on the ground and a large upper chamber where the missionaries might meet together.

Herr Waldmeier himself made the doors and shutters. He made a ladder that passed from the ground floor to the upper floor. The logs that held up this upper floor projected out between the stones at the front of the house. Herr Waldmeier placed planks across them and built around them a railing and so made a little balcony. The roof was steep and covered with thatch. Herr Waldmeier said it was a German house. Certainly it was unlike anything seen in this country before.

The kosso tree remained. Hagos lay in its shade, tied to its trunk by a long chain, and every day a goat was sent to him by the Emperor which Hagos ate.

When his belly was full and peaceful, Rosa rode on his back with her little hands knotted in his mane, beating his ribs with her heels as he paced round and round the tree on his long chain.

As Hagos had grown from a cub to a lion and Rosa had grown from a baby to a child, so I had grown from a child nearly to a woman. I taught the smaller boys their letters in the school and walked about the market in my new person with my eyes kept down but quickly glancing to see whose eyes followed me.

It was I who went to market because my sister was constantly in those years ill with child-bearing. These children were never born but died inside her long before their time was due, leaving her ill and weak and mourning as if for someone real to her. So the buying and the cooking and the caring for Rosa fell in a large part to me, although Herr Waldmeier could now pay for an old woman to grind the corn and a young woman to carry water and wood.

I was often in the market carrying Rosa on my hip, wondering if the young soldiers who passed through Gafat thought I was a married woman with my own child. And it was in the market that I learned about the crimes of the prisoners we had seen.

I learned that the Emperor had sent the British consul, Cameron, to England with a letter to Queen Victoria saying that he had heard from his friends that she was a great Christian Queen who loved all Christians and asking that she might provide a guarantee of safe passage along the roads of her country for the ambassadors which he hoped to send to England. But Consul Cameron had returned with no answer to that letter and then when, in the following months, no answer came from the English Queen the Emperor took this as a slight to his dignity and, becoming enraged against the consul, had him imprisoned in Meqdela.

I heard too how the missionaries, Mr Stern and Mr Rosanthal, who had worked among the Jewish tribes in the north-west, had had their houses searched, and writings had been found that appeared to mock the Emperor and on that account they too had been imprisoned, as well as Mr Rosanthal's wife and infant son. From Herr Waldmeier I never heard a word concerning these people.

One market day I walked down through the village carrying Rosa. The servant came with me with a jar tied to her back for honey and the bars of salt carried under her arm, for salt was more acceptable than money in the market.

The servant said that I should buy from a certain honey woman, for although she was not virtuous her honey was sweet, and being slovenly she was careless in her measuring so that one often came out well from the purchase.

The honey woman had a bold pleasing face. She squatted inside a circle of stones with her shamma folded over her knees and all about her in round shallow baskets were the yellow grains and red peppers that she was

57

selling, and two large bowls of honey. I squatted down and laid the salt in front of her and she tossed the shamma back from her plump arms and began to scoop the clotted honey out of the bowl with her hands and to smear it into a measuring jug. She slapped her hands in and out over the brim, slow and indolent. Flies buzzed in a swarm above the honey and clustered on her wrists.

A soldier passing behind me stopped to watch her. 'Where are you from?' he said to the honey woman over my head.

'I come from my husband's village,' she said.

Then he called out, 'Come and sell your sweet wares at Meqdela.'

The honey woman looked slowly aslant at him as if the sun were in her eyes and made no answer. Then she looked away and said scornfully, 'Have you let your prisoners escape yet?' The palms of her hands were stained red with henna and the thick honey shone on them.

'Not they,' said the soldier. 'They are all chained except the woman and the child.' Then he said, 'The child died. He escaped but they all wept. You should have seen them weep,' and he laughed shortly and began to sing under his breath.

I wished she would hurry. I said, 'That is enough,' and she looked at me then in slow surprise for it was less than I had said.

'It is not enough,' said the honey woman.

'It is enough,' I said sharply and paid her and walked away. I held Rosa on my hip with my arm tight around her waist. I pulled her little dress down over my arm so that no part of her showed except her feet and she cried all the way home because she wanted to walk.

*   *   *

Some months later another soldier passed through Gafat. He stood by the well and the headman came out and greeted him and asked him to repeat his news. The soldier said that three Englishmen had come to the base of the mountains and sent word to the Emperor asking for his protection through the passes held by the rebels so that they might come and speak with him.

These men were messengers who had come all this way to beg for the release of the European prisoners. They brought at last a letter to the Emperor from the English Queen and gifts that were very splendid.

The headman said what were the gifts? The soldier said there was a glass. He held his hands before him and slid them up and down a height as high as himself. That was how tall the glass was. When a man stood before it, there appeared, looking at him, a spirit with his own features and his own clothing, with the very pattern on his shield all identical. It was like gazing on still water.

'Water cannot stand upright,' said the headman. That was true. It was not water. If you touched it, it was hard and dry and if you walked quickly behind it—nothing; no one stood there.

Some weeks later more news came. The Emperor had met the Englishmen at A'shfa in Damot and accepted the gifts. It was said that Tewodros took great pleasure in the company of the leading Englishman, Rassam, who was of a pleasant disposition and sweet-tongued. There was also a doctor – a skilful hakim who cured the sick – and a young soldier like a stick, with an eye made of glass that flashed in the sun. As soon as I heard of them I began to picture these men, not like that poor chained man on the mule, but tall and powerful as I remembered my father.

The Emperor treated these people graciously, showing them many marks of favour and agreeing to the release

59

of the prisoners who, even now, travelled from Meqdela as swiftly as their health would permit, to join the ambassadors.

Herr Waldmeier, with the other missionaries, was summoned to the camp to help make his fellow Europeans feel at home, and I feared for him having to meet those prisoners we had never thought to see again, and I envied him greatly that he would see the new Englishmen.

They were away from Gafat for over a month. Then cholera broke out in the camp and the deaths mounted so rapidly that on the advice of the English hakim the army moved into higher ground and dispersed earlier in the year than was usual.

Tewodros returned to Debra Tabor, but to everyone's surprise he brought with him the prisoners and the three Englishmen who had come for them. For the rains would come soon and how were they to travel to their own country if they did not start now while the roads were still passable?

The day after Herr Waldmeier's return being a Sunday, he took Hagos' chain and shouldered his Bible as usual and set out for a village near Debra Tabor. I asked if I might go with him and he said that I might.

He was anxious at the weak and listless condition in which he had found my sister, uncertain whether he should have left her alone so soon again. 'I should have left you with her, Louisa. Perhaps Rosa will tire her.' Then I feared that he would send me back but he did not as we had already walked so far.

Outside the village he sat down under a tree to prepare his lesson. Hagos stretched beside him in the shade, folding one heavy paw across the other and hung his great sad head. Herr Waldmeier propped the Bible open on his knees and began to read. His lips did not move when he

60

read, as the village priest's did. The edge of his teeth bit into his lower lip. His hand hovered above the page, waiting to turn it. Then he snapped the Bible shut and came and squatted down by Hagos, digging his hand into his mane.

'Has he not grown? Do you remember him, Louisa, when he sucked at my fingers, so big?' He looked at me searchingly as if it were possible that I could have forgotten. I thought: have I changed in this short time that he has been away? I felt that I had grown unfamiliar to him.

'Yes,' I said, smiling at him.

'Does he not have a sad and wise face? Look, these are lines in his fur, but do they not make him frown? And below his eyes, on his cheeks, like the track of tears. Poor Hagos.' He stared into the unrevealing amber eyes. 'He is forever patient. I reproach myself, Louisa, that he is a prisoner, but how could I free him? For even if I made it appear that he had escaped without my knowing, they would say that the Emperor's favour had fled from me. Come!' he said. 'You may take his chain.'

The church lay outside the village in a thick grove of trees. Herr Waldmeier led the way towards it. Hagos padded gravely after him and I came last, carrying the chain. The village children that watched their goats by the side of the path, cried out, 'Lion! Lion!' and flung stones at the goats to keep them at a safe distance. One child ran ahead of us towards the church, shouting in as much fear, 'A white man! A white man!'

'I have been here before,' said Herr Waldmeier over his shoulder. 'Yet I am still a curiosity to them.'

The path led through the trees and opened into a clearing where the round white church stood hemmed in by green. The children had disappeared. The grove was empty and had its own silence. 'It is a holy place,' said

61

Herr Waldmeier. 'Can you not feel it?' Only the little metal discs that hung around the Cross on the church roof rattled together and caught the light. A dove worked a piece of straw loose from the thatch and flew with it through a narrow opening between the high wooden doors. It was true. Listening so intently, there was something I could feel that tolerated these small noises and our own intrusion.

The doors opened further and an old priest ran down the steps towards us, fumbling with one hand to fasten a rich green cloak around his shoulders. In the other hand he held out a little brass Cross that trembled in front of him. Behind him ran a young boy with a shaven head, holding open a book at a brightly painted page.

The old priest took Herr Waldmeier's hand, bowed over it and kissed it. Then he looked into his face muttering, 'Sir, this Cross, this book, take these. All our money we have given to the Emperor. Sir, this Cross, this book, are all I have.'

'Why do you think I wish to rob you?'

The boy answered, 'You are a white man, sir. The Emperor has said that we are to give our wealth to the white man.'

'I want nothing,' said Herr Waldmeier in distress. He reached out and tugged the old man's cloak back onto his shoulder, patting him roughly. 'I want nothing.' Then he dropped his voice and said, 'I want your blessing.'

The old man stared at him stupidly. Then he shouted to the boy who shut his book and ran back with it into the church. The old man gathered up the skirts of his robe and began to run after him, turning to beckon us on. Herr Waldmeier tied Hagos to a post.

Inside the porch of the church it was dark. Doves blundered and flapped in the high still places overhead.

Under our feet the ridges of the bamboo matting were rough with their droppings. Herr Waldmeier lowered his Bible off his back and knelt on the matting. I knelt beside him. 'I ask your blessing,' he said again. The priest hovered over us with his clothes smelling of dirt and incense. He pressed his Cross against Herr Waldmeier's cheeks and then cold against mine.

Herr Waldmeier continued to kneel, praying unhappy painful prayers that disturbed the dark porch like a current of air, while the priest stood anxiously watching him. At last he sighed and got to his feet.

The grove outside filled with villagers waiting for us and staring at Hagos. Herr Waldmeier sat on the steps of the church and opening his Bible began to read aloud to them. Then I saw by the entrance to the grove a European gentleman leaning on a rifle and watching with great interest the scene in front of him.

He must be one of the Englishmen. He wore a cloth helmet and boots that laced up the front of his legs to the knee. He carried a bundle of dead birds, holding them a little away from him so that the blood from their broken heads would not fall on his clothes. I could not take my eyes from him, so much was he my idea of what an Englishman should be: what my father would have been in his own country.

Herr Waldmeier saw him too and nodded. When he had finished reading he untied Hagos and walked over to where the Englishman waited.

'Good day to you, Herr Waldmeier. May I have a word with you?' said the Englishman. He removed his hat and now it was possible to see his face. It was as thin and sharp as a bird's and his nose narrow and curved standing out like a beak. When he smiled slightly and added in a lower voice, 'Away from here, I think, where we have less company,' wrinkles sprang out at the corners of his eyes and when the smile faded there were little white lines on the gold skin where the wrinkles had been.

'Indeed,' said Herr Waldmeier curtly and they both stood back to let the other enter the path.

'No, no. You lead,' said the gentleman, slinging his rifle over his shoulder and falling in behind. Hagos padded behind him and I followed Hagos. Behind me trooped the villagers.

For a time no one spoke. Then the Englishman said, light and high and little-caring, although it was clear he wished to be pleasant, 'What a capital country this is. Thick with game. It's not so in England, you know. Too many damned people about. Signs everywhere to tell you you can't do this or that. Why here the birds are so tame that when I shot these the rest settled and preened themselves right by the dead bodies. No fear at all. The country has not been touched.'

'Well, it has been touched,' said Herr Waldmeier. 'It scarcely knows yet what has touched it. The birds have not yet learned to connect the sound of the gun with the death of their companions. In a little time they will. Then they will fly away. So you are a sportsman, Dr Blanc?'

This then was the hakim of whom they had spoken.

'Well to tell the truth, Waldmeier, I'm not much of one, but it's an excuse to get on one's own, you know.'

'And we have interrupted your solitude?'

'No, no. I have been wanting a chance to speak with you.' But he had noticed the 'we' and now glanced uneasily back at me and stopped where he stood. 'My dear fellow, this is your wife. How very obtuse of me.'

'She is Mrs Waldmeier's sister.'

'Another of Bell's children?' And looking down at me, smiling, he said, 'She is a beauty. A credit to you.'

64

'Hardly to me,' said Herr Waldmeier.

'But you have brought her up?'

'She speaks English.'

'Good day to you, Miss Bell,' said the doctor as if only at that moment had I truly appeared. He raised his helmet in one hand and held out the other.

Because I had not expected him to speak to me, because he had so openly admired me, I looked now not at his face but at his dusty boots. I touched his hand quickly and because at that moment no English came to my mouth, said in Amharic, 'Thanks be to God I am well.' Then I drew my shamma over my face not wanting him to continue staring.

'Charming, charming,' said the hakim, half to himself.

We had come now to the tree where we had rested earlier and Herr Waldmeier now bowed the doctor to a place in its shade. The doctor hung his birds on a branch and Herr Waldmeier leant against the trunk. The villagers halted a little way away and spread out across the path, closely watching these two strange men. The doctor looked back at them. 'They cannot understand us,' said Herr Waldmeier.

The doctor propped his rifle against the tree and stooping picked up a stone which he threw at a dead tree-trunk some distance away. It missed and fell beyond the mark with a little puff of dust.

Herr Waldmeier smiled at him and he too found a stone and threw it.

'Oh, very good!' cried the doctor. 'Better than mine.'

Now they began a question and answer with every stone they threw, looking not at each other but at the dead tree as if their thoughts might meet more easily in the distance.

'You must feel great satisfaction at bringing Christianity to these delightful people.'

65

'Christianity was here many centuries before I was. I fear I have only introduced them to guns.'

'You are content with your lot here?' asked the doctor.

'Where else would I go?'

'You feel this now. Oh, very good!' for Herr Waldmeier had finally struck the tree. 'You feel this now, when you are young, but when you are older?'

'It is a good enough life. I don't complain.'

I was restless then, bored with their game. To what place should he go? What place was there but here? And 'here' had altered as they talked. Always before I had been absorbed into where I was, looking out from my own invisibility. Now I stood apart from stones and trees, seen, cut off from everything. They had looked at me and now ignored me. *I take no credit for her. She is Mrs Waldmeier's sister. Where else would I go.* Why talk of going?

When I listened again the doctor was saying in a sharper quicker voice, 'Do you think, Waldmeier, he means to let us go?' That was what he had sought us out to ask: if the Emperor intended to let him go back to England.

'He means to,' said Herr Waldmeier. 'I do believe he means to.' And now they stood together talking intently and quietly so that I must move nearer and strain to hear what they were saying to each other.

'It's not for me or Prideaux or Rassam, but there are others – you can guess who I mean – who cannot hold out if this cat-and-mouse game continues.'

'The prisoners.'

'The former prisoners. For what are we all? But they, good God, they can't survive much more. The Rosanthals are in the best shape though God knows they have lost the most. Their boy died, you know, and she lost a baby, a little girl.' I looked quickly at Herr Waldmeier and saw that this was no news to him. 'They're buried at Meqdela.

Poor Stern goes on about the grave not being dug deep enough because he was chained. He's half out of his mind you know. Talks like the day of judgement. At breakfast too. A bit much some mornings.' The doctor sighed. I could see that his face was pleasant by nature and given to laughter when allowed, but at the moment it was oppressed. 'The Rosanthals had each other of course and some shred of privacy. But Cameron and Stern were in the common gaol, packed in with those poor savages. God, what they've been through! No one would blame them for being half sane, but it's trying, Waldmeier, trying. They go on at each other so. Some incident, a year old, about a stolen piece of bread.' It shows what they were reduced to. And Cameron drinks like a fish. For God's sake don't repeat this, but between you and me and the gatepost, which Miss Bell here does not in the least resemble,' and here he sent in my direction the quickest and pleasantest of smiles, 'Stern plies him with the local hydromel and swears it's the only thing that keeps him quiet. To be honest, I'm not sure I've ever seen him sober enough to judge. He's quiet enough in his cups but his health's all shot to pieces. They must all be got out of here, Waldmeier.'

'I cannot speak for the Emperor,' said Herr Waldmeier, 'but you must understand that he has entertained great dreams of what he will do in his lifetime. He suffers much bitterness of heart that his people will not share these dreams but are in constant revolt. He feels most isolated, and now indeed he faces rebellion on many sides. He has persuaded himself that Mr Rassam is a great man in your country, close to the Queen, whom she has sent to help and advise him in his perplexities. That is not so, is it, Dr Blanc? He is deceived in that?'

The doctor sighed and took off his helmet. He slapped

67

in turn at each of his pockets and drew out of one a red cloth with which he wiped his sweating face and then patted around the inside of his helmet. At last he said, 'Mr Rassam has a particularly fine set of teeth. It strikes me each time he happens to smile, how blessed he is in his teeth.' Herr Waldmeier looked at him in surprise, his face caught wondering what expression best to assume. The doctor went on, 'He's clever. He's very charming. He speaks Arabic. But although I've never seen the English gentleman better played, he's not, of course, an Englishman at all and he's no more a friend of the Queen's than I'm a monkey's uncle.'

Here I began to laugh helplessly, stuffing the edge of my shamma into my mouth and biting upon it to stop myself. It seemed I had never heard anything so funny as this Englishman who said he was a monkey's uncle. Dr Blanc broke off to show that he was pleased though a little surprised that I should laugh so.

Herr Waldmeier scowled at me impatiently and said, 'It does not matter who he is. What matters is who the Emperor thinks he is. At the moment the Emperor thinks Mr Rassam is the friend he lost in Mr Bell. If Mr Rassam would consent to stay awhile I believe the Emperor might consent to let the prisoners and the rest of your party go.'

'Then I should say we haven't a hope in hell. Begging your pardon, Miss Bell. My dear fellow,' he said suddenly, impulsively taking Herr Waldmeier's hand. 'It has been more pleasure than I can tell to talk with a sane and happy man. It lets in the sun, you know. I feel we have a friend in you that we may well need. If I can repay in any way—'

'My wife,' said Herr Waldmeier quickly. 'She has miscarried several times. She is not well. Her strength is gone. If you could spare the time—'

'Indeed, indeed,' said the doctor. 'We have been

68

promised a visit to see the guns. A veritable Woolwich Arsenal I hear you've made yourselves. I'll make a point of seeing her then, and do what I can.'

He said goodbye to us, shouldered his gun and lifted his birds out of the tree. Then he set of to Debra Tabor with the stiff hurried steps that are his normal way of walking.

A visit from the Emperor

Three days later the sky darkened at noon and there was a smell of rain in the air. As I came from the market with fruit for my sister I found I must pass through a crowd of people going up the hill, and could see those ahead of me turning into the yard of Herr Waldmeier's house. The kosso tree swayed as if the storm had already struck it. Heads poked here and there among the leaves. And what was it, I wondered, they so much wanted to see that they had braved their fears of Hagos who lay stretched across the roots?

In the space before the house people squatted quietly in the dust, so close together that their haunches rubbed. It seemed that all the sick of Gafat were there. I went past a child with wasted arms crooked stiffly across his belly, and a woman in a litter who stared out between the dirty curtains with eyes as dull as stones, and children with a sickness of the eyes that left glistening triangles on the cheeks to which hung many flies. I did not want these people to be where Rosa was.

I said crossly to the old man who begged outside the foundry, 'Why do you wait here? What do you want?' He came towards me on his hands, trailing behind his useless twisted legs. He said, 'We are waiting for the English hakim who will make us well.' Then I knew that Dr Blanc had kept his promise.

The wind rose cold. The leaves of the kosso tree

trembled and turned up their white bellies like dying things, and sharp and cold the first shafts of rain struck at them. The people in the yard rose to their feet, swiftly unwinding their shammas and sitting upon them to keep them dry. I ran into the house, going straight to the room in which my sister lay and forcing the shutter closed against the wind. Then I gave her the fruit. She lay in the bed listlessly, holding the fruit in one hand. 'May God return it to you,' she said.

When her voice was so frail, I wanted to speak sharply to her to hear her voice sharpen in return. I said less kindly than I might have, 'The people in the garden say the English hakim will come here to see you. Will you try to sit up?' I began to jerk the cover straight on the bed and she said nothing so that the rain sounded as loud as a stick rattled on the shutters.

At that moment the door to the room was flung open and there stood the servant girl stretching open her eyes and beckoning to me. I went to her, half-shutting the door behind my back.

'The Emperor is coming,' she said in a whisper. 'He wishes to entertain the Englishmen in Waldmeier's upper room. He will bring them here when they have seen the foundry. All that is necessary to drink, the Emperor will provide.'

'Where are the Englishmen?'

'They ride from Debra Tabor. First they go to the foundry, but they say the Emperor comes on ahead to see that everything is prepared.'

At some sound behind her she turned, let out a cry and prostrated herself upon the floor. I, too, turned and saw, breaking through the curtain of rain that fell from the edge of the balcony, the slight domineering figure of Tewodros.

Often as a child I have stood and not wanted to lower my staring from the Emperor's face and felt the quick pressure of a hand, my father's or Herr Waldmeier's, forcing me to bow. Now, awe of him like a hand inside me drew me down, that posture being the only true expression of what I felt: all that I have ever had has come from him.

'Up, up,' said the voice impatiently. 'Where is the room?'

On my feet, my spine hard to the wall, I pointed up the ladder. His face as he lifted it was thin and anxious, aged in the many months since I had seen him. I thought with fear: his hair is grey. Then as he went past me I saw that the plaits of his hair that fitted tightly along the line of his skull were still black but covered with tiny beads of rain.

Behind him came another man whom I knew to be the interpreter, Aito Samuel. The Emperor peered quickly into my sister's room and seeing her asked Samuel, 'There is a sick woman here?'

'Waldmeier's wife is sick.'

'Has she a sickness that might be passed to Aito Rassam?'

'She has miscarried.'

'Oh well, there is no danger then. Keep the door closed and say nothing.'

He climbed the ladder swiftly with Aito Samuel at his heels. The servant plucked at my shamma, rolling up her eyes in alarm, and handed me a rag and a buzzard's wing. I scowled at her, knowing that this meant she had not cleaned the room, for this room was seldom used, and empty except for the gold saddle which Herr Waldmeier sat upon to read his Bible.

The Emperor's head was now in the room and I heard him say, low and sad. 'I had been told that Waldmeier's room was large, and furnished in the European manner.

72

How can Aito Rassam be happy here with no furniture? He will think it very strange that we have only this primitive place in which to offer him hospitality. Why should this be so in all my kingdom?'

Aito Samuel craned to see past him from a lower rung of the ladder. 'There is no other room so large in Gafat,' he said respectfully. 'The saddle is very fine.'

'What can be done,' said Tewodros, 'to make it acceptable to such a man? What can be done?' Then answering himself in quite a different rapid vigorous voice he said, 'Go now, Samuel. Bring carpets. Bring all that is needed. Quickly, quickly. You must be here before Aito Rassam arrives?' Then running out on to the balcony he shouted down to his guard below, 'Send to delay Aito Rassam on the way. Tell Waldmeier to show him many things. Urge him to take shelter at the foundry during the rain.' Then seeing me standing with my buzzard's wing, he ordered, 'Sweep, sweep!'

I bowed my head and swept, in great concern lest he should be disgraced in the eyes of this Englishman through carelessness of mine. The Emperor followed me about the room, breathing harshly and peering in the dim green rain light to see that I had missed nothing. 'There, there, look there! It must all be very clean.' As soon as I had swept the dust into a pile he knelt lithely and scooped it up into his hands and running again to the balcony he threw the dust over it into the yard below, calling at the same time to the watchers in the kosso tree, 'Who comes? Who comes?'

With the third handful of dust there was shouting from the tree, 'Aito Samuel comes with carpets!' and after more shouting the rolled carpets were slid up the ladder into the room. Aito Samuel followed and began at once to drag one of the carpets across the floor.

73

'Leave them. Leave them,' said the Emperor at once. 'You, Samuel, must prepare refreshment; they may be thirsty. Who are you?' he said suddenly, turning to me and shaking his head as if he had forgotten where he was.

'Bell's child.' I had supposed that he knew who I was.

'You must help me with the carpets. Samuel, go. Everything must be in a state of preparedness. Here, he must feel among his own kind, entirely at his ease. Everything must be done to make him happy.'

Samuel hovered at the top of the ladder, unsure whether to go at once or hear him out. Step by step his head sank lower, still obligingly turned towards his master.

One by one, we unrolled the carpets and he directed each unhesitatingly to a particular part of the floor. Then he slid his bare feet over any wrinkled portions until they lay pieced together so neatly that no wood showed. Finally he placed the saddle at the end of the room.

Now he began to look pleased, saying to himself several times, 'That is well,' and to me, 'Is that not more how Aito Rassam would expect to find it?' I nodded, not knowing at all. He said at once, 'Now I can take pleasure in his coming.'

Almost as soon as he had said that there were shouts of 'They come! They come!' Tewodros did not go to the window but sat down on the saddle, eagerly watching the hole in the floor.

There were sounds of mules in the yard, shouting, footsteps crowding on the floor below. A man climbed up into the room and stood shaking off his wet cloak which Aito Samuel ran forward to catch. He smiled at the Emperor and, hastily taking off his hat, bowed to him. His brown hair was curled very tight and close to his head with the wet. His lips shone full and pink in his brown beard. His

74

teeth were very white. This without doubt was Mr Rassam. I could see by little lines that came and went as swift as needles about his eyes that he was tired and did not wish to smile but made himself do so.

Behind him came Dr Blanc, dressed now in the red costume of an English soldier, and at his side another soldier, a young man, who stood very straight and wore a single eyeglass fitted into the skin around his right eye. After them came Herr Flad and Herr Waldmeier so that the room seemed suddenly small and crowded.

The Emperor's smile was of the greatest sweetness. His eyes opened large with pleasure and all the time he was watching with a remainder of anxiety to see if this man, Mr Rassam, were pleased. 'This is a poor place, not at all how I would wish to receive you, but it will be more convenient for you to rest among your own people. I have palaces but they are all in a ruinous state and I am a poor man. Your Queen, I know, has many palaces.'

'No place could be more welcome,' said Mr Rassam, who, anyone could see, was indeed sweet-tongued and of an easy disposition. Now he shook his tiredness from him as he had his cloak and continued, 'By Your Majesty's kindness it has been so pleasantly arranged that it would be quite impossible to make it more comfortable.' He spoke in Arabic which Aito Samuel translated into Amharic.

'Are you in jest or earnest?' said Tewodros suspiciously.

'In complete earnest,' said Mr Rassam, turning for confirmation to his companions and they smiled quickly at his bidding.

'Sit, sit,' said the Emperor, finally reassured. 'You must not stand in my presence. Also your companions must sit down. Now we will drink together and you will enlighten me on many matters.'

75

The Englishmen parted the backs of their coats and lowered themselves onto the floor. Herr Flad and Herr Waldmeier remained standing.

'Let me say,' began Mr Rassam, 'how very impressed we have been by all that we have seen at the foundry.'

When Aito Samuel had finished translating, the Emperor smiled and nodded to him and Aito Samuel hurried to the top of the ladder and called down for drink to be brought. The ladder and the floor below had become so crowded with people hoping to hear what was said that it was impossible for the servants to bring the mead but eventually it was poured out below and passed up the ladder from hand to hand.

Mr Rassam, when offered the mead, smiled and shook his head. The Emperor, once his own drinking bottle was filled, continued closely to question Mr Rassam about a war that had recently taken place in Europe at a fortress called Sebastapol. 'What guns did the English use for the siege?' he asked.

'Cannon and mortars,' said Mr Rassam.

'How heavy?' asked the Emperor.

'Really, Sire,' said Mr Rassam holding up his hands with a helpless laugh, 'I am not a military man. I know nothing of these mysteries. Perhaps Prideaux here can make good my ignorance.'

The young soldier poked his neck forward out of his coat as a tortoise will and said, 'They used all sorts. I believe, sir, the 13-inch is their heaviest.'

'Did the English cast the guns there, where they were fighting?'

'No, Sire, they carried them there in their ships.'

'And the carriages and mules to drag them?'

'They brought the carriages and horses too,' said Mr Rassam, 'all in their ships.'

From where I stood by the ladder I could hear whispers from below: 'What do they say? What do they say?'

The man on the top of the ladder whose head was in the room called softly down, 'There are islands beyond this land, scattered on a great lake. On every island is a different tribe and much fighting between them. Aito Rassam says the English take their great guns and fire them at the people of another island, the Muscovites.'

'Where are these islands?'

'Beyond Jerusalem.'

'Then you are a fool. It is well known that beyond Jerusalem the sun never rises and the land is occupied by serpents only.'

'Are the islands close together?' whispered another voice.

'No, far, far apart.'

'Wider than the plain of Debra Tabor?'

'Then you are indeed a fool. The guns cannot throw their balls from one island to another. We have seen the extent of their passage.'

'Aito Rassam says the English carry their guns with them.'

'Over the water?'

'They row them in their boats.'

'Then it is he that is a fool for everyone knows that the boat would sink if a metal gun is put into it.'

The mead was drunk and now Aito Samuel pushed past me to the top of the stairs calling, 'Hush! Hush!' for the Emperor had begun again to speak.

'And the Muscovites have the same guns, or were the English guns more powerful?'

'So far as I know they had the same.'

'But fewer?'

'No, I believe they were very evenly matched. Am I not right, Prideaux?'

'Yes, sir,' and again Lieutenant Prideaux's neck extended from his collar and retreated rapidly back inside it.

'How is it, then, that they did not win?' said Tewodros in a wondering voice. 'How, with such a fortress, being at no disadvantage to the English in the matter of the mechanical arts, with no lack of courage, could this be, when God must undoubtedly have been on the side of the Muscovites?'

It seemed that the room was hollowed out of the rain, all human sounds drawn in and stifled, only the one low voice in which strange and frightening forces marched.

'For the Muscovites were the more Godly of the two. They fought the heathen Turks so that Christian monks could worship in freedom in Jerusalem. That was a true and Godly motive.'

The Emperor looked about him in the silence and Mr Rassam, with a look of weariness like a man who gathers himself after too brief a rest and forces himself to walk again, said, 'Your Majesty has made a deeper study of these matters than I have. However I believe they fought on many issues.'

'There is but one issue,' said Tewodros fervently. 'But the English and the French allied themselves with the Turk to fight another Christian power. This I cannot understand, Aito Rassam. Why did they not join together, the English Queen, the Emperor Napoleon and the Emperor Nicholas, with their guns and their well-dressed and disciplined soldiers and sweep the Turk from Jerusalem?'

Aito Samuel began to translate this, straining to get the words exact for the Emperor speaks more Arabic than he will admit, and his eyes moved from Aito Samuel's lips to Mr Rassam's face as intently as a cat will watch a swinging object, determined that the sense should in no way be

78

altered. Towards the end he grew so impatient that he broke in before Mr Rassam had a chance to reply.

'Since my youth I have had great admiration for all things English and in Mr Bell I had a faithful friend, but the Englishmen who have come to this country since he died have abused me and reviled me to my enemies. And can you, Mr Rassam, who profess to be my friend, can you say that you do not hate me?'

The effect of his words reached us while Mr Rassam still sat smiling and waiting for Aito Samuel to translate, which, with some faltering, he did, watching not Mr Rassam but the Emperor, in great agitation at the turn his thoughts had taken.

'That is not so, Sire,' Mr Rassam exclaimed in some alarm. Then tempering his voice he added, 'I hope I have always treated you with the friendship I sincerely feel and the respect due to your high rank.'

I became aware by the sounds on the ladder that the very people who had the moment before strained into the room were now attempting to retreat down the steps, whispering urgently to the people who blocked their way.

The Emperor sat twisting his hand on the pommel of the saddle, sucking in his lips as if he fed upon them and staring narrowly at Mr Rassam. 'Why then have you read Stern's book? Why is it that when I gave Consul Cameron a letter to your Queen he returned to Abyssinia without an answer? Why is it that you seek to leave my country? Why do the French and English allow the Turks to remain in Jerusalem when by right that holy city is the birthright of the Emperors of Abyssinia, my patrimony? Why will they not help me, who am poor and weak and utterly encircled with enemies, to regain it?'

'Sire,' said Mr Rassam patiently, 'we have spoken of this before, and I have explained that only when the former

79

prisoners and ourselves are free to return to our own country can our Queen show you the friendship she is so graciously willing to extend. Then we can tell her of what we have seen today at the foundry, of the great efforts you have expended on your reforms, of the skill of your army, of your own great personal qualities. If you would allow us to return and explain your needs in person to Her Majesty she might then be willing to forward you any assistance she can, to help you strengthen your position.'

'Why is it that you so desire to leave me?'

'I do not, Sire. I am only offering to bear your message.'

Tewodros watched him, shrewdly. 'Then, my friend, I shall write the message now to you, but someone else shall bear it to the Queen of England. In that way you can enjoy our winter here with us.'

Immediately he ordered Aito Samuel to produce paper and pencil and began to dictate.

From God's slave and His created being, the son of David, the son of Solomon, the King of Kings, Theodorus.

To my friend and counsellor, the servant of the Queen of England, Aito Hormuzd Rassam.

My desire is that you should send to Her Majesty, the Queen, and obtain for me a man who can make cannons and muskets and one who can smelt iron; also an instructor of artillery. I want these people to come here with their implements and everything necessary for their work and then they shall teach us and return. By the power of God, forward this my request to England.

He sat forward tensely on the edge of his saddle, looking from one face to another. 'And so,' he said, 'whom shall I send with this letter to England?'

When his eyes reached Herr Waldmeier I was afraid but, after considering, he smiled and said, 'No. Not you, my son. For where I go, you go, and where I stay, there

80

also you will stay.' Then I was easy in my mind, for what greater guarantee of safety did I know?

I listened without concern as he spoke softly to Mr Rassam about an interesting observation he had made. 'You know, my friend, I have noticed that you Europeans attach particular importance to your women and children, and that, wherever you are, all your wishes are directed to returning to them. And so I think that if I were to select Flad to go to England, whose wife has no family here to give her shelter and who is dependent upon me for the support of her children, that he, of all people, is most likely to return. Therefore it is Flad that I shall send.'

Poor Herr Flad turned as pale as bread, and I felt an unexpected pity for Rita Flad, playing somewhere by her house, unaware of what had happened to her.

His cleverness in singling out Herr Flad had quite restored the Emperor's good temper and he now rose lightly to his feet saying, 'Now we are refreshed and will return to Debra Tabor,' and he crossed the silent room and lowered himself down the empty ladder while the others hurried to follow him.

Dr Blanc was permitted to stay. He spent some time with my sister and then before he went out to the crowd of waiting sufferers he stood talking quietly to Herr Waldmeier by the door. 'But if these gunmakers were sent,' I heard him say, 'would they ever return? That's the question I'd like answered. Will any of us return? And if he intends to keep us here, what can he intend to do with us?'

An incident at the foundry

Three days later, Herr Flad set out for England. He was barefooted and dressed as an Abyssinian but the Englishmen had provided money so that when he reached Massawa at the foot of the mountains he might buy boots and clothes like theirs in which to appear before the Queen of England.

Frau Flad wept a great deal that he must go and leave her. Rita and Martin held handfuls of their mother's long skirt against their cheeks and stared round-eyed at their weeping mother and their departing father.

I pitied them and pitied anyone who wept, for my sister lay gravely ill. The army had brought the cholera to Debra Tabor and from there it had spread to Gafat. The old woman who ground our corn was taken with it and died. My sister's strength had not yet returned to her and she too became ill and Rosa and I must not see her and must not listen at the door.

The Emperor sent each day to enquire after her and allowed Dr Blanc to remain in the house attending to her.

On the day following Herr Flad's departure a message came to Dr Blanc saying that the Emperor would come at noon to inspect the foundry. The hakim was to attend him there.

Dr Blanc did not wish to leave my sister but Herr

Waldmeier urged him to go lest the Emperor be angry and recall him to Debra Tabor permanently. Frau Flad would come and sit with my sister, and as Rosa and I were not wanted in the house it was decided that we should go to the foundry with the doctor.

There was a stone wall around the foundry with a big wooden gate. A crowd of people stood in front of the gate waiting in the sun to see the Emperor. Holding Rosa on my hip I pressed among the hot clothes of the people after Dr Blanc and found when he stopped that I must stand beside Mr Rosanthal, the missionary whose children had died. At the sight of him I felt cold shame and would have hidden Rosa, heavy and healthy, as she rode my hip, but he turned his worn face smoothly past me. I was no one to him. He said to Herr Saalmuller, who stood beside him, 'No rain today.'

'No,' said Herr Saalmuller. 'But later maybe.'

Then came the trample of mules. The crowd parted and moved back. Over the heads in front of me a bright green umbrella swayed against the blue sky. Quickly I set Rosa down in the space between my feet and pressed down her head and bared my own and bowed and saw nothing then but dusty clothes and dusty feet.

'Tewodros, Tewodros,' whispered the voices, and one cried out, 'Justice, justice!' but the Emperor's voice only called sharp and cold for the hakim to come to him.

Dr Blanc pushed his way forward with his helmet held to his stomach and his head bent over his helmet. A moment later we heard the foundry gates close.

The crowd spread out again, talking and covering their heads from the sun. 'He wasted no time,' said Herr Saalmuller.

Mr Rosanthal shrugged. 'How long will we be?'

'No telling.'

83

'Can we go, do you think?'

'No. Safer to stay.' They leaned their heads idly towards each other as they spoke and then turned from each other when they were silent. The crowd thinned. We stood nearer the gate now. Rosa fretted and pulled at my clothing. The mules curled up their hooves restlessly. The grooms led them away to the shade of a tree. They left a wide space of sunlight dotted with steaming piles of dung between the two halves of the crowd and, as we idly watched, the old beggar man dragged himself slowly across it to take up his post by the gate.

He moved sideways, using the stump of one arm on which a thick pad of flesh had grown and the hand of the other to shift himself along while his withered legs jolted after him. All the time he held up his face, smiling and nodding pleasantly to the people he hoped would give him money.

Herr Saalmuller said to Mr Rosanthal, 'Watch this,' and threw a coin. The instant it flashed in the air the hand that was a leg flung up and caught it before it fell. Then the old beggar squinted at it and bit it and called out, 'God return it to you, my lord.'

There was smiling and laughter at this. People turned proudly to see Mr Rosanthal's reaction. The old man sat still, waiting for the next coin. He did his trick three times and then the coins stopped coming and he cursed softly and dragged himself past the piles of dung to his corner by the gate.

A moment later the gate opened. 'That was short,' muttered Herr Saalmuller. The Emperor stood with the faces of his followers grouped over his shoulder. His own face was set and very pale. We bared our heads again and bowed.

The old beggar shuffled forward to hold up the dusty

calloused hand. 'Oh my King!' he called. 'Have mercy upon me.' But Tewodros did not look at him. Instead he walked straight to where Mr Rosanthal stood. The soldiers followed, trotting in a close pack at his heels, and after them, shuffling painfully over the dust, came the beggar.

The Emperor stood in front of Mr Rosanthal, staring angrily at him, and we saw Mr Rosanthal's gaze falter and fall to the ground. Fear like the first stirring of a wind moved among the group of people. The Emperor said in a loud and angry voice, 'When I came past just now you did not bow or uncover your head. What do you mean by this?'

Mr Rosanthal said nothing. He seemed by his face to be confused and unable to remember what he had done. But he was silent too long. The Emperor had his spear in his hand and now he struck the butt of it on the ground and spat impatiently into the dust. 'Did you not see me?' he shouted.

'Yes, Your Majesty,' said Mr Rosanthal, stumbling and confused by fear. 'I saw you but I did not think that you had seen me. You did not look in my direction.'

'Who are you to stay covered in my presence?' Each time he spoke the anger was more violent and firmly established like a mounting fever. The spear shook in his hand. His face was ash-coloured.

Mr Rosanthal stood looking down at his feet. His lips moved in his beard but made no sound. Behind his back his hands clasped and released each other wretchedly. The sweat off his palms darkened the cuffs of his shirt.

It had taken the beggar this time to reach the Emperor's feet. He had not heard perhaps, or seen the change worked on the Emperor's face, and now there was a silence he began again, 'Oh King, have mercy on a poor cripple.' He

85

paused. Silence. 'My lords, the Europeans, have always been kind to me. Oh my King, do you also relieve my distress.'

Now Tewodros saw him. He swung slowly on his heels, crouching, raising the trembling spear. His teeth showed to the gums. His lips were quite lost in his face. A whiteness like milk lay in the corners of his mouth. There was a great silence now.

'How dare you,' and all his rage fell molten on the old man's head, 'call anyone *lord* but me.' And then, in a voice which sounded like a whisper grown so loud we all could hear, he said, 'Beat him. Beat him to death.'

Without hesitating, two soldiers rushed forward. Their long sticks flung like flails in the air above their heads and we heard them fall.

'Mercy!' the old man cried out in a voice full of terror and disbelief. He was out of sight in all the legs. No one moved. Again the sticks high in the air. 'Mercy!' Fainter. And again fainter. They stood away then. The old man's rags lay heaped in the sunlight.

I had no weight. Even where Rosa's body pressed against mine I had no feeling. It was only a minute. For no reason. His body ever less human, dead. The sunlight did not falter. Staring stupidly at the thing that lay there, no one dared move or pray.

The Emperor did not glance at it but took another step towards Mr Rosanthal. He shouted again, 'You donkey! Why did you call me the son of a poor woman in your writings to your country? Why did you abuse me? Seize him.' The soldiers dropped their sticks and running forward caught Mr Rosanthal by the arms and pinned them behind his back.

'Seize the man called the hakim.' And more soldiers threw themselves in an instant upon Dr Blanc and pushed him forward out of the crowd to where the servants waited with the mules.

Tewodros ran past them, vaulted into his saddle and shaking his spear over his head as if he might throw it, pointed it finally at Herr Saalmuller and at Monsieur Bourgaud and Herr Moritz who had by now come running out of the foundry.

'You slaves, have I not bought you with money?' he shouted to them. 'You are proud, are you? Slaves! Women! Rotten donkeys! Poor men that I have made rich. Who are you that you call yourselves lords? Take care.'

He rode rapidly out of the courtyard towards Debra Tabor. Some of the soldiers mounted hastily after him. A mule was found for Dr Blanc and when he had mounted it his hands were tied behind his back. Mr Rosanthal's hands were tied in front of him with a long leather thong and he was dragged along on foot. The body of the old man was left where it lay, and who it was that in the end dragged it away and dug it a grave I do not know.

For I began to run through the scattering crowd, carrying Rosa. A minute later I heard a heavy running behind me and Herr Saalmuller overtook me without speaking, so that I ran behind him, panting and slipping on the loose stones of the path.

But before either of us reached Herr Waldmeier's house we saw him running down the hill towards us. The sun was on his face and I saw that he was silently weeping. When he reached Herr Saalmuller he took both his hands and stood shaking his head with the tears shining on his face. So full were we of what we had just seen, we did not grasp that his grief had a different source to ours.

'My poor wife,' he said to Herr Saalmuller.

'She is not dead?'

'No. But so ill, Carl. So ill. I am going for Blanc. Paulina is with her.' He stepped aside, letting Herr Saalmuller's hands drop, and stared past us down the road. Then turning to me he said distractedly, 'She asks for Rosa, but Rosa must not see her.'

'Waldmeier,' said Herr Saalmuller. 'Something has happened. They have taken Blanc to Debra Tabor. He is a prisoner.'

'I must go to him.'

'But you cannot. Theo, don't you understand? The Emperor has taken him and Rosanthal prisoner.' And leading Herr Waldmeier to the side of the road he gently forced him to sit on a stone and told him what had happened.

When he had finished Herr Waldmeier said wearily, 'Then I must go to Debra Tabor and ask the Emperor to release him.'

'No, no,' said Herr Saalmuller. 'It is not safe to go near him. What if he were to shut you up, too? What would that achieve? No, Theo, you must not leave your wife.'

'I will go,' I said loud and quick before I could lose courage.

'No, no,' said Herr Saalmuller again. 'It is not safe. His anger was terrible, terrible.'

'I am not afraid of him.' But as soon as I had said this I wished that I had said nothing, and when I saw the effect of my words in the relieved and eager expression on Herr Saalmuller's face I knew that I had gone too far. Still I thought Herr Waldmeier would forbid it.

He did say, 'How can I send Louisa if it is not safe for me?' but his voice was weak and confused. Also he had not seen what we had seen and so Herr Saalmuller who prevailed upon him in no other thing managed to prevail upon him in this.

88

'She does not look like a European,' said Herr Saal-muller as if I were already out of earshot, 'so she will have a greater chance of coming close to him.' Indeed I thought I looked like no one but my sister, being either darker or lighter in skin than everyone else I had ever met, and at that thought hot tears swelled from my eyes. Herr Saal-muller disregarded this. He spoke coaxingly to Herr Waldmeier, guiding him back towards the house. 'Once she is close to the Emperor she can make known to him who she is. In that way she is one of Bell's children pleading for another. We need not come into it. For don't you see, it was we, almost as much as Rosanthal, that seemed to enrage him. It was *we* that poor old man called lords.'

As we approached the house Frau Flad ran out towards us calling, 'You are back so soon. Where is the doctor? Why have you come without him?'

'Dear lady,' said Herr Saalmuller, 'there has been a misunderstanding. Dr Blanc has gone to Debra Tabor with the Emperor.'

'Why did you not stop him?'

'Wait, wait, I shall tell you. This good devoted child is going now to fetch him back. Fetch the mule, child. Should not your groom go with her, Theo?'

I set down Rosa and going behind the house called out to the groom to saddle two mules and ride with me to see the Emperor. He must already have heard what had taken place because when he led the mules around to the front of the house he trembled so that he could scarcely fit the holes of the saddlecloth over the wooden pommels. The missionaries waited by the mules in the high sun, impart-ing to me, as I could see by their solemn faces, motives of courage and self-sacrifice entirely of their own imagining.

'Quickly now, quickly,' said Frau Flad, fastening her

freckled and determined hand about my wrist. Perhaps I trembled or moved forward less eagerly than she, for she turned and said in a surprised, denying voice, 'You are not afraid, Louisa?'

I said nothing, it being obvious that I was afraid.

'You love your sister, do you not?' And not waiting for an answer she went on in a brisk and comfortable voice, 'Perfect love casteth out fear.'

Herr Saalmuller laced his fingers together to help me into the saddle and as soon as I had mounted Frau Flad caught the mule's bridle and jangled it. 'We shall pray for you continually until you return.' Brightly her lips and spectacles beamed up at me. The mule jolted forward, and so I set out for Debra Tabor, with the groom also praying aloud on the mule behind me.

The treasury at Debra Tabor

Before we reached Debra Tabor the setting sun touched a mountain to the west, breaking its dark outline with radiance as if it had burnt down into the solid rock. The mule began to strain up the last part of the climb. I let go the bridle and leaning my weight forward took a handful of its stiff black mane, guiding it this way and that up the stoney track. The sun was gone. The mountain whole again and black. The air cooled. The shadows in the folds of the hills were very blue, the hills increasingly black and massive.

I thought: He will kill me when I speak. Just as he killed the old man. But, although I thought it, I was not capable of believing that he would do such a thing to me, and recited in my mind the many gifts and honours he had given both my father and Herr Waldmeier, all tokens of his love. Such things did not alter. And then I found I did not believe that he had killed the old man. Although I had stood there watching, I did not feel it to be true. I thought in my confusion that by seeing the Emperor again I might in some way prove it untrue. Then I thought more clearly that I was going to ask for Dr Blanc to be released to help my sister and I began to hear in my mind what I should say to the Emperor and so filled my mind again with fear.

When we reached Debra Tabor the groom said that he

would take the mules to the well. I said, 'Then I will go alone and come back to you at the well.'

He said with gratitude, 'God protect you. Mary smooth your way.'

If ever I came back to the well, I wondered if I should find him there. I began to climb past the soldiers' huts, past houses that pressed on either side of dirty narrow lanes. All the time the place called and pulled at me, for here, and here, and over there, I had been a child, but then it had all been living about me. Not as it was now: no shouting, no laughter from inside the houses. Through low doorways I could see groups of people sitting on the ground, the firelight on their faces, the darkened huts pressing on their backs. They spoke low and never looked out at me. Only dogs moved importantly about the dark lanes, noses working over the ground on business of their own. What men I passed, walked quickly by in silence, sheltering inside their clothing. So, although I had meant to ask where the hakim was, I did not, but continued walking up through the village towards the high conical roofs of the Emperor's houses and the squat black shape of his stone treasury at the top of the hill.

There was a bamboo fence around the Emperor's compound but the gate was open. No one guarded it or questioned my passing. Ahead, across a wide open yard, was the great circular house where the Emperor feasted. I saw the shape of the doorway filled with shaking firelight and dimly, on either side, a row of six or eight men waiting and watching for what I did not know but told myself it could not be for me. I walked across the yard towards the house, looking fixedly at the firelight.

There was silence in which my feet made no sound. Then very near to me I heard again and again a clear hard scratching and chipping, and turning my head I almost cried out. There, by the path, on a stone, sat a man turned deep in upon himself in thought, all the time jogging his spear up and down so that the butt dug into the base of the rock he sat on. It was the Emperor.

My feet, all weighted as in dreams, held me where I was and my voice trapped in my chest swelled and pained me until without thought I cried out, 'Justice! Justice!' as if I had come asking him to act as my judge in some litigation.

He did not turn his head. Only the shaft of the spear moved quickly up and down. And now I wanted to be near him and called again more loud and urgent, 'Justice, justice!'

My voice penetrated to him and he raised his head, looking startled this way and that as if suddenly wakened, until his eyes fastened upon me and he called out, 'Come.'

And now it was a relief to run and kneel so that the ground bruised my knees, and to lay my head on the dust by his feet so that I felt the little stones press against my forehead.

'Rise, rise,' he said, turning to spit onto the ground beside the rock. I was standing, fearfully searching his face in the falling light while he searched mine with sad eyes from which all raging was far gone. 'Who are you?' he asked.

'I am Bell's child.'

'Ah.' His head sank onto his chest and he began again to chip restlessly at the edge of the rock with his spear. I thought he had forgotten me. 'You are married to Wald-meier?' he asked suddenly and spat again on the ground but through no contempt. I could see by the way his throat worked that the spittle was rising again and again un-bidden in his mouth.

'No,' I said. 'I am the younger. It was I who swept out

the room.' But this I could see meant nothing to him.

'Why have you come?'

'My sister, Waldmeier's wife, has the cholera.' For the first time, as I spoke these words, I began to weep for my poor sister, so that I began to speak looking at him and speaking clearly and I ended with my eyes seeing nothing and my voice so choked as to be hardly heard.

'She is dying, Negus,' for now I knew this to be true. 'Waldmeier says: for the mercy of God let the hakim come to her.'

The Emperor reached out and with his empty hand took mine and pressed it. All the time I heard the spear scraping on the rock and, when finally I looked up, his eyes, too, were filled with tears.

'Poor Waldmeier,' he said. 'My poor son, my poor son,' and he spat again into the dust. I remembered then how he had wept when my father had read him the poem about the king mourning for his queen, and I knew that he remembered his own grief, and that he would help Herr Waldmeier.

He made no attempt to wipe his tears but bent his head and let them dry on his face. Then he shook his shoulders and drew up his head. 'Come,' he said. 'I have treated the hakim and my friend wrongly. The others I either hate or care nothing for, but as Aito Rassam is my friend we shall go now and make him happy.' The strength had risen in his voice as his hard thinking had suddenly produced so simple and pleasant a truth.

He raised his hand above his head and instantly one of the watchers started out from the shadows around the house and came running towards us. I saw that he was no servant but the interpreter, Aito Samuel. I saw, too, from his eyes protruding and being ringed in white, that he was in great fear, searching out the Emperor's humour in his face as he ran, and flinging himself on his knees as I had done.

'Up, up, Samuel. You must write and take this letter to Mr Rassam in the treasury.' The Emperor rose himself from the rock and began striding impatiently up and down while Samuel crouched back on his heels and fumbled in his shamma for pencil and paper.

The Emperor dictated: *From Theodorus, King of Kings, the servant and creature of God, to his friend Hormuzd Rassam.* Here he broke off, waiting for Samuel to finish.

Why, I thought, is Mr Rassam housed in the treasury? Why does he send a written message to the treasury when it is only a few paces from where we stand? Why does he not go and say what he wishes to say to Mr Rassam? Then I remembered that there were no windows in the treasury. In my mind Mr Rassam again raised his hat and smiled, blessed in his teeth. I saw him shake off the wet cloak and force himself to talk pleasantly. It could not be that the treasury could be made a house fit for Mr Rassam to stay in. This however was a small part of my anxiety for I could now see that the Emperor had forgotten all about the doctor and thought only of Mr Rassam.

He continued dictating as if it were Mr Rassam and not Samuel before him. His voice was full of feeling, his hands lifted as if he argued with someone he loved. *I only want you to be happy. How could I go to sleep knowing you are unhappy, my friend? So I must come and cheer you up. I only await your permission to do so.* He stopped and spat again.

'That is all, Negus?'

'That is all. Quickly, quickly take it to Aito Rassam.' Aito Samuel sprang to his feet and he did indeed run in the direction of the treasury.

Now the Emperor turned towards his house and shouted for candles and arrack and mead. Servants came running with these provisions. The Emperor took the horn of arrack, slung it over his own shoulder and strode off towards the treasury. I was given the tapers, and two of the servants followed, one with the jar of mead and the other with a bunch of drinking bottles tied together by their necks and clanking as he ran.

It was dark now, the stone treasury only a square black shape. The guards had built a fire below the veranda that surrounded it. They sprang up stiffly as they saw the Emperor approach. He called out to them, 'Open the door,' and climbed onto the veranda.

'No, Negus,' said Aito Samuel. 'Do not go in there. Say who it is to whom you would speak. I will bring him out here to you.'

'Open the door,' the Emperor said again and the guard threw his weight against the heavy wooden bolt and slid it back. The door swung outwards, drawing with it the stored heat of the day and a stale sour smell that was unmistakably human. So, I thought, people are kept in this place.

The dark narrow passage opened almost at once into a room. Here a single candle had flickered somewhere near the floor. But at the Emperor's name there was a sound of shuffling and people struggling to rise and the candle fell and went out.

Now voices began to cry out and above them all the Emperor's voice calling, 'Light, light!' The tapers were snatched from my hand. The Emperor ran past me, lit one in the fire and was back in the room, holding it above his head. Flames began to spring up here and there in the dark space. I stayed by the entrance where the air was

96

fresher, understanding now, against belief, what I should see.

All the faces were the same. Hair, beards and clothes, all that made one distinct from another, were lost in the darkness and nothing left but pale repeated masks pierced with eyes in which the candle flames were emptily reflected. It seemed their souls were lost to them.

But as I stared and the Emperor lit more tapers this evil fancy left and I saw one after the other, Mr Rassam, Dr Blanc, Lieutenant Prideaux, Consul Cameron, Mr Stern, and Mr Rosanthal, but all so shrunken from what they had been that I wondered if the doctor were released whether his skills would be left to him. They stood pressed together while the Emperor settled himself on a bench which the guards had dragged in from the veranda.

He lowered the horn of arrack from his shoulder and pouring some into a bottle held it out to Mr Rassam saying in a pleasant voice, 'I know you do not usually drink but I feel sure that you will not refuse to drink on this occasion to make me feel happy.'

Mr Rassam, as if given back his pleasing voice and soul and boots and long English coat, stepped forward, bowed, and thanked the Emperor politely and when Tewodros had poured for himself they toasted each other and then they toasted Queen Victoria.

'Come, come,' said the Emperor, impatient that the happiness he had requested had not been produced. 'Come. Hakim and the soldier must drink with me, too. Come, come,' and he turned towards them his smile of particular warmth and charm. They, too, must irresistibly smile, not out of pretence but because they had no power to fight his demand that they be pleased. Ignoring the others, he poured arrack into two more bottles and

97

gave them to Mr Rassam's friends, so that they, too, came partially to life again.

Dr Blanc, as he stepped back with his bottle, saw me and looked puzzled and then eager, thinking perhaps that the Gafat people must also be with me and that help might be at hand. Then my face must have told him that I had not come offering help but asking what he was now powerless to give. I could do nothing but lean against the doorway and wait.

I thought of Herr Waldmeier waiting minute by minute, and the long time there might be before we set out for Gafat, if indeed we did, for the sad and gentle mood that made me think the Emperor would release the doctor was fading in his vigorous efforts to make Mr Rassam happy.

'Why do you stand?' he urged. 'Sit, sit.'

Immediately there was a shuffling and a wavering of the candles as the crowded air shifted and everyone sat on the floor. They moved cautiously, glancing at one another. Even though he had spoken, they could not be sure that this was a safe course of action.

Only Mr Stern remained standing. With his arm leaning against the wall and his head buried against it, he began to pray under his breath but loud enough so that we all could hear what he was doing.

'Shut up, Stern. Sit when a gentleman asks you,' said the Consul Cameron, rather loud, in English, and I saw Dr Blanc shake the consul by the arm and low out of sight pass on to him his bottle of arrack.

'How are you, Stern?' called out the Emperor cheerfully. 'Why are you standing and always in such a miserable mood? Sit, sit.' And turning to Mr Rassam, he said with a happy intimate laugh, 'Think of some way to comfort Mr Stern so that he does not moan so.'

He offered Mr Rassam the arrack again and when that gentleman smiled and refused, he filled his own bottle and began to drink it quickly, all his attention now taken up with his pleasure at being in Mr Rassam's company.

'Do not regard my face,' he said to him, reaching out and laying a hand on his arm, 'but trust to my heart, because I really love you. It is true that I have behaved wrongly to all of you this afternoon, but I have an object in what I do.' Here he broke off and looked vaguely at the group of staring faces as if for a moment he had forgotten what that object might be. Then he quickly drank from the bottle again and said in a low significant voice to Mr Rassam, 'Because there were people watching I had to appear angry.' He paused to drink again. 'Oh, my friend Rassam, how can it be that I have treated you so ill? I tell you this. I have in my time killed hundreds of people but I have never had a feeling of remorse for their death, because I knew I was doing the will of my Creator in punishing them as they deserved. But with regard to yourself I feel that I have done you wrong and my conscience has suffered ever since.'

The breathing in the room was low and stifled. Even Mr Stern was quiet now for it seemed that the Emperor struggled inside himself with the desire to release them.

Until now all his efforts had been to gain a response from Mr Rassam, but now he seemed to forget the existence of the group of men staring so closely and desperately up at him, and they, as soon as he forgot them, seemed to fade again to indistinction as if one by one the candles were going out. Although Aito Samuel had no choice but to continue translating, the Emperor spoke aloud to himself, considering the words slowly as if they were still in his mind. 'I used to hear that I was called a madman for my acts but I never believed it. Now, after the way that I

99

have treated my friend this afternoon, I think perhaps I really am.'

Mr Rassam cried out, 'Pray do not say such a thing.'

'Yes, yes,' he repeated sadly. 'I am mad.' He got to his feet and absently shouldering the horn of arrack, looked slowly about the room. 'But as fellow Christians we should love and forgive one another. Is that not so?' Then straightening himself he walked suddenly out of the room.

The door remained open but no one attempted to move towards it for this room was only an inner chamber of their imprisonment. The Emperor's will, the nature of the mountains, the rain which could now be heard beating against the walls of the treasury, all held them captive beyond hope and I, too, out of hopelessness remained where I was, never considering that at any minute the door might be closed upon me.

But that did not happen. Instead Aito Samuel returned running and called out, 'The hakim must come.'

Dr Blanc turned in great agitation to Mr Rassam saying, 'Ask him where he is taking me. What will happen to the rest of you? I cannot leave you.'

'Come, come,' said Aito Samuel urgently. 'Before his mind changes. Some other place will be found for them. Tomorrow the army will leave and you will leave with it, but tonight you are to go to Waldmeier's wife.'

I ran forward then and took the doctor's hand to pull him to the door, and Mr Rassam said, 'For God's sake go. It may be the means of delay or of winning back his favour if you save the poor woman.'

'Very well,' said the doctor quietly. 'God knows when and where I shall see you,' and he came with me outside the treasury and the door was closed behind us.

A mule was waiting for the doctor. The groom waited with my mule by the well and together we set out in the rain and the dark, riding as quickly as we dared along the steep track to Gafat.

Our haste was of no use. My sister was dead when we reached Gafat. And as soon as the dawn broke the soldiers came to the house and took Dr Blanc again to Debra Tabor. From there a few days later he and all the English prisoners were sent to the Emperor's fortress at Meqdela.

'There is no God in Abyssinia'

I wept for myself and not for my sister, nor did I think at all of what might become of those poor Englishmen.

I wept for fear that they would take me away from Herr Waldmeier, and at the same time I turned away from him and from Rosa and hid myself in my room and feared the sound of every footstep lest it be someone come to take me from him, and so I continued until I thought: who bakes the bread?

No one but I was to feed him. Frau Flad was not to enter our house as other than our guest. I got up and dressed cleanly and going quietly to the empty kitchen I washed my face and began to grind corn. I rocked to and fro on my knees, rubbing the corn until the stones rang hollow against each other. Then I ground more corn. Only when my arms ached and the sweat ran down my breasts did I feel any kind of comfort.

When the bread was baked I took it to Herr Waldmeier. A bed had been moved for him into the upper room. There he lay exhausted, trying to sleep with Rosa climbing on him and picking up his eyelids to see where he hid from her. I thought: how dirty she is.

When I had made them eat I brought water and told Herr Waldmeier to wash in a harsh old voice that seemed no part of me. I picked up Rosa and stood her naked in the yard and scrubbed her all over and rubbed her fiercely dry. Then I unplaited and plaited all her hair close and tight to her head so that she cried, but she cried at least for a simple pain that would come to an end.

When she was all clean and quieted I felt that I had made her over into something of my own and she felt so too, and walked all day with her hand knotted in my clothes and I must walk always as slow as she. But this I did not mind for I thought: the harder that Rosa clings to me the more necessary I become, and the harder it will be for Herr Waldmeier to send me away.

The day of the burial came and with it my mother and her family, more unfamiliar now than strangers. They wept and flapped their garments and went away again with nothing said. Each day I thought: he will forget that I am nothing to him. He will grow so used to having me here that he will forget to send me away. But of this I could never be entirely sure. I felt that anything I neglected would be taken from me. The days were numbed with working.

All around there was great sadness. The epidemic continued and many people died. People lay dead by the side of the road and no one came to search for them. Every day, going slowly with Rosa to buy food, we would pass processions of mourners. There was a smell of death when the sun was at its height. There was too much death to feel.

They said, 'The cholera will go when the rains are over,' but Mascal came and went and nothing changed. Herr Waldmeier worked at the foundry making gun carriages for the Emperor to take into Gojam on his next campaign against the rebels. In the house he read constantly, committing portions of the Bible to heart and seldom speaking. He took into himself all sorrows. He mourned every body he saw and could pray and weep for each one, but I shrank

103

away from other sorrows and worked and worked to keep the house and kept Rosa close, and watched his sad face for any sign of what might become of me.

At that time Herr Waldmeier made me learn by heart the King's song in the Book of Ecclesiastes which begins, *Remember thou thy Creator in the days of thy youth*, and to please him I learnt it in a day. At first I thought: life is not so bad as this poem says it is. He makes me learn it because I am young and he is growing old.

But when after the rains the troubles remained and intensified I walked through Gafat slowly, leading Rosa and saying these words inside my head:

And the doors shall be shut in the streets, when the sound of the grinding is low, and he shall rise up at the voice of the bird, and all the daughters of music shall be brought low;

Also when they shall be afraid of that which is high, and fears shall be in the way, and the almond tree shall flourish and the grasshopper shall be a burden, and desire shall fail: because man goeth to his long home, and the mourners go about the streets.

For I noticed now how many of the doors were kept covered with cow hides and the sound of grinding muffled inside them. And indeed there was no singing to be heard, only the sound of lamentation as the mourners went about the streets. It seemed that the great king, Solomon, had prophesied what was happening even now in Gafat.

And more and more I said in my head: *When they shall be afraid of that which is high, and fears shall be in the way*, for not all the deaths at that time came from the cholera. Tewodros executed many of the Galla prisoners he held at Debra Tabor and left many to starve even to death. The people who had come to the mission no longer came, fearing the hatred he had begun to show for

104

Europeans. Now all news was of what the Emperor had said and of what he had done. Even when at last the cholera weakened and left us, the cloud of fear remained.

When the rains were over the Emperor had not taken the guns to Gojam as he had planned. For the first time he left the rebel, Tedla Gwalu, unchallenged and stayed on in Debra Tabor through September, October and November.

The loyal chiefs of this district of Begemeder, where Debra Tabor lies, had paid their year's tribute of three hundred thousand dollars and supported the Emperor's camp throughout the rainy season with grain and cows. Now they must find more grain and cows to support him through the months of the campaigning season as well. His army then numbered thirty thousand fighting men as well as their dependents, and daily the people prayed that he would lead this army into Gojam and feed it on what they plundered from the rebels.

But the Emperor delayed, riding each day to the foundry at Gafat and saying that he would not go until more mortars were cast and more carriages made. Herr Waldmeier said that the true reason was that he dared not take the guns out of Begemeder which was now the last province to remain loyal to him in all the land and so he delayed, feeding his army on the remnants of that loyalty.

He forced the chiefs to pay their tribute in advance, promising that soon he would move and stay away a long time, and they struggled to meet his demands, but all they could provide was not enough.

Then word reached Gafat at the end of November of signs in the camp that the army was preparing an attack. On the first evening in December, hearing the sound of many horses, we ran out of the house, looking towards the road from Debra Tabor. Herr Waldmeier with his small

German Bible in his hand for it was his time of the evening to read, Herr Saalmuller with his sleeves rolled up and fresh lather withering on his wet arms, Herr Moritz clutching the neck of a drinking-bottle, stood together watching down the road.

A crowd gathered. The women gave their shrill *Lil lil li* to wish the army victory and as well to express joy at their departure. All the dogs in Gafat barked.

But it was not the entire army, only a large troop of horsemen riding furiously to the north. The beat of the hooves and the faint chinking of harness were the only sound they made, and they rode without the flicker of a torch in the rapid-falling darkness.

The sight of that swift and violent purpose, after so many months of inactivity, excited people and left the paths between the huts in Gafat crowded and restless. Herr Waldmeier turned back to his house, and Herr Moritz and Herr Saalmuller, without being asked, fell in behind him and followed him up to his room. I came and stood by the top of the ladder to see if I were needed to wait upon them.

'Ach, it is too warm to stay inside,' said Herr Moritz. 'Will this balcony hold me, Waldmeier?'

'Of course, of course.' He moved irritably about the room, opening and shutting the Bible in his hand, shifting the saddle away from the door. I knew he did not wish to waste the remaining daylight in talking, and that he wished they would leave him. Nevertheless he leant in the doorway while they settled themselves on the planks of the balcony and began to pass the arrack bottle back and forth.

'None of us can make arrack like you, Moritz,' said Herr Saalmuller. 'I will get your secret from you someday. It is superb, is it not, Theo?'

Herr Waldmeier grunted, his mind elsewhere, and

passed the flask on without drinking. I sat quietly down on the floor where I might hear them but my mind was still full of the soldiers riding in haste and secrecy through the dark night. For always Tewodros led his army faster than men believed possible and struck where they did not expect him. The soldiers were in their minds, too, for Herr Saalmuller now said, 'Well, where is he off to?'

'Gondar. Where else?' said Herr Moritz.

I thought of the soldiers riding just after dawn through the gates of that unsuspecting city. The fat Moslem merchants lie in bed and feel their houses shake, and hear them clatter past, and tremble. For Gondar is the richest city in the land and Tewodros hates it. There, are the ruined palaces he spoke of to Mr Rassam. Once the Emperors of Abyssinia lived in them, sealed away from their people as the sacred Ark is kept hidden in the churches. Now it is the trading centre for the Moslems who come up the dry river valleys from the coast with their mules loaded with muslins and calico and velvet and beads and spices.

'It must be Gondar,' said Herr Moritz wisely, although no one had contradicted him. 'If it saves us from starving, I'll drink to success. I'm all belly, you see,' – raising his voice he looked sideways up at Herr Waldmeier to see what effect it was having – 'and do not trouble my conscience much as to how I fill it.'

'He has wrung the Moslem merchants there time and time again. They've nothing left,' said Herr Waldmeier quietly.

Herr Moritz said, 'There are forty-four churches in Gondar ripe for picking.' He looked slyly over his bottle. 'How would you feel about our Christian master if he took to desecrating churches?'

'He would not do that,' said Herr Waldmeier in such a

tone that everyone could know at once it was exactly what he feared.

'Waldmeier, you are a child,' said Herr Moritz, wiping his lips impatiently. 'He hates the priests. He would bleed them to death without a qualm.'

'He does not hate God,' said Herr Waldmeier looking earnestly down at him. 'He would not desecrate His house.'

Then Herr Saalmuller who had been nervously rolling and unrolling his damp sleeves, made this statement: 'I cannot believe, Theo, that you, even allowing for your sympathy with these people, could equate these trumpery storehouses of a superstitious and ignorant priesthood with the true house of God. God's house is in the pure and blameless mind as Christ has revealed to us by the cleansing of the temple. These so-called churches are mere temptations to avarice and so we shall pray – those of us who do pray –' (this to Herr Moritz) 'that it is enlightenment that turns him against the churches.' Now he was on his feet speaking only to Herr Waldmeier. 'Thus the young Hezekiah to protect Jerusalem from the Assyrian cut off the gold from the doors and doorposts of the temple of the Lord and yet he remained strong in the favour of the Lord.'

Herr Waldmeier merely stood back to let him pass and Herr Moritz, too, rose to his feet and came into the room. 'He will lose everything if he does that,' said Herr Waldmeier.

'Ach, Theo, you brood too much on every little thing. You should marry again. Come away, Moritz. He does not want us.'

'No, that is not true,' he called down the ladder after them.

'Of course, of course. But you brood. It is a sad time
108

for everyone. You must not brood, Theo.'

They had gone. The quiet room absorbed the gaps they had left. It was pleasant now. I said, 'Shall I bring you food?'

'No, no,' he said. 'I shall finish my reading.'

'It is too dark for you to read.'

'I can see.' Nevertheless I went to the shelf and lit the lantern and stood beside him holding the lantern so that its shape of light slanted over his page. He smiled at me and then said, 'You will tire your arm. Put it on the floor.'

I set the lantern down beside him and went again and sat quietly, away from the light, knowing that if I made no sound he would not think to send me away. He continued to stare down at the words but he never turned the page. After a while he closed the book and laid it on the floor and blew out the lantern. At first the room seemed dark but then the light from the window asserted itself again. I could see his face and he was talking to me. So I sat watching the light fail on the wall and Herr Waldmeier's lips move in his beard and heard him say, 'If he does indeed do this thing, he is ruined. Until now I could believe – did I not believe, Louisa ...'

See, it is to me that he speaks. He appeals to me as if I were involved in his beliefs. His servant, his child who is not his child, his sister whose blood is so apparently different from his own, he is saying to me, 'Did I not believe, Louisa, that he, at least, believed himself to be a great Christianising and enlightening force in this land, and that all this sad cloud that has fallen upon him was merely bitterness of heart that his people would not support him in his great enterprise? So Saul ...'

His beard has many variations of colour. It is lighter and more golden around his mouth. The hair on his cheeks is thin and curling but I can see how hard is the bone and

109

how rapid and feeling is the flesh above it as he speaks of Saul.

Happiness is in the room as stray as a wind, having no part at all in what he is saying. He leans forward on the saddle, speaking earnestly as if my understanding is of importance. His big hands are held out clasped before him and I know by the whitened weaving of his fingers that all is earnest and important and serious. I cannot help but smile and he will see and think I am not listening to what he is saying. '... and if he does this thing my position here becomes a mockery. Then I shall do what I do merely to keep alive, to curry favour. I will no longer serve God at all and you, Louisa, must not stay with me. You must return to your mother's village before I lose his favour.'

I heard these words that I had been afraid of. I watched them shape and leave his lips but they seemed never to reach or touch me. The happiness drifted undisturbed in the room. And now I realised that he was not speaking but staring at me, waiting for his reply. All expression was smoothed from his face by the loss of light. I thought if I lit the lantern now, how dark the room would seem. 'I will not go,' I said.

'Louisa, it would be wrong of me to keep you. It may soon no longer be safe to be associated with me.'

I was aware that the pleading accents in his voice pleaded against these words, not with them, and that he did not know this and that I scarcely understood. So there was a troubled quality in this happiness and it must be dispelled.

I stood up and took the lantern and went with it to the shelf. With my back to him I lit it. Then I said calmly and in many ways deceitfully although the words themselves were both truthful and correct, 'I stay for Rosa's sake. My sister would have it so. Also my mother. When you
110

marry again I shall return to my mother's village. Until then, I stay with Rosa.'

Herr Waldmeier, blinking and uneasy in the light, passed his hands over his face. 'Then we must both pray that the Emperor has restrained himself from doing this thing.'

Two nights later the horsemen rode back, their torches blazing from a long distance and their progress much slowed by the mules they brought with them, laden with what they had plundered.

The Europeans in Gafat, in order to be seen to greet the Emperor and rejoice at his victory, ran out along the road waving torches and shouting 'Hezekiah, Hezekiah!' But Herr Waldmeier would not join them and kept me in the house with him and made me pray that God would forgive the Emperor. For messengers riding ahead of the main force had spread the word that Tewodros had burnt above forty churches and thrown the priests into the flames to die. The women who had ululated at his arrival, thinking to please him, he had accused of betraying the secrecy of his attack and they, too, were thrown into the agony of the flames.

And then we must pray for ourselves and for all the Gafat people and ask forgiveness for our cowardice, for it was out of fear of their lives that they had called him Hezekiah.

I feared the Emperor would have noticed that Herr Waldmeier was not among them. When a messenger came from Tewodros ordering Herr Waldmeier to the foundry he dared not refuse but went at once, shutting Rosa and me into the house. Later he told me how the Emperor came to the foundry and had emptied on the floor skinfuls of thick silver dollars and bells and crosses and silver and brass vessels: all the treasure of the churches of Gondar. How the large dark pupils of Tewodros' eyes were entirely ringed with white, and so bloodshot that he could imagine the sacrilegious flames still reflected in them, and how the gold and silver shone in the torchlight, and how the Emperor shouted in a voice so hoarse that it was scarcely human, 'Burn it in your fire, Waldmeier! Make it into a gun.'

From that day the Emperor's cause was lost. All things turned against him and men said openly, 'There is no God in Abyssinia if he allows Tewodros to live after burning churches and keeping in prison the messengers of a friendly Queen.'

Captivity

At first it seemed, when we knew of the extent of the sacking of Gondar, that something immediate and terrible must happen in our lives to match it, but very soon I could believe again that our lives would continue as they always had. The work on the gun-carriages continued at the foundry and Herr Waldmeier worked there from morning until the light failed. When he had eaten he went alone to the upper room and read by the lamp, for by a silent agreement I did not go with him into that room nor did he ask me again to leave him. And so our lives passed for several months without my knowing fear that anything would change.

One afternoon – it was the 13th of April – I sat in the patch of sunlight that the window made in the room I shared with Rosa. She sat between my knees and with a pin I separated thin lines of her stiff coppery hair and worked them into plaits close to her head. Herr Waldmeier sat beside us and read from the Bible about Daniel not being eaten by the lions. This is Rosa's favourite story. She likes to think how she would befriend the lions and go to sleep along their warm backs with her head on their manes. Herr Waldmeier read it to keep her still and thoughtful, as it takes a long time to plait her hair and she becomes restless and twists her head and the long pin I use might hurt her.

Outside, Hagos growled over his latest goat and fumbled its torn head between his great paws. We sat in the house because we did not like to see him eat the goat and because for some reason he disliked it very much if we should look at him while he ate.

Herr Waldmeier said that as long as a goat was brought each day and Hagos left with us we need have no fear that he had lost favour with the Emperor. So the sound of the lion's growling seemed a surety for another day as well as adding reality to the story.

I finished one plait at the nape of Rosa's neck. I felt her shiver with pleasure as I slid the pin between the tangled hair at her forehead and began to work another parting. I looked up with her hair twisted in my fingers and saw through the window soldiers running up the yard to the door of the house. They seemed to be repeating actions that I had seen in my mind again and again.

A man stood blocking the door and read down to us from a paper, as I seemed to know that he would, this message from the Emperor: *From Theodorus, King of Kings, to his paid servant Waldmeier. I have heard that the Europeans in Gafat are in correspondence with England, therefore you are prisoners.*

When he had finished the message, he raised his musket and pointed it at Herr Waldmeier. He had a heavy cruel face. Then he stood back and swinging the muzzle around he aimed carefully and shot Hagos through the head.

I stood at the window. I had jerked my hand free from Rosa's hair for she had cried out. Hagos whimpered like a small animal and then lay still on his side in a way that no living animal would have slept.

Rosa was screaming, 'Papa, Papa!'

Herr Waldmeier was bent over, his arms hooked behind him by their arms. They dragged him out of the room and held him in the yard, tied with his arms behind him by leather thongs. Rosa ran after him, clamouring and dragging at his clothes but he could not lift her or hide her face against him to prevent her seeing Hagos lying with the flies already crawling on his muzzle and the goat's head still caught in his limp paws.

I ran in and out of the house. I ran to where Herr Waldmeier stood and hid Rosa's head under the hem of his shamma and made her fasten her arms tight about his legs.

I ran into the house, although Herr Waldmeier shouted at me to stay beside him, and in the doorway I met a soldier coming out with a pile of books and he pushed me aside so that I fell and bruised my shoulder, which then I did not feel at all. In spite of Herr Waldmeier's shouts, I ran into the house, fighting my way between the soldiers, and ran into my room and took the cloak in which years ago I had arrived in Gafat, and from there I ran to the kitchen.

The soldiers had not yet come to the kitchen. I ripped the lining of the cloak and turned it inside out so that the rich part did not show. Then I began to fill the space between the cloak and the lining with grain from a jar. Again and again I dug my hands down into grain and emptied them into the cloak. Then I rolled it like a sack and dragged it back through the house, between the soldiers' legs, and outside, and put it down by Herr Waldmeier. And then I ran back and all the time he was shouting at me, but his hands were tied. He could not stop me. I was still in the yard; I did not know what to do. I thought about the golden saddle. I had no intention towards it, only it suddenly filled my mind entirely in all its parts. The pattern of the gold work and the tassels of monkey fur were all very clear to me. I began to run to where it was, pushing my way between the soldiers, and again no one stopped me. I climbed the ladder.

Herr Waldmeier's room was empty and undisturbed. That surprised me and made me stand still. The saddle stood by the door of the balcony with the box of sunlight falling half over it. It irritated me that the saddle did not fit exactly into the shape of the sunlight. I looked at the glittering parts of the saddle and knew that I hated it.

I began to drag and push it through the door. Then, levering it against the wall of the balcony, wedging my knees under it, I pulled it upwards with my arms and when with great effort I had raised it onto the highest rail, I toppled it over. It fell out of sight making a great thud onto the ground. A voice screamed with pain. I stepped back into the room and went and stood by the ladder, winding my shamma which had become torn, around my head.

I heard angry voices and three soldiers came up the ladder and ran past me, crowding each other to get out onto the balcony. They shouted to the people below who shouted up to them. I climbed down the ladder and walked out of the house past the soldier who lay moaning on the ground, past the hated saddle, past Hagos at whom I would not look, and went and stood beside Herr Waldmeier without a word.

I stood beside him and trembled, not because I was afraid but out of anger and tiredness, and he leant down and whispered urgently, 'Run Louisa, run. Before they see you with me. Run now, while you can.'

Without looking at him I knelt down on the folded cloak which still lay at his feet. I buried my head behind Rosa's small neck and held with my arms around her sobbing body and Herr Waldmeier's hard leg until the trembling ceased. Then I stood and leant against him and
116

when he said, 'Why will you not go?' I would not answer.

We waited there a long time. The yard was littered with things which had been ours but now seemed valueless, strewn about in the sunlight. My sister's clothes I once had envied. Herr Waldmeier's books, flung open on the ground, flapped their leaves over and over. The man who had shot Hagos has sent for his servants to skin him, and as they set about their work three vultures flew heavily down and hunched themselves in the kosso tree, waiting until their feast were left to them.

More soldiers brought Madame Bourgaud into our yard, red in the face with anger and driving her three larger children before her as if they were the cause of all the trouble. Each one was brushed and dressed and carried a neat bundle. Monsieur Bourgaud walked behind her, looking shrunken with fear and carrying the two smaller children. Madame, who turned repeatedly to tell him to hurry or to adjust the babies, carried over her arm a large basket covered with a clean cloth. She said to Herr Waldmeier, 'Why were we not told sooner that this would happen?'

Then came Frau Flad in a fainting condition supported on each arm by Herr Saalmuller and Herr Moritz, who also each dragged in their hands a large sack of the Flads' possessions. Rita and Martin followed, white and scared, more at the condition of their mother than through any understanding of what had befallen them.

Frau Flad's front hair had fallen loose and wisps of it were stuck to her wet face. Her spectacles were unsettled on her nose which gave a drunken appearance. As she was helped past Herr Waldmeier she suddenly cried out, 'I am utterly defenceless. Who will answer to Herr Flad for this?'

When the soldiers wrenched the sacks from Herr Saal-

muller and Herr Moritz and emptied on top of our possessions silver-mounted daggers and pistols and shields and
silks as well as a great many dollars, she burst into uncontrollable tears. Herr Moritz, against whose shoulder she
had elected to weep, managed to settle her upon a stone
and so release himself, while Rita and Martin tugged and
patted anxiously at her hands and cheeks.

Now came Frau Moritz and Frau Saalmuller, struggling along with their own bundles, and Mrs Rosanthal
who alone of all these seemed composed and quite indifferent as to what might happen to her.

'What does he mean to do with us?' cried Herr Saalmuller. 'What does this mean? Are we all prisoners or are
we not? What will happen to our possessions?'

'I ask you,' said Madame, 'how long is it that we are
to stand in Herr Waldmeier's yard doing nothing at all?'

When no one had an answer for her she laid down
her basket, gesturing Monsieur Bourgaud to stand over it,
and seizing the smallest of her children, undid her bodice
and gave it suck. Frau Flad turned from this sight, wheel-
ing her children rapidly around the rock on which she
sat but her disapproval restored her somewhat, and she
ceased her crying. The older Bourgauds stood in a row
and watched the soldier's servants skin Hagos.

After more waiting, our mules and the mules of the
other households were driven into the yard, and each of
the women, myself included, was told to mount with the
children in her charge, Frau Saalmuller, Frau Moritz and
Mrs Rosanthal helping out with the additional Bourgauds,
and Rita Flad being allowed a mule to herself. Herr
Waldmeier's arms were released, but now he and Herr
Saalmuller were forced to walk side by side with their
inner arms tied together and so too Monsieur Bourgaud
and Herr Moritz.

118

In this way we left Gafat, glad to be moving, freed of all our possessions, unable to form clear thoughts of where we might be taken or for what purpose, dazed rather than fearful, too inexperienced in our captivity to know what we might have lost. As we went through Gafat we passed the schoolmaster, Debtera Sahaloo, being led up the hill by soldiers. He turned up to us a face stiff and grey and did not speak. I wondered why they led us one way and him another, why they troubled with him at all since he was not a European.

Surrounding the thought of Hagos there was a great pain in my mind for undoubtedly it was our fault that he had lain there, chained and trusting, when the gun was raised against him. At the same time I thought there is no worry now about whether the goat will come tomorrow.

It was clear now that we were being taken along the road to Debra Tabor. Rosa's hands were gripped around the pommel, my arms on either side of her held the reins. Ahead of us rode Mrs Rosanthal holding the strong little Bourgaud child in her arms as once she had held her own, but that was not to be thought about. Instead I thought: perhaps Mrs Rosanthal had neglected to bring grain for her child. I have brought grain. For I had slung the rolled-up cloak over the mule's neck. That foolish thought comforted me completely, as if that small amount of grain was a barrier against anything that might happen.

We were led through Debra Tabor with all the people watching us by their fences but making no sound. In the open ground outside the Emperor's houses, tents had been prepared for us and hides provided to sleep on. In the tent allotted to Herr Waldmeier I spread a hide for him and one for Rosa and myself to share. The cloak I spread under our hide. I thought: tomorrow I shall dig a hole and bury the grain, for I did not think of eating it, only of having it. Then I went outside and stood holding Rosa's hand by the tent, and so each family stayed by its own tent and watched one another at a small distance, too troubled to speak.

Women came carrying water and faggots. They left a pile of wood between the tents, but although several people started forward they stopped again for there was clearly only enough for one fire.

'Bourgaud,' commanded Madame, 'out here. Build a fire for all of us.'

At once not only Monsieur Bourgaud but also Herr Saalmuller and Herr Moritz sprang forward to arrange the logs. They discussed among themselves in loud voices where to put the fire, where the wind was, where the smoke would go. They referred often to the ladies and how they must be protected from the smoke. Herr Moritz and Herr Saalmuller knew different ways of constructing a fire. 'You build for a forge,' said Herr Moritz. 'I build the true campfire.' In time they reached an agreement. The fire began to smoke and little portions of flame moved inside the black twigs.

'Come, come,' called Herr Saalmuller. 'Warm yourselves.'

When I began to move towards the fire my legs stumbled, seeming without bone or power, and now my arms and my back ached violently. There was a sharp pain in my shoulder and I thought: what has happened to me? For until I saw the fire I had felt none of this. Then, as if from a long time ago, I remembered that the soldier had put his hands on my shoulders and flung me to the ground so that I looked into the leaves and felt the impact of the stone against my shoulder and heard my teeth clank

120

together. Also the saddle had been heavy as I lifted it. That was what had hurt, but the pain had waited until now.

Now the little groups moved and sat beside the fire, holding out their hands and talking softly, soothing the children who had begun to whimper with hunger. I sat and shivered, cold with pain. Rosa twisted and fretted beside me. 'Be still,' I said. 'You hurt me.'

Then she butted her head against me and whined, 'Bread for Rosa.' And when none came, 'Please, bread for Rosa.'

'Hush,' I whispered. 'Later there will be bread.' But I did not see now where I should find the strength to walk back to the tent and how grind it and bake it without the others noticing and demanding it from me. How I was to do this lay all confused on my mind.

'They will surely feed us,' said Frau Flad sharply.

'Usually some food was brought,' said Mrs Rosanthal.

Darkness fell, and staring at the fire shrank our eyes so that turning behind where the soldiers stood, there seemed to be nothing but shadows and each of those dim movements one could imagine to be a man bringing bread and meat.

A hyena wailed outside the village and one after another the village dogs howled in answer, catching at the sound and dragging it down until once more the cold wail rose above theirs. There was singing from the Emperor's house.

Herr Waldmeier stood up, and taking Rosa in his arms walked over to the guards. When he came back he said, 'The Emperor has made no mention of food. We are to eat our own.'

At first no one spoke. Then Madame Bourgaud said, 'Who has brought food?'

'You have, Madame,' said Frau Flad. 'In that basket I saw you carried!'

'That was bread for the journey and beer for Bourgaud. It is gone.'

'Your children have eaten. Mine have had nothing.'

'And whose fault is that, Frau Flad? Am I to be punished for providing for my children when you do not?'

Herr Waldmeier bent down to me. 'Did you bring food, Louisa?'

I said, 'No,' but when he continued to look at me I stood up and went to the tent. I felt that he had been unjust to me. My body pained me so that I could scarcely lift the cloak. It hurt to stoop through the opening of the tent and the fire seemed further away than I had just come.

Then Herr Waldmeier, seeing how I walked, was running towards me. He struck his hand against his head and cried, 'You are hurt. They hurt you. I had forgotten.' He took the cloak and dropped it by the fire, looking only at me and saying, 'Where, where did they hurt you?' while the other people rolled out the cloak and I heard the lining rip and thought: now we have nothing. I would have cried then but I thought: perhaps I will need to cry more later. 'My shoulder,' I said. 'The greatest pain is in my shoulder.'

'There is little enough,' I heard Frau Flad say. I turned in surprise for it had seemed just now so heavy and I had reached my hands again and again into the grain jar. But whether there never had been very much or whether some had fallen away, only a small pile lay in the middle of the cloak with all the people kneeling around staring and moving their hands towards it.

It was decided that there was only enough for the children and that Madame should have a portion as she must provide milk for her baby. Madame produced from

122

her basket a little tin cup, and Herr Saalmuller, as he had no child of his own, measured the grain in it while each child made a cup of hands to receive it.

When it was my turn to be fed, Frau Flad said that I was not a child.

'Of course she is a child,' said Herr Waldmeier.

Frau Flad said, 'She does not look like a child.'

But Herr Waldmeier said again in anger, 'I say she is a child.'

Herr Saalmuller hesitated and then, holding out the cup, said encouragingly, 'Also, it was Louisa that brought the grain,' and I held out my hands and received it from him. Frau Flad turned away, pulling at her loose hair and snatching it behind her ears. She did not speak again. When Rosa's hands were filled, Herr Waldmeier, repenting of his anger, enfolded hands and grain inside his own and said grace with her. Then the other children were made to stop eating and say a grace too and a more Christian attitude prevailed. We held our hands to our faces and licked the grain with our tongues, crushing the kernels in our back teeth and enjoying the flavour but receiving little satisfaction.

At Debra Tabor

That night through hunger I did not sleep. Only Rosa slept. I listened in the close tent for Herr Waldmeier to breathe as sleepers do but all night he was restless, turning and sighing on the hard ground.

The hyenas continued to howl. The dogs howled in chorus back at them and before they were silent, before the patch of sky through the top of the tent had lightened, the cocks in the village began to crow. Once, Herr Saalmuller who lay in the next tent cried out, 'Oh Lord, deliver us,' but whether in sleep or prayer I could not tell.

In the morning every man in the village brought a bundle of thorn and spent the day building a thorn fence around our tents so high that we could not see out. At noon they brought us food. The following day the tents were replaced by straw huts which provided far more room but at the same time gave our camp a disturbing look of permanence.

On the days that followed, the guns that were still at the foundry and the carriages were dragged up to Debra Tabor, and with them the tools that had been at the foundry. These were returned to their respective owners, but none of our other possessions were seen again except some of Herr Waldmeier's German books, although in these many of the pages were torn or missing.

On the fifth day, when the last of the guns were brought

up, one of the boys from the mission school managed to come inside the thorn fence. He mingled with the women who brought fuel and water, and taking a bundle of faggots upon his own back came through the gate bent over so that no one should see his face. Nor did anyone notice him until he went to Herr Waldmeier and tugged at his shamma. Herr Waldmeier knelt quickly in front of him, gripping his shoulders. His name was Wastefan and he turned his head away not wanting to meet Herr Waldmeier's eyes. Herr Waldmeier said. 'What has happened to the school?'

'There is no school now.'

'And the boys?'

'Some have gone away.'

After a silence Herr Waldmeier said softly, 'And Debtera Sahaloo.'

'He is dead, Waldmeier.'

'How is he dead?'

'The Emperor, Waldmeier.'

'How is he dead?'

'They took off his hands and feet, Waldmeier, in the school yard.'

'And left him?'

'They left him in the school yard but they stayed with him to see that no one gave him food or drink.'

'How long?'

'For one day and a half he recited the Holy Scriptures as you had taught him, Waldmeier. Then for one half a day his voice went away and he made no sound. Then he was dead.'

Herr Waldmeier turned away from him and covered his eyes with his hands. He said, 'That martyrdom was mine but the Lord found me wanting and gave it to his more deserving servant.' Tears ran from under his hands

125

down the crevices of his cheeks. Then he wiped his eyes on the edge of his shamma and thanked Wastefan for the risk he had taken in coming, and told him to return to Gafat.

Two days later when the guards brought us food one of them said, 'Tewodros is gone.'

'Where is he gone?' said Herr Moritz.

'To Foggera to bring more food.'

Although he had not once come near us, the relief of knowing that Tewodros was not in Debra Tabor was great. No one would dare kill us without his orders. Immediately the news came, we were filled with a feeling of security and well-being greater than anything we had been conscious of in the days of our prosperity. Otherwise it is impossible to understand the peculiar happiness of those few days. For we were left with nothing, after possessing so many rich articles, and we were hungry with little confidence that the food would continue to be provided. But above all the greater fear, which we had not mentioned even within ourselves, was removed: that in some empty and ordinary portion of the day the gate would be thrown open and the Emperor appear as he had at the gate of the foundry at Gafat, saying, 'Kill them.'

Herr Waldmeier is sitting on a stone. His eyes are hidden by his straw hat. All of his face is hidden by his hat or his beard. He is looking intently at the thing he is making in his hand. His bare blackened feet are pressed into the dust. No part of him is at rest. All of him works the little tool in his hand as it digs into the wood. He talks rapidly all the time, telling Rosa and myself and the little Bourgauds what he is doing. His words come in little thrusts like the tool's. Fragments of wood leap out of his hand. We squat at his feet and stare. He is making a toy.

126

All day he spends with us.

For since he heard of Debtera Sahaloo's death he was like a man recovering from an illness or a wound. He walked slowly as if he feared to tear at some part of himself not healed. He spoke quietly and kept with the children.

He held out the wooden animal he had made, turning it over in his hand and looking at it, pleased. Rosa took it, laughing, and trotted it up and down in the dust. Robert Bourgaud crouched and stared at it gravely. 'What animal is it, Herr Waldmeier?'

'Of course it is a cow!'

'But it is not correctly done, Herr Waldmeier.'

He lifted it off the ground frowning at it. 'What is wrong? It is a fine cow.'

'But its horns are upside down.'

I said, 'It has no hump and its neck is skinny.'

'Ah,' cried Herr Waldmeier in dismay, 'I have made a Swiss cow!' And he laughed and, speaking over their heads to me, said, 'Always one thinks the cows of one's own childhood are the only cows. This is not a cow to you at all.' After that he tried to carve an Abyssinian cow but it angered him that he could not make it well. 'I cannot do it,' he said. 'I was only taught to carve Swiss cows. That is all I am good for.'

Rosa accepted both cows and made many more by asking the Bourgauds to spit in the dust. This they willingly did, each trying to place his spittle exactly on what was already there. Then they helped Rosa shape small lumps of mud which were also perfectly acceptable to her as cows.

'The guns were the temptation of the Devil,' said Herr Waldmeier to me. 'Had I kept to the Lord's work, Debtera Sahaloo would not have suffered for me.'

127

'You would now be dead.' It was on this occasion that we spoke these words, I am sure, for I connect them with Rosa's hand grasped around the belly of the wooden cow. Other people are there. Frau Flad sits on a stone by her hut and sews a tear in Rita's dress. Rita must sit inside the hut until the dress is mended and Martin must hold the parasol between his mother and the sun.

Two village women squat in the open gateway, staring in at us. They lean together so that their shoulders touch. Their empty baskets rest on the ground and they lean on the rims of them propping their chins on their hands. Their mouths are slightly open. They stare and stare. A little naked boy runs from behind them into our prison and squeals with daring. His back is brown. His buttocks are grey with dust.

Herr Saalmuller and Herr Moritz dig latrines. It is their constant preoccupation since the tools have come from Gafat. Their spades scrape on the stony ground.

Madame Bourgaud, with a cloth about her head and her long skirt pinned up with a thorn, stirs at a pot of gruel over the fire. The sunlight is so brilliant that it obliterates the light of the flames. One cannot see their extent. Only when Madame passes behind them her skirts become insubstantial and the smoke causes her face and arms to lose their solid shapes.

Perhaps it is these effects of light that give the other people their remoteness. The enclosure was small; we can only have been near to one another. But, as if the light fell between, Herr Waldmeier's presence is of a nature separate to theirs. He is whittling the remainder of his wood with strong aimless strokes of his knife and all the time he is talking to me.

'It was a dream, Louisa. How can I explain to you the strength of my feeling? All the opposition we had expec-
128

ted to meet from the Emperor fell away. He was so eager to accept our skills and to offer his help and, I swear, his true friendship. And the work at the school and the work in the foundry, all of it so new and of such peculiar interest that I cannot describe it to you.'

He catches the wood between his knees and pushes up the brim of his hat with the back of his hand. His thick hair falls down. It is lighter now than his skin. I see, too, that his lashes are paler at their roots, and accept, and now seem to possess, all these things, as I do his words.

'Do you remember it, Louisa? Do you remember building the house and the excitement of that time? But it was also a Godly time. I felt continually in His presence – that minute by minute I was doing His work with my mind, my hands. I am not a thoughtful man. I find it hard to pray. Would you believe that? In that empty room in Gafat I often found my thoughts uncontrollable, but was never unmindful of Him in the school or the workshop. There, I felt in a constant state of prayer, liberated of the need for words, and it was felt: you could see it affect the people working with me. They, too, felt there was something exalted in the work they were doing.'

He lowered his eyes and began slowly to carve again. 'I have always felt a great grace in being taught the skills of carpentry for it was through those same skills that Christ learned to live among men, and often in those early days, when the workshop smelt solely of wood and those dark faces watched me so eagerly, I thought of that other carpenter's shop and felt the sympathy of God about me. And perhaps there was sinful pride enough in leaving His craft and striving to master another. Perhaps there was an evil inherent in the guns.'

And now, when his voice was most rapid and filled with

129

feeling, it suddenly slowed and seemed almost to have lost the meaning of what he was saying. The tool moved more and more slowly across the idle lump of wood. He stared at me. All these words thrown at me, even when he appealed to me to answer and then did not wait but threw between us more and more words. Now they all fell down and he stared direct at me. But I lacked the courage to remain silent. I said, 'You did what was right. If you had not made the guns he would have closed the mission long ago.'

'Ah, if I could believe that was the simple truth.' He stared, surprised, at the wood in his hand which he had forgotten, and so at me as if I had altered before him, and I saw Madame lay her spoon across the pot and call that the food was ready, and Frau Flad hand in the dress to Rita, and Martin sent back to ask Mrs Rosanthal whether he should bring her gruel to her hut, and Herr Moritz and Herr Saalmuller lay their shovels neatly side by side, and Rosa within reach of my arm, clutching the wooden cows.

At night, when the food was eaten, Herr Waldmeier or Frau Flad led us in prayer. We prayed that we might be safely delivered, that our lives would be spared. We prayed for Herr Flad and for the soul of Debtera Sahaloo. We prayed that the mission might yet be restored and the Lord's harvest field yet reaped and garnered. Sometimes we sang hymns.

The stars were very large and bright, as if they might merge together like molten metal. Several in an evening would break away and fall great distances across the stationary stars. I thought to ask Herr Waldmeier whether there was a space between the edges of the sky and earth where they fell. Or did they hit the earth? And did they burn with heat, or had, as it appeared, the sky chilled them?

But in the moments that I thought about these things, I did not want to remind him of my presence lest he send me inside the hut. The children fell asleep, sunk against their parents by the fire, and one by one were taken away but the men stayed talking, and often when I had laid Rosa on the cowhide I crept back near Herr Waldmeier but out of his sight and listened to the deep German voices.

Dogs from the village strayed in through the open gates and moved like shadows outside the circle of firelight. By day you could see how thin they had become, for they had in the past made a livelihood of scraps and now, with the shortage of food, people ate what they had once thrown outside their doors, so that the dogs' ribs were like the sides of baskets and their haunches so sharp as if they would break the skin. In time they all died or were killed and eaten in their turn but while the Emperor was at Foggera they prowled about our fire, hunting for discarded bones with some goodness left to them.

Once I saved a scrap of goat's meat and used it to tempt a dog towards me, I held my hand out into the dark where the firelight did not reach and heard the dog sniff and saw it lower its head and swing it from side to side, reluctant to come into the light. But it was hungry, and as I drew my hand back it came cautiously until its forepaws were on the line of firelight. Beyond that it would not go. I gave it the meat fearfully for I thought it would snatch and bite my hand, but although the scrap was so small, it tilted its head and took the meat delicately so that its teeth did not touch my fingers at all. I should have liked to do that again and perhaps someday to stroke it but afterwards I felt guilty that I had not given the meat to Rosa and I did not spare any to the dog again.

131

'He means to kill us,' said Herr Saalmuller. They never spoke of the Emperor by name because undoubtedly the guards were listening and would have caught that sound although the rest meant nothing to them.

'But why?' said Herr Moritz. Again and again they held this conversation. 'We have shown him no disloyalty. We have built his guns. Why does he now turn against us?'

'Now he has the guns,' said Herr Waldmeier. 'If Flad is successful, he will soon have trained British artisans in the country; perhaps unknown to us they are already in Massawa. If that is so, what need has he of us?'

Frau Flad began to weep like one who has run a long way.

'Comfort, dear Frau Flad, comfort.'

How is that I could see her face shine with tears, and understand the causes of her distress and share many of them, and yet be unconcerned and wake in delight at the day and measure out that time in events that no one else knew of, although we rose and ate and slept all in sight and hearing of each other?

'Why have I taught you German? What madness is it? Of what use? We should never have come to this country. We have interfered. I have taken you from the home you knew, Louisa, and made you into something you would not have been.'

These are Herr Waldmeier's words in the dark hut that still smells close of fresh cut grass. I sit cross-legged on my hide with Rosa's sleeping back pressed against the base of mine. Herr Waldmeier lies on his side of the hut and makes an end to the solid shape of dark between us. His head is propped on his arm. He is talking to me very low so that no one will be disturbed. 'Can you remember? Can you remember the first time you heard my name?'

132

'Yes.' Ras Ingada had said my sister was to marry a European, Theophilus Waldmeier, who spoke many tongues and shaped wood into useful devices. My sister covered her face and hid behind the house.

'And what did you feel when you heard about me?'

'I do not know what I felt.'

'Did you want to see me? Admit that you had no desire to see me.'

'But then I had not seen you. I did not know you.'

'You neither wanted me nor needed me.'

'I did not know you.'

'Can you remember that time before you heard my name?'

'Yes.'

'Were you not happy? Think, think how happy you were.'

'No.' I had no special recollection of happiness.

'You are mistaken. You think because your life was very simple it was not happy. But I say that in that simplicity you were more happy than ever you have been since I touched your life. I did not know that you were coming that day. I did not understand who you were. You will not remember, but no one had thought to mention you to me, and you came, a little dark thing all wrapped up on a mule. I thought: my God, what am I to do with a child? I was frightened enough at the thought of a wife. I did not want to marry. I thought: the child is too much. What does it eat? I thought, as if you were some strange animal. I did not know what to say to you.' He is laughing. The memory of not wanting me is absurd to him.

I say, 'My life is simple now.'

'But it is not. There is no place now in which you truly belong. That is what I fear.'

'There is this place.'

But now I am aware of a stiffness and silence where he is. I have displeased him by my answer. He stands and stretches and goes to the open doorway. He leans against the doorpost and says quietly into the room, 'You are still a child. You do not think ahead. This is enough for you?'

'Yes.'

After a while he says, 'He will never let us remain like this.' He means the Emperor and as he finds relief in thinking of me as a child, I shall answer as a child.

'Why should he not let us stay here?'

'Don't you feel, Louisa, that this is no time at all?' He is dark against the open door. The stars are behind his head. 'The time does not move. This is a waiting, and nothing is satisfactory. I do not like it, do you see? I am unable to wait. I am irritable and depressed.' How can he say this, when this has been a most happy time and he feels it so as well as I? Yet he is saying, 'I am irritable and depressed, not because of what I have lost, but because of this not-moving. This idleness. And so it must be made to move.'

'What will you do?'

Herr Waldmeier said, 'I shall build another gun.' This seemed to me so harmless a suggestion that I felt nothing but relief. 'Is that not right, Louisa? Is that not all that is left me to do? Then at least each day will have its task and something – even a useless thing – will grow and people will see it grow and at last it will be complete and I can say, "I have accomplished this thing and time has moved forward. We are not where we were." Is that not so?'

'Yes.'

'I tell you this, Louisa, because I would be truthful with you. I thought that by building the guns I protected the mission. But it was vanity. God held our lives in His hand and while we prospered it was His strength not ours.

134

But He knew our vanity – our love of wealth, our pride in our achievements. My pride, Louisa, my pride and my love of the work that I did with my hands that I had not been sent to do. And so He has destroyed us. He has turned from me and left me helpless in the hands of a madman, helpless in my passions, Louisa. Nothing is left for me but to keep alive, as I am not worthy of martyrdom. And that I will contrive by the building of this gun.'

He did not say any more but told me to sleep and, coming into the hut again, took his hide and dragged it out after him. After that he slept always by the embers of the fire and grew wilder and more unkempt in his appearance than any of the others, and silent and inaccessible, thinking always about his gun.

'What if he does not want a gun?' said Herr Saalmuller. 'What if he would rather wait until the English artisans come before he has another cast?'

'They have not come yet,' said Herr Waldmeier, 'and, besides, we shall build him such a gun as the English would not think to build. A great gun will, in his eyes, set him up above all the rulers of the earth. It must be big, Carl. Larger than any mortar in Europe. Of a twenty-inch calibre. What do you say to that?'

'I say it is absurd. We cannot do it.'

'If we can build little mortars, we can build great ones. You will see. You will see.'

On the day that they held this conversation, the headman of Gafat came to the enclosure bringing us a small bowl of honey.

'May God return it to you,' said Herr Waldmeier. 'I know it was given out of your own need.'

The old man continued to draw his whisk to and fro over the basket as it lay in Herr Waldmeier's hands. 'It would be more, if there were more to give. May Tewodros return with plenty.'

'Will he return?'

'Oh yes,' said the old man resignedly. 'He will always return to where the guns are and where the white men are.'

'After he returns, how long will he stay?'

'They say he has ordered two roads to be built. One leads to Gojam and the other leads to Meqdela. They are wide enough to carry the guns. But which road he means to take is a secret in his own heart. Perhaps he does not know himself.'

The following day a boy who had come in carrying faggots as Wastefan had done, lingered by the woodpile until Herr Saalmuller came for wood. Then he bent down and ripping open a patch on his ragged trousers he drew from inside it a letter and pressed it swiftly into Herr Saalmuller's hand.

The letter was from Herr Flad. He had been received kindly by the English Queen Victoria and had returned to Massawa with a party of English workmen. In a few days he would begin the journey up into the mountains to ask Tewodros to exchange the prisoners for the English artisans. They were to stay at Massawa until this arrangement was agreed.

On the day following that, the Emperor rode again into Debra Tabor leading a long train of mules laden with food and that peaceful time was over.

136

Herr Flad returns

Herr Waldmeier still had in his possession a single silver dollar. He showed it to one of the guards, saying, 'By the death of Tewodros, it is yours if you will take this paper to the Emperor.' On the paper were the drawings of the giant mortar.

The guard took the paper and returned for the dollar. That evening as we sat to our food the gate was thrown open and Tewodros stood in the gap. In the dark no one doubted that it was he, feeling at a distance the force in him although he made no move. He called in a low and pleasing voice, 'Waldmeier, my son.' When Herr Waldmeier went to him, the Emperor embraced him, laying his head for a moment against his shoulder and then, straightening, said softly, but so penetrating is the quality of his voice that we all can hear, 'Tomorrow, my son, we begin to build this gun together.'

The Emperor's house is at the highest point of Debra Tabor. Behind it the mountain falls away but here and there are spaces of flat land and on one of these they dug a pit for the gun and fenced it around with bamboo so that no animal would fall into it at night and break its leg.

Then Herr Waldmeier made a wooden wagon with heavy wooden wheels which later he would use for a gun-carriage for the great gun. He harnessed it to eight oxen

137

and set out along the rough road cleared towards Meqdela, to the banks of the Djedda where he might quarry pure limestone for the furnaces. This stone withstood the fiercest fire he could put in it, and never gave way and mingled with metal as had the first furnace at Gafat.

Herr Moritz went to select the stone and Herr Waldmeier went with him lest the wagon need repairing on the way. They were accompanied by a troop of musketeers, for now rebel bands might attack the Emperor's men even between Debra Tabor and Meqdela. Herr Waldmeier rode first, with a saw and an axe strapped to his back and bags of nails hanging from his saddle. He turned away and the clouds of yellow dust took him from us even before the bending of the road.

For three weeks I did not see him but lived out the days with Rosa in the prison compound. The gate in the fence was left open after work had started on the gun but we continued to live as we had and seldom went into the village. Then one afternoon the guards called to us that the wagon had been sighted. I took Rosa through the market and sat with her on a stone overlooking the road. We heard shouting and the grating of great wheels on the road. Then the oxen strained around the bend with the unsteady pile of stones tied onto the box of the wagon. Soldiers ran behind, wedging stones under the wheels to prevent it slipping back. Urging them on was Herr Waldmeier, covered in dust, riding his mule, alive, returned to us.

In the market at nightfall the oxen stood steaming and trembling. Foam spattered on the dust in front of their hooves. One of them fell. Its knees folded and only its head was held upright by the harness. The soldiers seeing that it was dead freed it and cut it to pieces and roasted it on a fire and ate it.

138

Herr Waldmeier, through exhaustion, could not eat or scarcely speak, even when he had washed away the dust in his throat. He fell on his hide by the fire and slept. Yet at dawn, when I woke, he was not there but at the new foundry already directing the building of the furnaces.

And now, so that Rosa might see him, I took her each day to watch the building of the furnaces. I would take food and water and sit with Rosa under a tree. Herr Waldmeier directed the workmen who sat in a half-moon, chipping at the blocks of limestone and tossing the chips into a great pile in the centre.

The sun is brilliant all about them. The dust rises off the stones like steam. Far away the lines of the long mountains are very clear. Hunger, which no longer affects the belly, presses like hard hands against the temples and it seems the head is hollowed of all that has happened before. The pictures made by that time are clear and at a distance. In none of them have I any part.

The Emperor sits upon a stone. His spear is propped beside him, his hands clasped together on the shaft, his cheek resting on his hands. He studies intently the plans of the gun laid out with stones at his feet. He lifts up his head with some question. Herr Waldmeier stands bareheaded at his side and stoops to point out some part of it with his finger. The thick straw hair falls over his face.

Or they walk beside the growing walls of the two furnaces. The Emperor's hand is upon Herr Waldmeier's wrist, black and crooked like a bird's claw, and gripped so tightly that when he releases it there are red marks where his fingers have been.

The Emperor stands with Herr Moritz and Monsieur Bourgaud, sampling with his fingers the pans of different clay brought from different rivers to see which one will

139

be the most suitable for moulding the cope of the gun. And this, he says, is the fattest and best, and he looks shrewdly at Monsieur Bourgaud to see if he has chosen well.

Ah yes, it is indeed the best. Has he not chosen the best clay before the Europeans have given him any advice? He gives orders for two hundred men to go to that portion of the river and fill their buckets with as much clay as they can carry. And although this place is not far from Debra Tabor, as many armed soldiers go with them.

The Emperor kneels and measures with the shaft of his spear the depth of the pit in which some day the gun will be cast. Then, holding that place on the spear, he carries it to where Herr Waldmeier shapes the core of the gun from a stout tree trunk propped on trestles. He measures· the spear against the core. Herr Waldmeier never glances at him, but continues to move the blade of his axe rapidly over the surface of the log, frowning, clamping his teeth over his lower lip in his concentration, squatting down until his eyes are on a level with the surface of the wood so that he can judge its straightness.

The Emperor watches him, leaning on his spear, his hands high on the shaft so that he seems to hang upon it. The shamma is lifted by his arm, revealing the dark rib-bones as prominent as the dog's had been. Herr Waldmeier's face is thin. His eyes appear larger and darker than they were. The lines between his eyes that once came and went are fixed there. The bone stands out on his wrist as he guides the axe blade.

As if this gun were an evil thing he must cast out of himself, Herr Waldmeier will not rest, but puts himself into all its processes. He hefts the stones, although there are a hundred men to do it, and lifts the core onto the trestles. Throwing the shamma clear of his arms he kneels among the women showing them how to knead

140

the clay. The muscles stand out like bones, the flesh all fallen away.

If it were an evil thing, would he not hate it? In all the movements of his hands and eyes about the gun I cannot mistake his love for it. When he comes to bathe his hands in the water I hold up for him, he looks all the time over his shoulder at the finished core which is now bound neatly with its long plait of yellow straw, waiting for its cope of clay.

At night he comes back from the foundry and when I have bathed his feet and brought him his food he sits by the fire indifferent with weariness, eating rapidly without hope of satisfaction and shortly afterwards stretches out where he is and falls at once into a cramped and leaden sleep.

I cannot sleep. The moon fills the camp with cold daylight. He lies by the fire. His naked feet rest one on the other, hard and blackened but in the arches pale and defenceless, so that I feel pity like a contraction of the flesh in parts of me I did not know had feeling. I should not have seen him so, and begin to cry slightly against my arm: to comfort him in his condition being the only comfort left to me and that in some way denied. To talk with me no longer gives him pleasure.

One morning after the men had left for the foundry, a guard ran in among the huts shouting, 'Flad has come. Flad has returned.' We stood like enchanted things, holding whatever was in our hands stiffly before us. A crowd of people passed the open gate, descending and waving their sticks about a rider on a mule who wore a high cloth helmet. Frau Flad gave a cry and ran through the gate in pursuit. The rest of us, gathering up the smaller children, followed.

Herr Flad had dismounted outside the fence of the Emperor's compound. He stood there, a smaller man than I remembered, with a full well-fed face and European clothes, patting helplessly at the shoulder of his wife who clasped him to her and wept more copiously at his return than at his departure. Although pressed in on every side, the great distances he had travelled surrounded him with an air of separateness. All that had happened to us had no place in his mind, nor had we access to all that he had seen and heard in that outer world.

Two servants came from the Emperor's house and spread a large carpet on the dust under a tree, and before we had time to speak with Herr Flad, Tewodros himself appeared with Ras Ingada, his servant, Walda Gabir, holding above his head a bright green silk umbrella. Herr Flad knelt awkwardly in the dust while the Emperor settled himself cross-legged on the carpet.

'Well, well,' he said to Herr Flad. 'Where are the English artisans? Why do they not accompany you? They are behind on the road? Unused to this country, they could not keep pace with you?'

Herr Flad spoke nervously but with surprising firmness for one whose news must disappoint the Emperor. 'Sire, I have letters from the British general at Aden which explain why they are not here, also from the general this gift,' and he drew from his jacket a number of papers and a leather case.

The Emperor handed the papers to Ras Ingada without looking at them. He began to fumble impatiently with the fastening of the case and in a minute drew forth a telescope. The crowd that had gathered at a respectful distance from the edges of the carpet released a sigh, for the sun glittered brightly on the brass making them suppose it was gold.

142

Tewodros too, looked pleased at first and turning to the distant mountains he raised it to his eye, but at once he could be seen folding his lips in irritation and twisting the tube this way and that. Then, turning angrily to Herr Flad, he said, 'It is not a good telescope. Why has it been sent to me?'

Herr Flad offered to adjust the focus for him but his hands trembled and were clumsy. He, too, raised it to his eye and frowned and lowered it again, attempting to adjust it with unsteady fingers.

'Give it to Ingada,' said the Emperor. 'There is no time. I know it is not a good telescope. I know it is not sent to me for good.' He waved Ras Ingada back and beckoned Herr Flad to sit with him on the carpet, saying, 'Have you seen the Queen of the English?'

'Yes, Sire,' said Herr Flad. 'She has sent a verbal message to Your Majesty. She was most gracious ...'

'What is the message?'

Herr Flad tightened his shoulders and holding out his chin recited in a tremulous voice but with brave resolution, 'The Queen of England has told me to inform Your Majesty that if you do not at once send out of your country all those you have detained so long against their will, you have no right to expect any further friendship from her.'

Tewodros leant towards the words, his eyes very bright. As soon as he realised that Herr Flad had finished, he said, 'Again.'

Herr Flad repeated the message.

'Again.'

A third time he repeated it.

When he was silent the Emperor continued to watch him intently, letting the breath slowly out of his thin body. Then he said quietly, 'I have asked from them a sign of friendship but it is refused me. If they wish to come and fight...' This phrase passed around the crowd like a wind, *If they wish to come and fight ... if they wish to come and fight ...* for he had extracted more from the message than we had. Herr Flad made no move to contradict him. 'If they wish to come and fight, let them come and call me a woman if I do not beat them: warriors that have allowed themselves to be dominated by a woman.' Then he shouted out, 'Bring me the telescope.'

Ras Ingada ran bowing forward, proffering the telescope. Tewodros snatched it from him, lifting it again to his eye and twisting it violently this way and that. 'It is not sent for good,' he said loudly, glaring at Herr Flad, who though he trembled visibly did not lower his eyes but sat there on the carpet, fortified by the memory of some power more tangible and less remote than God's. Now, he even ventured, 'Indeed, Sire. It was sent with all ...'

'The man who sends me this telescope only wants to annoy me. He wishes to tell me, "Though you are a king and I send you an excellent telescope, you will not be able to see through it." Is that not so?'

'It is true, Sire,' said Herr Flad his voice now scarcely audible, 'that if you do not comply with the Queen's request you will certainly involve your people in a disastrous war.'

There was then a long silence in which came to us the singing of the women performing the final kneading of the clay. The Emperor regarded Herr Flad coldly. At last in a curiously flat and quiet voice, as if these matters had passed long ago outside his interest, he said, 'Do not be afraid. The victory comes from God. I trust in the Lord and He will help me. I do not trust in my power. I trust in God who says, "If you have faith like a mustard seed you can remove mountains".' He handed the telescope over his shoulder to Ras Ingada so carelessly that

144

it almost fell. 'If I had not chained Mr Rassam, it would all have been the same. The English are not my friends. They would never have sent me the workmen. Bell was my friend and because of the esteem I bore him I humbled myself before the English Queen.' When his voice is gentle and low as it was now, it draws people to him and so the crowd pressed in to the very edges of the carpet leaning their heads forward to hear his words. 'Even as the great King Solomon, when he would build the temple to the Lord, humbled himself to send to Hiram of Tyre and asked for workmen skilled in metal, so I knelt at the feet of a woman to ask for workmen, but they are denied me. Since Bell was killed I have had nothing but scorn and discourtesy from the English but it is of little matter. I leave it to the Lord. He will decide it when we fight on the battlefield.'

Scarcely looking at Herr Flad he rose and walked away in the direction of the foundry.

When Herr Flad was shown his new home in the enclosure he said in disbelief, 'You live here? For how long has this been? What has happened?'

Looking from one to another, as he did, we were aware of our hungry and dirty condition. 'Did they not tell you?' said Frau Flad. 'Everything we had was taken.'

'They told me nothing. That you were here for your own safety. I thought he had treated you with honour.' He raised his hand to Rita's sharp chin and said in bewilderment, 'How tall you have grown. I remembered you a little girl. I brought you a plaything. Quite wrong, quite wrong.'

'And look at little Martin,' said Frau Flad. 'How they grow and all day it is, "We are hungry, Mama. What is there to eat, Mama?" and there is nothing to eat. Tell

145

me, how much do you think is the price of bread in the market?'

'I have no way of knowing,' said Herr Flad looking at her in the same bewildered way.

'A dollar. A whole dollar. Would you believe such a thing?' They did not ask him at all about his journey.

'I have some money,' he said. 'We shall manage. This cannot last for ever.'

At that moment Herr Waldmeier came running through the gate of the enclosure. His arms as he held them out were coated in grey clay that had puckered and cracked as he ran. He brought them towards Herr Flad's shoulders as if to embrace him but drew them away again. 'Forgive me, Martin! I am so very dirty. Louisa. Water.' But I had already fetched it from the fire and stood at his side holding the bowl of warm water up to him. 'You have come back,' he said, beaming down at Herr Flad. 'What a brave soul you are!'

Herr Flad dropped his head modestly, 'You are grown so thin, Theo. I should scarcely have known you. It grieves me to find you all like this.'

'Yes,' said Herr Waldmeier, scraping away the clay down his wrists into the water, 'we fell on evil times after you left, but I do not think of that now. We manage. We manage. And the work goes well. Of course I had heard that you were here but I could not come at that moment. This very morning we put on the first layer of the cope. You know how delicate a process this is on such a very large calibre. Did they tell you, Flad, it is nearly twenty inch? What do you think of that?'

Herr Flad's face had stiffened. He looked oddly at Herr Waldmeier and answered with caution, 'I had heard nothing of this monster.'

'Well, well,' said Herr Waldmeier, 'there is a great
146

deal to tell. But you, dear Flad, what miles you have travelled. It is so good to see you. The others will come directly they can be spared.'

'Theo,' said Herr Flad, smiling affectionately at him, 'we must talk.' Instinctively Herr Waldmeier's head turned towards the foundry but he turned back, patiently forcing himself to listen. Herr Flad cautious for his fine suit, spread his handkerchief over a rock and sat upon it. Herr Waldmeier folded himself down onto the ground close at his side for he lowered his voice to such a tone of secrecy that it surprised me they did not send me away. 'What exactly is the position here?' said Herr Flad.

'We will cast it next month. Almost there is enough metal. There is much from Gondar and he did manage to bring a large amount from Meqdela but the road is no longer safe.'

'Do you mean there are now rebels in this province?'

'There are rebels everywhere. You were fortunate to come safely through.'

'Does he not attempt to put them down?'

'Not now, but perhaps when the rains have come and gone and the gun is cast.'

'The gun? The gun?' This talk of the gun displeased Herr Flad. 'Why must it wait upon the gun? Always before he moved without the guns.'

Herr Waldmeier slid his hands over his eyes and down his cheeks as if these questions were asked him in a foreign tongue, forcing his mind to more effort than he could give. 'We cannot leave the guns behind. To guard them adequately he would have to cut his force in two. He has not sufficient men left.'

'You mean he fears an attack on Debra Tabor itself.'

'If he left it and left the guns here.'

'But how has this come about?'

147

'Well, men must eat, and in the end he had to plunder the countryside all about here. So now we are surrounded by his enemies.'

'Then there is nothing left him?'

'This hill and Meqdela.'

'And the land between hostile to him. Theo, what will he do?'

'He will do nothing until the gun is finished.'

'But he cannot stay here. If there is no food in Debra Tabor. I have seen the country is desolate for miles around. He will starve. We shall all starve. He must be made to move.'

'Well, he will not.'

'Why, Theo? Why?'

'Because of the gun. Flad, I do not know. Can you not understand how it is? I know only that each day I must build the gun. That so long as I do that another day and another day are added to our lives. I cannot think beyond that now.'

'And when this marvellous gun of yours is cast? What then?'

'Ah, then you will see. His strength and courage will come back. Now he is defeated but then he will shake off his despair – this rage against his people. His old aspirations will come back to him.'

'And then?' asked Herr Flad.

'Ah, I do not know. I do not think a day ahead.'

'Now I shall tell you.'

'Ah yes,' said Herr Waldmeier. 'I talk so. Tell me. It is you that must have news. They say you saw Victoria.'

'Yes, yes,' said Herr Flad with sudden enthusiasm. 'She was most gracious. So simple it was incredible to me. So small a person, so unaffected in her manner. Even I might speak to her. But such power, Theo. We have lived here

148

so long. We have been so dominated by the one man that we have forgotten what true power really is. They mean to send an expedition. At whatever cost they mean to bring Cameron and the others out alive.'

'But that is inconceivable,' said Herr Waldmeier.

'Ah, to you here. But had you been there, as I have been. They are a deeply militaristic people and their wealth beyond belief – and their pride. They will not tolerate what has been done to Cameron.'

'They have managed to tolerate it for four years.'

'Then, there was hope that Rassam might succeed. But now at last they realise that Tewodros will only understand superior force. If you could see their troops, Theo. Men like giants. I saw them on parade in London. Moving in a great long line they did not look like men at all : long bands of red, white and black, heaving like the stripes on some great serpent. An extraordinary sight. And the number and the precision of all those thousands of boots made the most extraordinary noise as if they were crunching over broken glass. It was a revelation to me to see such an army. And their weapons, Theo ...'

He looked away from that distant parade ground, the sight of which had given him the courage to bring unpleasant news to the Emperor, and saw the dust blowing between the mean huts and Herr Waldmeier's thin and haggard face watching him with no comprehension. He said then, very gently for he is a kind man, 'Theo, you have had such troubles – and your wife, my dear fellow, I have not said – how very sad for you. But do you not see you are making this monstrous gun to fire on the English?'

'Sebastapol'

Each day more clay was prepared and another layer smoothed carefully over the cope. Under it a charcoal fire was kept constantly alight between the trestles so that each layer would dry. The pit was lined with stones. In the treasury the metal was weighed and sorted and the ewers and trays and church vessels were crushed so that on the day of the casting all could be fitted into the two furnaces at one time.

Herr Flad who had now been told of the sack of Gondar cried out in distress. 'Theo, think what it is you use!'

But Herr Waldmeier only answered, 'There is a great deal of metal needed.'

At this time a fence was built around the hill of Debra Tabor and it was whispered that the Emperor had had it built more to keep his own followers in than to keep the rebels out, for large numbers of his soldiers had deserted him and even after the wall was complete took every opportunity to escape back to their villages. The pasture lands for miles around Debra Tabor were quite devoured, and now the last of the animals died and were eaten, or, if they were too emaciated, were left to rot where they fell, so that the air stank.

Now, when foraging parties left the camp they were no sooner through the fence than lights sprang out on the distant hills: beacons lit to warn the villagers, so that when the soldiers arrived the grain was buried in the fields and the cattle driven into hiding places. Often the soldiers returned with nothing but a rabble of peasants, who having lost everything came in despair to the Emperor for food and protection, and he continued in the midst of all his cruelties to take these poor people in so that the lanes and hovels of Debra Tabor were as crowded as ever, but whereas once they had been filled with soldiers now not a fifth of the mass of his followers could carry arms, and those that did were made weak and discontented through hunger and sickness; the rest mere mouths and empty bellies.

Only the gun continued to grow. The clay blackened and hardened over the fire. Herr Saalmuller welded iron bands around it to strengthen it for the casting and to hold the core more securely in the centre. Then slowly and with great caution the entire mould was lowered into the pit and supported on every side with stones to help it withstand its ordeal.

Then the crushed metal was brought from the treasury and heaped into the furnaces. We heard it rattle down and the bells from the Gondar churches cry out flat and final as they fell, for it had been impossible to break them. Herr Flad knelt at the sound and prayed aloud. For two days and two nights the fires burnt, reducing all these items into one, and the next day the molten stuff was to be released into the pit.

On the afternoon of the day before the casting, the Emperor sent to our encampment the gift of a goat. A guard dragged it in by a leather thong tied to its horn. Everyone who was in the enclosure ran forward and stood together, staring at the goat. Rosa stroked it and turned to smile at me, but even she did not think of it as anything

151

but meat. The goat sensed what was intended and bleated shrilly and continuously.

As all the men were working at the foundry, the guard offered to kill it. We watched how it lay staring, with its severed throat sunken and brilliant on the dust, and saw the shining silver belly and the fibrous silver fat as the skin was torn off it, and smelt the blood with pleasure.

Madame said that owing to uncertainty about the goat's age and the state of its health, it must be boiled. All afternoon the smoke from the pot was a torment to us. Madame took tiny segments out of the pot on the point of a knife and blew on them until they were cool enough to put in her mouth, cocking her head intently as she chewed and saying again and again, 'Not yet, not yet. It will be wasted if it is not just so.' It grew dark. Herr Saalmuller and the others returned one by one from the foundry but no Herr Waldmeier. The meat was pronounced ready. Madame began to ladle it carefully onto the plates.

'Why has Theo not come?' said Frau Flad. 'There is no need for him to work by night as well as day.' For since the fires had been lit he had stayed beside them and not allowed himself to sleep lest the workmen neglect them and the heat be lost.

I said, 'I will go to him,' and before she could object ran out of the gate. Beyond the guards' fire the lane was deserted. I ran past the fence of the Emperor's compound towards the foundry. The great fires glowed around the two furnaces. Black figures crouched in front of them, tossing faggot after faggot onto the flames from the piles of fuel beside them.

Between the fires, kneeling alone by the pit in silence, I found Herr Waldmeier. I thought: perhaps he is in prayer, but immediately he called out, 'Who is there?'

'Louisa.'

'Oh,' he said in a happy voice, 'Louisa, come here and see. It is in the pit.' I walked to him through the heat of the fires. 'Come,' he said, rising back on his heels. 'Come and kneel down. You will not fall.' He reached out his arm behind my shoulders not touching me but to me it felt as surely as if he had. He was whispering as if we were in the presence of a living thing. 'Tomorrow the metal will be molten. We shall open the doors and it will run down those channels into the dark mould. Do you remember, Louisa, the first time you saw that brazen serpent? Pray God tomorrow we shall see it again.'

The fire breathed hot and dry against my face. I could not look into the heat. I shut my eyes and felt my lids close coldly onto my hot cheeks. It was many weeks since I had been alone in his hearing. Now I could not find again the voice in which I spoke to him, but began in a rapid childish manner, 'You are to come. Frau Flad says you are to come now. There is a goat. The Emperor has sent it and the guard killed it and Madame has cooked it all afternoon. She has sampled it several times but no one else has been allowed to touch it. Now she says we may eat.'

'A goat,' he said. He was laughing. 'A living goat.'

'It is not alive.' I, too, laughed like a child. 'It is dead and Madame has cooked it for a very long time.'

'That is good.' For a moment his hand smelling of fires rests under my chin and he says quietly, 'It will nourish you.'

'And you,' for I had felt his hand shake.

'God forgive me,' he said, 'but I have loved and needed this work.'

Frau Flad's voice thinly called my name from the gate of the enclosure, 'Louisa, what keeps you?'

'Go, go,' he said in a whisper. 'Perhaps someone will take your portion,' and all the time that I do not wish to

153

leave him, the water collects again and again around my tongue and my stomach gathers up at the thought of the meat.

The meat that night by the fire was hot and sweet and fell easily from the bone. Its goodness spread itself through the whole body. When the bones were licked smooth, we cracked them on stones and sucked them again. Even after I lay with Rosa on my hide in the hut there were the fibres caught between my teeth to be sucked out and relished. Why with all that feasting was I not satisfied? Something, unnoticed, unrecognised, had been there and now was lost. I did not know what made me feel so and thought: perhaps I am afraid. They said in the village that when the gun was finished the Emperor would take the Europeans down onto the plain of Debra Tabor and there have them slain.

I remembered the mould lying in the dark pit. Now Herr Waldmeier had cast it out of him. It was no longer a partial thing, half within his mind. For three days, once the metal was poured into the mould, the gun would work its cold completion in the earth, and then, I thought, it will be no part of him. It will not need him. The Emperor will not need him.

Even in the dark with the hyenas howling unchallenged by the fence, when thoughts were at their worst, I could not say to myself with belief: I will be taken out and killed. For how? By whom? Yet, I thought, lying a year back on a mattress in Gafat would I have believed any of this? I thought of the soldier who with an empty face had pointed his musket at Herr Waldmeier's head and then swung it so small a distance and killed Hagos. It was done as simply as that.

*   *   *

As soon as the sun rose we went to the foundry and found there the Emperor standing leaning on his spear and staring fixedly at the channels that led from the two furnaces into the pit. Then Herr Waldmeier knelt and swiftly drew back the door and the bright brass sprang free, gliding thickly down the curve of the channel into the dark pit.

There it stayed hidden for two days and two nights and on the third day the mould was raised again out of the earth and laid quite cold upon the trestles. Then Herr Saalmuller severed the metal bands and Herr Waldmeier lifted his hammer and chisel to strike away the cope, but at the last his hands trembled so that he lowered them again helplessly.

He was not afraid that Tewodros – who looked so brilliantly upon him and now took his hands between his own and said calmly and gently, 'Courage my son, courage. Rest now and in a moment your strength will return to you' – meant within the day to have him killed. He trembled only for the gun.

In time his hands grew steady. He placed the chisel against the blackened mould and raised the hammer and struck it. A curved segment of the mould like a dark rind fell away.

Then there was a great drawing in of breath and a cry from the crowd that had gathered. For from where the clay had fallen away the golden flesh of the gun was revealed and flared in the sun.

Then Herr Saalmuller and Herr Moritz, grinning like wild things, joined in breaking away the rest of the mould until the gun stood entirely free. The Emperor ran forward, sliding his hands over its surface while the core was extracted. Then he peered down its emptied mouth. It was perfect in all its parts.

The Emperor seized Herr Waldmeier's hands and kissed them repeatedly, for chiefly they had worked this miracle. His thin lips moved in shapes of words but did not speak. A darkness was taken from his face and there came a rare return of his smile of such particular beauty. Almost at once it turned to an expression of intense sorrow. Tears now covered his cheeks and fell onto Herr Waldmeier's blackened hands which he still held palm upwards in his own, saying, 'Now I know that you can do everything but escape death. Oh Waldmeier, my son, the pity of it that these hands which work such wonders must also lie at your side in the grave.' So he wept for him and called him 'My son', and although he talked of death, whatever he may have intended before he saw the gun, there would now for a while be no more thought of killing.

The gun was a thing of great strength and beauty: thick and wide-mouthed, straight along the side except where two wide bands of metal were raised on its surface, rounded at the end. At first it was gold in colour and shone brilliantly in the sun, but in time its skin changed to a green in which little flecks of gold were still visible, running this way and that.

To the Emperor it was a source of great wonder and joy, as if it gave him a proof of his power which the fence and the hunger and the warning beacons continued to deny. He called the giant mortar 'Sebastapol'.

'For God's sake,' said Herr Moritz, 'what does he know of Sebastapol? Does he know what will happen if he fires that damnable thing? Does he know what guns are capable of doing? Sebastapol, my God, Sebastapol!' It was generally believed to be at that place called Sebastapol that Herr Moritz had ended his association with the Russian army.

156

They did not, however, test the great mortar as they had the smaller ones at Gafat. At first the Emperor repeatedly asked Herr Waldmeier to have it removed to the plain and there fired. But each time Herr Waldmeier persuaded him against this, saying that the sound would so terrify people that many would die and that all pregnant women for miles around would miscarry. Each time the Emperor conceded, until it seemed superstition had grown in his mind that the first firing of Sebastapol would coincide with some momentous event and that it must be saved for that. What that event might be, or where it might take place, we did not know.

The rains had come. Work on the two roads, to Gojam and to Meqdela, was discontinued. The Emperor ordered Herr Waldmeier to start at once on the conversion of the wagon into a gun-carriage for the great mortar, but along which road he intended it to travel he did not say.

The march to Meqdela

The rainy season is always the saddest portion of the year. Its dreariness seeps into the mind. There is great discomfort, and at this time evil spirits most commonly reveal themselves.

Added to this was a growing lassitude caused by the lack of food and the difficulty in maintaining our life in the enclosure, and a general hopelessness at our condition. For the ring of rebellion tightened around Debra Tabor and it seemed each day that the possibility of leaving that place, which could no longer support us, became less.

Even the potency of the gun on the Emperor's imagination seemed to have failed. He drank more and more heavily when he retired to his house at noon. He emerged in the evening in dangerous erratic moods and people prayed for him to sleep again. Long before dawn he woke and sat on the stone where I had once found him. Here, at this early hour, people formerly had flocked to ask his judgement in their litigations. Now no one dared approach him, and he continued to sit alone, hour after hour, sometimes in drenching rain, rapt in thought or prayer.

Mascal came, but looking out from Debra Tabor the land was all dark; the bonfires kept in readiness only as a warning.

The rains ceased. The gun-carriage was completed. On
158

October 1st we received the order to march out of Debra Tabor : forty-five thousand people on foot, not knowing where we were being led, moving in a loose mass out over the plain with the great glittering mortar in our midst. In addition to the mortar, fourteen other guns travelled with us, some on the loud wooden wheels of their carriages, some in wagons with the gunpowder and stone shot. As no draught animals were left alive, the wagons and guns were dragged by men. Five hundred hauling on five plaited leather ropes dragged Sebastapol alone. Within a few days their grunting as they heaved it forward and their panting as they gained new footholds came no longer to seem the voices of many men but the single sound of the gun itself.

When the edge of this great crowd had moved off the slopes of Debra Tabor, sudden bursts of flame and smoke appeared one after the other on the crest of the hill. Tewodros was firing the town. Knowing that the rebels would enter the place as soon as he left it, he burnt it all sparing only the church he had built in expiation of his crimes against God at Gondar. There was to be no returning here. In this way we knew that he must be attempting to lead us through the mountains to the only place of safety left to him : his fortress on Meqdela.

The dust already in our throats and caked at the corners of our mouths and at the edges of our nostrils, the voice of the great gun, the grating of the wheels, the smell of burning, all seemed sensations particular to that moment when the feeling of release and the excitement of moving forward were strong in us. We did not recognise them as the daily unchanging parts of a new life. Nor did we know at all how long that life would be ours.

On a mule it is a week's journey from Debra Tabor to Meqdela. Tewodros has led an army over that ground in less time, for it was his ability to inspire his men into marching at great speed and arriving before expectation that first gave terror to his name. So, in the year that Rosa was born, he marched into Gojam and arrived so rapidly on the field of Injabara that Tedla Gwalu fled and his followers threw down their arms in terror and stood without resisting, waiting for the slaughter: seven thousand killed like sheep. So, he had ridden against Gondar in eighteen hours. Now for the first time he must travel at the pace of the guns. It took us six months to complete that week's journey.

For each day's march Tewodros divided his army into two. Half his soldiers set out at dawn, taking in their protection half of the wagons and guns and half of the followers, women carrying children, women carrying against their breasts the grey matted heads of babies born to them in the night, old men carried on the backs of their sons, sick men on litters. After a march of one and a half or two miles, they would halt and make a camp of huts from the bundles of sticks they had gathered on the way. At noon the second half of the army would set out to join them. When they met, the soldiers who had accompanied the early march and since had rested, moved forward again, with the Emperor and Herr Waldmeier, to clear a road over which the gun must travel on the following day.

In this way we travelled through Begemeder and although we often saw clusters of riders on the hilltops watching us, the rebels never once attacked, fearful still at the very name of Tewodros. Perhaps, too, seeing his great horde at a distance or the glittering city of campfires at night they were deluded by memories of his former power.

When there are clouds in the sky I have watched their shadows move slowly along the sides of the mountains,

160

and so, if I moved with the dawn march and found myself standing with Rosa at the top of a rise looking back the way we had come, I saw the dark human shadow creep over the land, and sometimes through the haze of dust the bright speck at its centre.

Look ahead, and there might be a valley with terraces of green running along the sides of the hills, and patches of bright crops growing between the shrunken channels of a stream, a village with smoking huts, the cross on the church-top shining above its dark grove of trees, goats grazing among the cattle. Such places I saw but never reached. Even as I stood and looked, the great shadow spread about me and ahead of me down the mountainside, and when I came carrying Rosa to the place where the village had been, it was deserted: the green fields cut to a dusty stubble, the stream trampled dry, the huts burnt down to circles of blackened stones and in an hour no trace was left, all overlaid by the sudden city of stick and grass huts. No place could support us for more than one night. In the morning we fired our huts and moved into unwasted country and laid that waste in its turn.

Each day the Emperor looked at the land ahead, the shape of which he knew very well, and pointed with his arm like a charred stick the way that the road must go. Then Herr Waldmeier would show him where the edge of the road must be strengthened with stakes, where the land must be built up with branches and stones, where boulders must be cleared away. When the rocks were too mighty for the soldiers to move, Herr Waldmeier hammered holes into them with a metal spike to the size of a thumb. Into this he poured gunpowder and let fire run along a straw rope to meet it.

Then the powder made its great sound and, bursting free, tore the rock to fragments. At first the soldiers

161

cheered whenever this was done, but soon, as they came to know the nature of the task he had set them, that always the way would be barred by another rock, their cheering ceased. So he scarred the land ahead of us, and along this wide scar, on the following day, the guns crept with the great mass of people all about them.

In this way, in two months, we journeyed out of the province of Begemeder and came to the steep ascent up to the Zagite plain and the plateau of Wadela. Here the road must be blasted through the great compacted columns of black rock that make these mountains and it was said openly that it could not be done, that we would starve where we were, with the wasted land at our backs and our faces to the wall of rock. But the Emperor showed no sign of doubting. On the first evening that we camped in that place he sent men with every available saw to cut wood and branches so that work on the mountain road could begin without delay in the morning.

That night a man we had never seen came and sat quietly by the missionaries' fire. Then everyone shifted on the ground to make room for him, grudging him this intrusion but not daring to deny him. His buttered hair stank in the warmth of the fire. His clothes were torn and filthy. Gravely he bowed to each one of us. Then from out of his rags he handed Herr Waldmeier a written message saying that the British force had landed at Zula and was preparing to march inland to Meqdela.

Then we were filled with wonder and an unreasoning joy, turning to one another, touching hands in our excitement. I looked with love on Rita Flad. Frau Flad and Madame Bourgaud silently embraced and wept.

'You have seen them?' Herr Waldmeier asked the messenger.

'With my eyes,' and he drew in his breath and rattled his fingers in the air as if his eyes still burnt with such sights.

'How many men are there?' asked Herr Flad who felt responsible for this wonder.

'Oh, many, many. Not as many as this, but all soldiers. Their coats are red, one like another's. Some wear brown. Some have brown faces.'

'And guns?'

'There is no gun so large as Tewodros' mortar, but there are many guns and oh, lords, they are carried on the backs of such beasts as have never been seen.' He drew a great shape with his arms about his head. 'A tail before and a tail behind. Surely it looks both ways. It is very large yet its skin is loose upon it as if once it had been larger still. It moves on legs like the trunks of the cedar and on its back is the gun, and there are many of these creatures.'

'Do they build a road?'

'They move along the dry bed of the Tacazze.'

'Does Tewodros know?'

'Surely he knows, lords, for I was delayed with fever at Gondar and since then I was forced to hide in a cave from rebels and was misled as to where to find you. The news will surely have reached him by this time.'

Yet the Emperor had shown no sign of rage and so we were in great uncertainty as to whether he knew or not. For who would dare carry such a message to him? And if he did not know, perhaps the raging lay ahead at some uncertain date when he would first hear of that other road forcing its way into the mountains.

Two days later the Emperor sent for Herr Waldmeier and said, 'Some donkeys have come to my country to steal my workmen. Now, for your safety, I will chain you.'

163

Herr Waldmeier had been ill that day with fever, so that the soldiers who brought him to the Emperor must hold him upright lest he fall.

'Look at him, Negus,' they said. 'He is too weak to move. How could he run away? Besides you can chain him when you reach Meqdela.'

And so he was not chained. Instead the Emperor had a red silk tent pitched beside his own and there at night Herr Waldmeier, Herr Moritz, Herr Saalmuller, Monsieur Bourgaud and Herr Flad were made to sleep under guard. All day they toiled, cutting the road out of the side of the mountain, and in all that time I could not come close enough to Herr Waldmeier to speak with him. He was ill and I could not go to him, but could only stand by the roadside with Rosa at dawn and see him carried among the workmen in a litter up the mountain, and wait again at night until I saw torchlight down the completed road and he was carried past again to the guarded tent.

They toiled like this day after day and slowly the mountain began to yield to them. The Emperor worked at their side, helping to haul the rocks off the road, driving in the stakes at the roadside that would hold the earth and stone revetments, until the light was quite gone and the men could not see where safely to place their feet, but staggered like drunken men on their return to the camp through hunger and exhaustion.

One night as they returned in this condition two men fell from the road and were killed. When their bodies had been carried back into the camp a voice cried out, 'The mountain is angry. It will kill us all.' Then Tewodros climbed on a stone and shouted out to them, 'I know that you all hate me; you all want to run away. Why do you not kill me? Here I am alone and you are thousands.' He flung
164

out his arms and stood with his lips drawn out of sight and his teeth bared, defying them. A great sigh rose and fell about him but it caused no motion. Then he shouted again across that silent flinching multitude, 'Well, if you will not kill me, I will kill you. You need not fear the mountain. It is I you need fear. I will kill you all, one after the other, and the blood will flow like a torrent in the rains.'

The next day they followed him again onto the mountain and from the camp below we saw again the white cloud float away from the rocks with the black specks of birds rising more rapidly past it. Then the dull thud of the gunpowder reached us and the rocks poured in a smoking stream down the mountainside. The dust cleared. The edges of the raw crater crawled with little creatures the colour of earth, and when the next cloud of smoke rose it came from higher on the mountain, and so in time they reached the top.

When the road was complete the Emperor began without a day's rest to haul the cannon up it, first the lighter guns and mortars and, at the last, Sebastapol. Then we fired that city of huts we had thought never to leave alive and followed after.

We could hear Sebastapol's slow ascent above us. The vast crowd of men straining on the ropes grunted like some great beast. From time to time one of the leather ropes would snap. The sound rang out like a whip cracked repeatedly against the mountainside. We were told that when this happened Tewodros would spring forward with the new rope and fasten it swiftly and haul upon it himself until those men who had not been hurt in their fall returned to the rope and began again to pull upon it. Then he was at the front of the procession, spilling water on his shamma and wiping the leading soldier's face. Then

165

he was at the back, helping to wedge stones under the gun-carriage wheels so that they might not slip.

When at last we reached the top of the pass there spread before us a great cultivated plain. The harvest crops were thick in the fields. Already stacks of garnered straw stood like brilliant yellow huts among the grey huts of the villages. By every door were high baskets filled with grain. The cattle trampled round and round the yellow circles of the threshing floors and great flocks of sheep and goats were scattered widely about the fields. The people of Zagite, never believing that Tewodros could reach the top, had hidden nothing and although that countryside was destroyed as we passed over it, from that time we were no longer hungry.

Once, travelling near the front of that army, we reached a village where the huts still burnt. There an old man was found hiding in an underground grainstore and when he was dragged out and told that he would not be killed, he told us how in the rains before the last rains six Europeans had been brought through the village on their way to the prison on Meqdela. He counted them off on his fingers. There was a man with a black beard who sang songs deep in his throat and a quiet man who rode with him. A twisted man who saw visions. A great hakim who had cured the eyes of the headman's grandson. A man with an eye that flashed fire and another man who gathered the honeysuckle just coming into bloom and pressed it in between the pages of a book. When he was asked why he did this he had replied that he would send the flower to a lady in a far-away country. He was a pleasing man and most sweet-tongued.

On Christmas Day we camped at Bet Hor which is no

more than fifty miles from Meqdela, but the land ahead was cut by two deep gorges which the road must be made to descend and climb again. By late January we were camped beside the river Jiddah and we waited there a month while the road was blasted up to the Dalanta Plateau.

Towards the end of February, when we had climbed to Dalanta and were waiting for the second march of the day to begin, soldiers who had left at dawn came running back, pointing behind them and shouting, 'Meqdela! Meqdela!'

That evening, leaving Rosa with Madame, I followed the Emperor and Herr Waldmeier to the edge of the plain and saw Meqdela standing between us and the high flat-topped mountains to the south.

The mountain did not tower above us. Its summit was on a level with the place where we stood, but it was severed from us by the deep-cut rivers that had carved it out of the surrounding uplands. The sun no longer shone upon it. It was a solid featureless blue. It appeared so near to us that with only my eyes I could see the pointed huts lining the edge of the fortress, like teeth. Rising from them were thin straight lines of smoke. It seemed that by merely walking out along this spit of land we must surely find another such reaching towards us out of Meqdela and, within the hour, walk among those blue jagged huts. The desire to reach them was very strong. It was the place of safety towards which we had marched. It would bring a final end to the time we had passed. For beyond that there was no place that we might go.

But as we walked to the end of that field, the land became broken and fell away. A little way ahead, the Emperor sat on a rock at the edge of a small grove of trees. His attendants stood at a distance but Herr Waldmeier kept at his side, staring with him downwards. Coming closer to where they were, it was possible to see further and further over the edge of the land to the great depths below. There, far below, infinitely farther it seemed than the smoking huts on Meqdela, among small broken foothills was the grey road of the river-bed and all that was left of the parched Bashilo running like a thin line of molten metal from one to another of its withered pools. That river must be reached and crossed before ever Meqdela could be climbed.

I came as close as I dared and squatted down on the brittle leaves that had fallen from the trees. With my shamma all around me so long unwashed it was the colour of earth, and I so silent, they never noticed I was there. So I waited to hear Herr Waldmeier's voice and accustomed myself to the scars of his illness. His hair which had hung stiff and thick from his head like a lion's mane had all fallen away, leaving his head shrunken to the very skull. He was like some other person and I invisible as a ghost to him.

The Emperor had the telescope Herr Flad had brought him and, wasting no time looking at the fortress, he pointed it down the gorge, searching out the existing tracks to see which might be the best for his road to follow. His servant, Walda Gabir, came forward then and, cupping his hands to his mouth, let out a long wavering cry. Everyone was silent; even the Emperor, holding up his head, listened for an answer. The evening stillness filled with an indefinite humming. Far away a dog barked. We heard no human sound.

Then Tewodros held his telescope so that the setting sun made bursts of light along its surface, and minutes later tiny flashes of light came and went along the fortress. Someone watched for us and knew that we were there.

Herr Waldmeier smiled ruefully at the Emperor and said, 'They are very near.'

The Emperor merely grunted and trained his telescope down into the gorge again. Then there was a cry from Walda Gabir. We saw him standing on a rock, pointing away from the lowering sun into the mountains to our left and, following his arm, there in the thin evening light were other flashes, rising again and again from out of some distant hidden valley.

'What is it?' said Tewodros in a loud and challenging tone. No one answered him. 'Who will tell me what it is?' But he, as we did, realised what it must be.

'It is the light reflected off the English guns,' said Herr Waldmeier at last but he did not look at Tewodros as he said it.

The Emperor sighed, moving his telescope restlessly about the wide distance. Then he called out to Herr Flad who a few minutes before had joined the group attending him. 'Flad,' he said as if the subject were quite a new one, 'the people from whom you brought me a message and whom you said would come, have arrived at Zula. They are coming up by the salt plain. Why did they not take a better road? The one by the salt plain is unhealthy. The English are unused to such heat – are they not? – and will die rapidly.'

Herr Flad said, 'Many of their troops are from India, Sire, and so are accustomed to heat. This is their quickest entry into the highlands.'

'Oh, oh,' he said absently. 'Is that so? I had not known they had sent Indian troops. Oh, my son,' he said sadly, turning to Herr Waldmeier, 'we are making this one road with such difficulty, you and I. For them, with their acquisition of the mechanical arts, it is only child's play to make roads everywhere. They move with great rapidity.'

169

Here, Herr Waldmeier's hand stretched suddenly out to Tewodros but fell again helpless to his side. There was concern on his face that bordered on love, for their long labour on the gun and on the road had brought them close in a way that discounted many things.

The Emperor did not respond to him but continued in the same melancholy tone, 'It seems the will of God that they should come. That at last I should have provoked them into bringing me an answer to that letter I wrote so long ago. I see the hand of God in this. If He who is above does not kill me, none will kill me. And if He says, "You must die," none can save me.'

His voice had grown slow and gentle and the fear that had sprung up around him softened. 'You think that I am not afraid,' he said, smiling a slow and beautiful smile at Herr Waldmeier. 'I tell you I long for them to come, as much, perhaps, as you do. I long for the day when I shall have the pleasure of seeing a disciplined European army. I am like Simeon. He was old, but before he died he rejoiced his heart by holding the Saviour in his arms. I am old too, but I hope that God will spare me to see such an army before I die. My soldiers are as nothing to it.' Now he turned his face from one to another as if engaging each in separate conversation.

'For when I was young I thought it was a mark of cowardice when each man did not fight out his own battle to win his own glory, but now I see the wonder of it: where thousands obey the command of one man. My soldiers would never consent to this. They say that the English soldiers can be made to move their feet at one time and so fight as a single giant. One line kneels down, another fires over its head. Is that not so?'

Herr Waldmeier nodded his head at Herr Flad and
170

said, 'Yes, Sire, it is so. Flad has seen these soldiers in England.'

'And they are dressed as one man and move as one man?'

'Yes, Sire.'

He said again in a happy voice, 'I pray to God that my eyes shall be opened to this wonder before I die.' Then, folding his shamma across his mouth, he withdrew into thoughts of his own while everyone remained as they were, fearing that any word or movement might destroy this peace in which at the moment his mind kept balance.

Then Herr Waldmeier, whom I have seldom seen kneel to him, fell on his knees at the Emperor's feet and said in a shaken voice, 'I beg of you do not fight them.'

Tewodros stared at him for a moment in astonishment. 'What do you mean?' he said.

'I beg you not to fight them, but to send now and negotiate. They will treat you honourably if you return the prisoners to them.'

'And if I do not?' He whispered this, but dark cords stood out in his wasted neck as if he shouted, and at the corners of his pale and scarcely moving lips a little line of white collected as if he had drunk milk.

'If you do not,' said Herr Waldmeier in a despairing voice, 'they will fight you and you cannot win against them. Do you understand? You *cannot* win and there will be more and more bloodshed which is entirely needless.'

When Herr Waldmeier had first knelt to him, the Emperor had been sitting on a stone. Now he sprang lightly to his feet and, standing crouched like a hunter, he backed away, balancing on the balls of his feet, breathing heavily and watching Herr Waldmeier as if he were a dangerous prey.

'For God's sake,' cried Herr Waldmeier, 'do not bring this thing down upon yourself.'

Then we heard the breath he drew in, its long passage like a snake, and heard it issue forth in slow and venomous words. 'Who are you, dog? A poor man. Come from a far country to be my slave, whom I have paid and fed for years. What does a beggar like you know of my affairs? Are you to dictate to me what I am to do? A Queen is coming to treat with a King, as Sheba came seeking my ancestor, Solomon. What do you know about such matters?'

All the time that he spoke he groped with his hand below the cloth of his shamma, at the belt of his shirt. The cracking of little twigs on the ground beneath the tree came between his words as he moved warily about. We saw what he intended but could not move. And Herr Waldmeier saw and still compelled to speak cried out, 'I know it will destroy you. Make peace.' Out of stubborness or courage or pity, or desire to be free, or thirst for martyrdom, he cried again, 'Make peace.'

The pistol shone in Tewodros' hand. The trigger clicked and slow words, 'He will kill him', are in my mind accompanied by no sensation. There is another click and now I think: why does he not fall but continue kneeling there like one alive? Without understanding, I see the Emperor shake the pistol and squeeze it in fury in his hand. All this time his other hand reaches back to Walda Gabir, gesturing, and Walda Gabir stares, his face all lined in dismay, but compelled by that greater will than his own he stretches out his spear to the hand that grabs it.

As soon as the one hand grasps the spear, the other flings away the pistol. Now, hissing in his throat, he crouches down shaking the spear above his shoulder. He draws it back. It balances in his hand. I do not think. I am not aware of moving. Only I find I am between them. I stare

172

into the dark consuming eyes ringed with white and at the line of foam that completely obscures his lips.

I see his eyes see me. I hear the spear sing in the air. I am watching it throb in the ground where my hand could touch it. There are voices behind me. Herr Waldmeier is behind me. His hands are on my shoulders. He shakes me. My teeth rattle in my head. I bite my tongue. There is salt in my mouth. It bleeds. He says again and again, 'What have you done?'

I think I have taken from him the thing that he wanted. But that is not why he is angry against me. It is no more tolerable that I should die than he should. I am surrounded by him, involved in his trembling, his sweating, the running of his heart, caught between his hard arm and his hard side, looking out to see what will happen.

The Emperor stands a little way before us, watching the spear steady itself and frowning as if in bewilderment at the sight. Very slowly, never taking his eyes off his master, Walda Gabir, goes to the spear and pulls it from the ground. Tewodros stoops and picks up the pistol and looks at it, idly tossing it once or twice on his open palm as I have seen a man pick up a stone and consider its shape, whether it will be of use to him, and then cast it aside. So he handed it back carelessly to Walda Gabir.

As soon as it left his hand a confusion of voices was released from the little knot of soldiers who watched him. They discussed among themselves and with him whether we should be killed. Like some conversation overheard, it seemed to concern people remote to ourselves. Yet they bore our names.

'Do not kill Waldmeier, Negus. Without him the road cannot be completed. At Meqdela you can kill him.'

'She is the daughter of your friend Bell who took the gunshots into his head for you.'

I heard the Emperor say, 'Bell was a fool. He would never learn to use a shield.' Then he turned his head to where we stood, and came rapidly and knelt on the ground before Herr Waldmeier, saying, 'Take my spear then and kill me but do not mock me.'

'I have never mocked you,' said Herr Waldmeier. 'I have been your faithful servant.' But in their voices I could hear that neither truly asked forgiveness or forgave.

The Emperor was on his feet again at once, looking shrewdly at Herr Waldmeier, saying, 'I know now why you wish me to negotiate. You would have been my messenger to the English would you not?'

'I am willing to do that.'

'And when you have gone, like all the others you will not return. I see in your eyes that you think constantly: how can I run away to these red jackets? But I am not finished with you yet. I cannot spare you until the road is complete and the guns are safe on Meqdela. Then what happens to us both is in the hands of God and of little concern to ourselves. This woman is Bell's child?'

'Yes.'

'Then she belongs in my protection, not in yours. Where is your own child?'

'In the camp.'

'It is not enough to guard you with the eye, and they tell me you are not strong enough to carry chains, but I see how it is with you, my son. It is in the nature of your people. Where this woman and that child are, you must go, and therefore I can hold you by the heart. Tomorrow I shall send them on ahead to Meqdela as a surety that you will build the road. Unless you build the road and travel along it with the gun you will not see them. Follow me now.'

I felt him release me and felt that he had gone. I heard
174

bare feet move across the crumbling leaves and twigs and was aware of faces turned towards me as they passed. Herr Flad said gently, 'Come with me, Louisa.' But I shook my head and he, too, passed.

Then I sat down on a stone and felt a great weariness of mind and body. I was unable either to recall or to think ahead. I seemed to be a part of the rock. The warm soft parts of me, alien to the rock, did not exist. The hard bones at the base of my haunches and the base of my wrists touched directly on the rock. Nothing protected me from it. In time Robert Bourgaud came looking for me and said that his mother had food for me, but I shook my head dumbly for it seemed that I could not rise from the rock. He went away then and when it was dark Madame herself came with a torch, leading Rosa who climbed onto my lap and immediately began to cry. Then I was able to stand although I felt stiff and strange and so, carrying Rosa, followed her back to the camp.

In the morning soldiers came to the tent at dawn, leading a mule, and Rosa, when I told her that we were to ride upon it, held up her arms unquestioningly for me to lift her into the saddle. Only as we rode out of the camp with four soldiers trotting on either side of us did she say once, 'Papa.'

I said, 'He will follow. He will come.' But in a little while we passed a group of men walking along the track and recognised the missionaries among them, setting out to start the road down the side of the gorge.

Rosa seeing Herr Waldmeier cried out, 'Papa,' and bounced excitedly on the saddle in front of me. He stopped and lifted his hand and stared at us through the dust as the others continued to jog past him. Then he called one of our guards over to him and I saw something white pass

175

between their hands. It was a letter, and in the time it took for the soldier to return I believed that the letter would contain words of his to me, but when it lay in my hand I saw the name on it was Dr Blanc's. I must turn my head to see him now, still standing staring after us as I continued to stare at him, in silence, and so was taken slowly from him.

A visit to the captives

I have heard a soldier say that a wound often does not hurt when it is received, the flesh around being for a time quite dead, and so a man will continue to walk and even fight and wonder why he feels nothing, and so perhaps it was with me.

I wondered at the great silence and stillness inside me and in the cool towering light all about me, and all that day felt in a mood of gentle obedience. If the soldiers told me to dismount and walk, I did so and thanked them, and when they told me to mount again I let them lift me into the saddle and settle Rosa in front of me and thanked them again.

So we moved deeper and deeper into the ravine, climbing down into cold shadow for it was still early and the sun had not yet penetrated the valleys. The land rose up on either side of us but it did not in any way press in upon us. The Bashilo is a great river and its valley is wide and spacious, and as the sun rises filled with light. We crossed the grey stones of its bed at noon and watered the mules in the shallow stream still running at its centre. Then we began to climb among the flat-topped foothills at the base of Meqdela.

The mule's feet picked over the stones. It turned its head to find the best way and jerked its body up the steep path. The harness clanked. The soldiers' muskets moved stiffly with the shifting of their shoulders. The muscles sprang and shone in their thin bare legs. Their bandoliers rattled as they climbed. Our ears were empty of the great roar and hum of the army so that single sounds struck with great clarity out of the spaces around us: a shepherd's flute, shouts from the rocks above us, the bells of herds hidden in these small hills.

Sometimes the mule pushed its way ahead and then I saw over Rosa's head no living person, but moved along this great wall of rock with its green branching plants and yellow and orange flowers and could imagine myself alone in all the world. I touched the letter in my belt. And indeed looking back we had left no trace of our passing more than a thin steam of dust.

When we came to little groups of huts no one ran away. Here, a woman stitched a basket under a tree and turned to stare with the straw held between her teeth, and, there, a child milked a goat and squatted motionless with his hand still gripped about the teat. When we passed, they moved again at their tasks, in the trust that life might never change.

I thought: perhaps the letter is of no importance. Perhaps I will keep it.

We climbed above the cultivated fields. They stretched out below us in all directions, like soft brown hides pegged out in the sun. Now, the villages and scattered herds were easily seen. Only the top of the mountain was hidden from us. But moving along its flank we felt its strength and benevolence and offer of safety.

The track grew steeper. The mule's hot flanks worked in and out, pushing my bare ankles with them. The air cooled on my arms and face. I thought: I will not read the letter but will keep it because it contains his voice.

And now we could see people waiting on the rocks

above our heads, and some came running rapidly down unseen tracks and gave the soldiers mead which they drank and offered to me but I refused. They all began to run now, although the climbing was so much steeper, laughing and talking among themselves and slapping the mule's rump to make it move more quickly.

At the last they made us dismount and let the mule climb on its own while we scrambled along the track it took, and so we came to the place where the first gateway to the fortress clings to the edge of the mountain.

When the gate was opened and we had passed through it, the world of the mountain revealed itself. In the centre, below the walls of the fortress, the thin crescent-shaped central plateau, Islamagee, curved away, golden, blurred with smoke from evening fires, rising at the far end in the flat peak of Selassie. The fortress of Meqdela is built upon just such a flat-topped rise, but is walled in black cliffs too sheer to climb at any point other than this narrow path. The mountain sides were invisible now. The curve of Islamagee floated in the fading air as if no other place existed.

And now a second gate led us through the fortress walls and here was another separate world of huts and fires and animals and people, confusing in the coming darkness.

We were taken to the house of Bitwaddad Damash, a commandant of musketeers, and there I spoke quietly and in the correct forms to his wife and ate what she gave me to eat and watched Rosa did not eat too rapidly. Afterwards we were taken to a small red tent pitched by their house and guarded by a soldier crouching over a little fire. I spread the hide that was all we had brought with us, and prayed as I had been taught, folding my hands over Rosa's and speaking slowly so that she might recognise the

179

words and say them with me. I lay beside her and when I saw the lids had closed down onto her cheeks I took the letter and laid it carefully under the edge of the hide, where my hand could touch it but where my body would not crush it nor the oil on my hair stain it, for I knew that in the morning it must be parted with.

Before I slept, the shadow of the guard moved between the tent and the fire. I heard his shield grate on the ground by the tent-flap, and saw the shadow lower and heard the shield grate again as he settled his head upon it.

When I woke there was no light. I did not know how near or how far away morning might be and so I felt afraid. The flap of the tent was closed. No stars. The greyness inside it contained no shape. With my eyes strained open, knowing the roof of the tent to be red I could only see it grey. I could imagine no event in the day that was ahead. I had no purpose in it. I felt its emptiness and shapelessness inside me. Then I remembered the letter and touched it with my hand.

Outside the cloth of the tent the guard's breath rattled in his nose. He shifted and the tent bulged where he lay against it. Now the tent began to redden and the line of the pole became clear. Rosa moaned and twisted and dug her sharp elbows into my side. Her small back breathed against my back. I lay very still then, not wanting her to wake before she must.

Later I heard the guard rise and clear his throat and spit, and in time he opened the flap of the tent and handed in two flat rounds of bread and water in a glass bottle. I said to him that I must see the hakim, and feared as I said it that he might tell me that the hakim was dead. Instead he said, 'Are you sick?'

I said, 'No. I am the hakim's friend.'

Then he pointed to a group of huts surrounded by a fence and said, 'That is where the European prisoners are kept.'

'They are well?'

'They are well enough for the moment.'

When we had eaten, I spilled the last of the water on the hem of my shamma and wiped carefully around Rosa's eyes and under her nose. I shook out her little shamma and wrapped it neatly around her, and when we had relieved ourselves in a ditch behind the tent I took her by the hand and we began to walk slowly towards the Englishmen's huts. The guard made no attempt to stop us or come with us, but stayed as he had been, crouched over his fire.

I walked in this new place with the strangeness I had felt the day before still strong about me, placing my feet carefully, one before the other, as if the surface of things was brittle and I might damage it. I broke the air ahead of me and felt it close behind me. Yet I was a very insubstantial thing, most real at the point where my hand gripped Rosa's. These huts I knew by their size and by the number of storehouses behind them, must be the Emperor's. There was the gate we passed through the night before, with a crowd of women waiting with baskets to go down to the market on Islamagee. And that narrow plateau that I had seen so briefly the night before now seemed as far away as the river or the Emperor's camp, for because of the stone walls built around the edges of the fortress you can see nothing from it but the sky.

As we came closer to the prison compound, the pictures I carried of the Englishmen came again into my mind: Dr Blanc, with his gun on his shoulder, swung the dead birds; Mr Rassam threw off his wet cloak; the stiff young soldier extended his neck when they asked him about the mortars at Sebastapol. At any moment these pictures would be overlaid, I did not know by what, and so began to hurry in my anxiety, dragging Rosa faster than she wished to go.

The gate into the compound was open. When I asked the guard if I might see the hakim, he merely pointed to one of the huts at the farthermost end of the enclosure. Here I went with Rosa, and squatted down on the dusty ground and watched.

Smoke rose straight into the air from the summit of the doctor's hut. The cramped spaces around it were filled with little fences no more than a handspan high, made of pieces of bamboo crossed this way and that to form a pattern. In amongst them a few dead plants lay stretched out on the dried ground.

An Indian servant in a turban appeared with a bowl from which steam rose and, with a quick look about him, stepped deftly over all the little fences and disappeared into the hut next to the doctor's which was covered with a thick green vine. Then the hide over the door of the doctor's hut lifted and a man with chained ankles shuffled out into the sun.

I had no difficulty in recognising Dr Blanc for although there was a dried and bleached look about him he was very little changed. He carried a walking stick in his hand which he leant on like a crutch. He wore a shamma thrown over his shoulders and native trousers. He was barefooted, and the rings on his ankles were bound round and round with dusty bandages. It was sad to see how slowly and painfully he moved. In that he was most altered. Yet his face was clean-shaven and I thought fuller and fatter than I remembered it.

I stood to my feet and would have called out to him but his glance ran over me without any recognition. He
182

had turned away and now called furtively through the doorway:

'I say, Prideaux, come here a minute.'

The hide lifted again and there appeared Lieutenant Prideaux, dressed and chained exactly as the doctor was.

Dr Blanc then raised his stick and pointing to the vine on the neighbouring hut said in a satisfied voice, 'I do believe it's dying.'

'By Jove,' said Prideaux squinting eagerly towards it. 'I do believe it is.'

'You haven't done anything to it, I suppose?'

'No. Of course not. But won't it just vex him?'

From behind the vine a voice shouted, 'How do you expect me to shave in this damned tepid water?'

'It seems that things are not going so well in any case,' said Lieutenant Prideaux. The Indian servant burst through the vine and the two Englishmen turned quickly away shuffling between the little bamboo fences. The doctor poked at the dead plants with his stick. Their eyes travelled across me without curiosity.

I called out to them then, 'May God open you.' But out of shyness and unaccustomedness I spoke not in English but in Amharic. Lieutenant Prideaux nodded curtly but Dr Blanc looked at me as if some recollection moved in him.

'May God take pity on you and release your chains,' I said more loudly, forcing myself to find the English words. As no one was in sight at that moment, I held out the letter.

Immediately they both began to hobble towards me, inch by inch for the link between their feet was no wider than a hand's-breadth, the doctor in the lead, stabbing the earth with his stick and twisting his mouth as if the movement pained him. He never took his eyes off my face.

183

'Miss Bell, is it not?' he said quietly, taking the letter out of my hand, and while he slid his finger under the seal and tore it open he said rapidly in a whisper, 'Why are you here? Are you a prisoner? Where is Waldmeier?' Then he opened the paper and let his eyes run over the words.

By now the young man had come up behind him, saying also in a whisper, 'What is it? Is it from Waldmeier? What does he say?'

'It is a private matter,' said the doctor, folding the letter and putting it quickly away inside his clothing.

'What do you mean it's a private matter?'

'Oh for God's sake, Prideaux, there still are such things. Now, where are your manners? Surely you remember Miss Bell?'

'Oh, yes indeed. Good day, Miss Bell.'

'Forgive him, Miss Bell. The truth is the ladies usually pass us by and make straight for the Residency,' and realising at once that this word meant nothing to me he gestured to the vine-covered hut. 'We call Mr Rassam's quarters the Residency.'

'Have they told you that Tewodros has had him unchained?' said Lieutenant Prideaux to me.

'There's nothing like friends in high places,' said the doctor.

'Look here, Blanc, surely Waldmeier says something about us. Where is the army? Oh, it is a shame not to tell. He must know what is going on.'

'He does not know any more than we do.'

'Oh, come,' said the young man disbelievingly and then, turning to me, 'Can you imagine what it means to us that we have not been forgotten? What it means that we and England's honour will be avenged even if they come too late to rescue us?'

'Yes, quite, quite,' said the doctor. 'It is a most anxious

time for everyone. Come, Miss Bell, I think you should pay your respects at the Residency.'

'Oh, I say, Blanc, you're not going to call on him first. It will be a fearful loss of face.'

'I look upon this as a diplomatic call not a social one,' said the doctor firmly. 'You must understand, Miss Bell, that there is a certain unavoidable coolness at the moment between ourselves and the Residency. Nevertheless it is clearly my duty to escort you there.'

'I suppose there's no need for me?' said Lieutenant Prideaux.

'None at all.'

The doctor took my arm and began to shuffle forward but in a minute turned, frowning, and held my arm out before me in both his hands and gently pushed the folds of cloth back from my wrist. 'You are half starved,' he said, it being more than a statement of fact.

'It is better now. Since Zagite there has been food.'

'And Waldmeier?'

'He, too, is very thin. He has been ill.' And then, looking at his kind face, I laughed and said, 'All his hair has fallen out.'

'Oh,' said Dr Blanc. 'Poor fellow. Has it really?' And he laughed too and, hiding my arm under his, again continued slowly forward. 'It does not trouble you that Waldmeier has lost his hair?'

'No.'

Rosa had run ahead and come back. Now she walked backwards just in front of us, staring at the doctor's lame motion. He made as if to poke his stick at her. 'She was scarcely more than a baby. That measures the time we have been here.'

'You are well, God willing?'

'Oh yes. Quite well. Devilish irritable but no one ever

185

died of that. The trouble with this damn mountain is that you can't see off the edge of it. I dare say we're all a little odd by now. At least the others seem damned odd. Prideaux's not so bad.'

'He, too, looks well.'

'Oh, he's well enough. The truth is, Miss Bell, he is so very like so many other young men that at times I feel I have a whole regiment at my back. A great comfort. Untroubled in his imagination, that's his chief strength. None of this fuss about dying. He's saved his boots, you know. They're as good as new. Sleeps on his uniform trousers to keep the creases in. All waiting for the day the Army comes and finds him here. That's keeping things in proportion is it not?'

Outside Mr Rassam's hut there were other garden plots dug and fenced, but the earth was all cracked and dry and the plants withered. Only the vine grew thick and green. As we pushed between its leaves it let off a strong disquieting smell like human skin. Dr Blanc shook a mulebell that hung by the open door and called through it, 'Mr Rassam, sir. I have brought you a visitor.'

Mr Rassam rose smiling in the speckled light of his crowded hut. His face was plump and shining. There were white dabs of soap at the edges of his thick brown hair and the trim little beard confined to the lower parts of his chin. 'My dear fellow,' he cried. 'Any time, any time. Come in. Come in.'

My hand he pressed confidingly, saying, 'This is indeed a pleasure, Miss Bell. I remember you most clearly. And how fortunate that Subhan has been baking. I am expecting company this afternoon and if you will risk burning your fingers I think we can provide an apricot tart. Subhan! Subhan, coffee and tarts for one lady. Tell me, Miss Bell, do you like apricot tarts? We shall wrap up one for this

186

dear little child and let her take it outside where I am sure she would far rather be.'

As this was the first occasion on which I had eaten an apricot tart I could find no words to answer, nor had any place I had been in previously prepared me to understand the home that Mr Rassam had built himself on Meqdela. It was a large hut. In the middle of its crowded room stood a table and four chairs. On the clean white cloth that covered the table stood a plate with a very small spoon and an empty eggshell resting in a very small bowl that exactly fitted it. Everywhere there were stacks of printed papers and books. The blue uniform he had once worn hung near the wall from a beam. On the central tree-trunk of the hut was nailed a picture of a lady's face, as like as if it lived although there was no colour in it. The skin of her face was all one white and the skin showing on her breast, surrounded by flowers. Her pale hair was in great quantity about her head; light caught in it like fire. Her lips were parted in a bold and foolish smile.

'Come, come be seated, Miss Bell,' said Mr Rassam. 'We must not keep the doctor standing any longer than is necessary.' He held a chair towards me and I sat cautiously upon it, this being an entirely new experience for me. The seat was made of cloth and swayed beneath me. There was nothing to grasp with my knees. Only my hands grasped the narrow wooden frame. I thought: I will fall to the ground. It made me want to laugh.

Now Mr Rassam hovered about Dr Blanc, pulling a chair towards him and attempting to take his arm. 'Oh for God's sake,' said the doctor. 'There was none of this fuss before.'

'No, no, of course,' murmured Mr Rassam and so I understood that the coolness between them was because they were chained and he was not. I looked politely away and breathed the mingling smells of the vine and Mr Rassam's shaving soap, and stared again at the picture of the woman. Was she Mr Rassam's wife? Was she beautiful to him? She was not so to me. Was she very sad now that he had been taken away from her? Did she never smile? And he? But Mr Rassam gave every appearance of enjoying himself.

The servant laid the plateful of little pies upon the table. Rosa was dispatched into the dead garden, holding one in each hand, and Mr Rassam held the plate towards me saying, 'Oh, please, try one. They really are delicious.' Yet all the time I was aware that in the shelter of these friendly words he was collecting his thoughts. Suddenly his face sharpened. He said to the doctor, 'But where is Waldmeier? If she is here, where is Waldmeier? Surely the road has come no further than the Bashilo?'

'She has been sent on ahead. Waldmeier is with the Emperor at Dalanta. The road isn't down to the river yet. Won't be for some days, would you say, Miss Bell?' I shook my head.

'Ah,' said Mr Rassam with relief. 'Well, help yourself, Miss Bell, and tell us all that has been happening to you. We hunger and thirst after any scrap of news that we can get. Do we not, Blanc?'

I tried to turn my mind to the camp and to what had happened on Dalanta. I thought: if that were real, then this is not, and if this is real that cannot have been. The little tarts were filled with sweetness like honey and the more I ate the more it seemed to please Mr Rassam, the more smilingly he handed me the plate. 'These are a great favourite,' he said to Dr Blanc, 'among the ladies here, although I find their husbands prefer tipsy pudding, and for some reason no one can abide Subhan's exquisite egg custard. We have been most fortunate – have we not
188

Blanc? – in having our Indian servants still with us. It has helped us to keep our standards. Now tell me, Miss Bell, where exactly is the Emperor and what chances are there that the British army might reach us before he does?'

My mouth was full of sweetness. 'She brought a letter from Waldmeier,' said the doctor.

'Well, my dear fellow, where is it? Let me have it.'

'It is a personal letter addressed to me, but he says he thinks Tewodros will be here within two weeks. Judging from the difficulties they have had in making the road, he does not think our fellows could be here for at least a week after that.'

'But surely the British army has the means to build a road at twice the speed that ...'

'That is what he says.'

'You can imagine, Miss Bell, how much safer we should feel if the British were to intercept Tewodros and, well, perhaps we had best say, negotiate for our release – before he reaches Meqdela. No doubt Waldmeier is aware of that.'

'Waldmeier has fallen from grace,' said the doctor in a lowered voice. 'The Emperor has made an attempt on his life.'

Mr Rassam made little noises with his tongue and said quickly, 'Yes, yes, and yet I trust he continues to cooperate with us. We have heard about the gun he has made, Miss Bell. Of course I am quite sure that at the time he and his friends made it he can have had no idea against whom it would be used. That is so, is it not, that it was cast before anyone knew of the British expedition?'

I remembered the sound of the women singing over the clay as Herr Flad first announced that a British army would come. But no one had believed him then. 'Yes,' I said. 'It was cast before that time.' Then, as he remained

189

watching me attentively with his shiny lips parted, waiting for more words, I said, 'It was to take against Tedla Gwalu, the rebel of Gojam, and another road was to be built for that.' But even as I said it, I could scarcely remember if this had ever been intended, so little had any practical use for Sebastapol ever been discussed.

'Tell me more about this wonderful mortar, Miss Bell. The casting I hear was successful.'

'Oh yes,' I said with pride. 'It was perfect in every part.'

'It fires a very large ball?' Here with the slightest of movements he shook from his cuff a pencil and a piece of paper and without removing his friendly brown eyes from my face prepared to write.

'Oh, very large,' I told him.

'You don't happen to know how large?'

'Oh yes,' and with my hands I made out of the air the very ball I had seen Herr Moritz chip out of rock. The pencil jerked back and forth above the paper but did not touch it.

'And the weight,' said Mr Rassam patiently. 'Did Herr Waldmeier chance to mention the weight?'

'Everyone knows,' I told him, 'that these balls are very very heavy.'

'And do they travel very far, Miss Bell?'

'They travel in the wagon.'

'No, no; when the gun is fired.'

'But it is never fired.'

'Why is that?' said Mr Rassam looking quickly from me to the doctor and back again.

'Herr Waldmeier says that pregnant women will miscarry and old men will give up their souls at the sound it will make. He says that to the Emperor.'

'And what does the Emperor say?'

'He says that the voice of Sebastapol must first be heard

190

at some great event. He says it must not be coaxed to speak for men's amusement, like a child or like Aito Blatto who tells funny stories.'

'Ah well,' said Mr Rassam with a sigh, swinging back in his chair and pushing the empty paper from him. 'Sebastapol's great event is coming very close. And now, Miss Bell, we can look forward to your company for a little while yet. It is seldom we have a visitor so charming as this, is it not, Blanc? You must share a meal with us now and then. Of course all our poor vegetables are dead now, but until a month after the rains we had peas and beans in our little gardens. You have no idea, Miss Bell, how a mouthful of garden peas alleviates the tedium of this endless meat diet.'

'I think you will find,' said the doctor rising unsteadily to his feet, 'that Miss Bell has remarkably few opinions on the tedium of meat diets. Come, Miss Bell. Our visit is at an end for today.'

'But of course you will return. We can always offer you tomatoes from our faithful vine.'

'I thought,' said the doctor beginning to shuffle towards the door while Mr Rassam's hands again started towards him and hesitated and withdrew, 'that the vine did not look so healthy as it has done.'

'What do you mean?' said Mr Rassam quickly. 'It is in perfect health.'

'Good, good,' said the doctor. 'Prideaux was anxious too. He'll be relieved that you have noticed nothing amiss.'

'But nothing is amiss,' said Mr Rassam, laughing slightly but looking swiftly at the rim of leaves around the door.

'Crop not down at all?'

'No more than is quite in order at this time of year.'

'Good, good,' said the doctor again, pushing me gently

191

ahead of him through the door. 'It was such a pretty thing in its prime. Good day to you, sir. Good day.'

'You must come some day with little Rosa and help me feed the birds,' said Mr Rassam to me. 'Come in the mornings. The afternoons are thronged with visitors.'

When I had found Rosa the doctor took my arm again and began his shuffle back towards his own hut. 'Do you know what Waldmeier wrote to me about?'

'No.'

'Not at all?'

'No.'

'Well, Miss Louisa, in the midst of all his trials he chose to write to me about you – and Rosa of course, but chiefly about you.' In that letter he had written my name. 'It appears that when your sister died he took the wise step of putting himself and Rosa under your protection, but that now even that may not be enough to save him. You know, do you not, that he expects to die when the road is finished.'

'Yes.'

'He wishes in the event of my outliving him – which is a doubtful one at best – for me to have you safely escorted to your mother's village. Rosa will go with Frau Flad.' Rosa looked up at him then, hearing the names but not understanding the words that linked them. 'He thinks she will be made very unhappy to lose you but what life is there for her here? These are sad matters to discuss are they not, but you must be told by someone what is to become of you. All this is coming to an end. It must be. Not to think ahead is to accept death too readily, as Waldmeier does. No doubt his being a missionary, after all, affects him in this and he thinks in terms of martyrdom. I do not understand that being martyred is so very different from being simply killed, as I may well be, but somehow it
192

always involves so much more upset. Oh well, it is the cause and not the blow, as the good bishop said. I imagine the cause in this case has become more than a little confused.' He poked angrily about him with his stick. 'Do you know what I should say to Herr Waldmeier if I had him here? I should say, "What do you intend to do with Miss Bell if you live?"'

The guns on Meqdela

Now Holy Week is come again and we have reached this present. Before, I was remembering by months and years; now day by day. Tewodros has come to Meqdela. His followers are camped on Islamagee. Only half the soldiers remain below to guard the guns while the road is blasted slowly upwards. For the last two days we have heard the thud and echo of explosions and know that soon it will be complete.

Then the guns will be dragged to safety up the mountain and Herr Waldmeier will be returned to us. When the sun is risen and Meqdela isolated in light, who can doubt its power as a refuge or that its rock will nourish the withered root and send the plant spreading out again over all the land? So once, as a child, I heard the Emperor say. Then I wake at night when the distances are shrunken to the close-breathing tent. I think: *when the road is complete there will be nothing left that he can do for the Emperor.*

On sunny days the flashes are visible of the English guns. Then for a day or two the sky will be overcast, and when the flashes are seen again they are nearer.

'If they don't come soon we shall plant another garden,' says Mr Rassam. The little brown envelopes of seeds, sent to him from the coast, are laid out tidily on his table, marked *cabbage, beans, peas*. They will plant them as
194

they did last year on the 24th of May which is Queen Victoria's birthday and, although they cannot really believe that they will still be there, it is a kind of superstition with them to talk constantly of their gardens and to plan where each vegetable will go.

'At least if we plant them we shall know we are alive,' says the doctor.

For since the Emperor has pitched his tent on Islamagee, and in spite of the fact that he has exchanged many exceedingly polite letters with Mr Rassam, the Englishmen are very anxious to know what he intends to do with them. There is anxiety everywhere in the fortress, for who, in Tewodros' long absence, has not fallen short or laughed unwisely or whispered a real or imagined insult in the wrong ear? And now, hour by hour, people ask, 'Is Tewodros well?' 'Does he sleep?' 'May he wake well.' And every message that comes from the camp is told and retold and examined minutely in the fear that someone's fate is hidden in the words.

Holy Tuesday

Today a message came early from Dr Blanc, asking me to come at once to the Residency. I picked up Rosa and ran to the gates of the compound and saw the doctor walking towards us between the rows of huts. He wore his red uniform. Then I noticed the strangeness of his moving, for he walked like a man who wades through water, and, coming to a stone lying in his path, I saw him lift his foot over very high as if it had been a rock. Only then did I realise that his feet were free of chains. I ran to him then, taking both his hands in mine and laying my forehead upon them out of pleasure for him, saying, 'Praise God that He has seen fit to open you.'

'Yes, thank God, indeed.' Holding on to my hands and

195

keeping me close to him he went on in a low voice, 'The Emperor has sent word that Prideaux and I should come with Mr Rassam to watch the arrival of the guns. Aito Samuel thinks that as Mr Rassam is in such favour at the moment, the more you are seen with us and become associated in people's minds with our party, the better things may be for you. The consul and Stern and Rosanthal are still chained so there is nothing we can do for them, but won't you come with us now?'

It took a long time to pass between the two gates of the fortress for the Englishmen's wasted legs would scarcely bear them, and they walked like little staggering children. The guards laughed but with no malice, and lent them their walking sticks. Mr Rassam was scarcely stronger, for his delicacy had forbade his walking too conspicuously about the prison compound. Nevertheless he managed to walk by himself and hold his own umbrella. They had not been outside the fortress for eighteen months, and stopping frequently to catch their breath they stared in bewilderment at the steep track leading down to Islamagee, and Selassie at the far end, saying, 'Was it really so large? I do not remember it so.'

In time we reached the level of the plateau and found it all overlaid with the huts of the army. Then we were led to a place where we could see the fresh wide scar of the road running along the southern flank of Islamagee. It climbed along a sloping ledge with black precipices rising above it and falling away below, until at last, where we halted, the trace turned sharply and the road was blasted through rock and rose steeply to the level of the plain.

Here the Emperor sat waiting on a pile of stones, watching intently for the first appearance of Sebastapol. A great crowd of his warriors were grouped around him, and
196

all along the cliff-tops, in lines of white and brown, their families waited as on a festival day for the procession to arrive. From far away over the drop of the mountain came the sound of the men dragging the gun along some invisible stretch of the road. At such a distance it sounded no more than some little creatures panting, but I would never have mistaken it: a sound to which my ears had grown so long accustomed that to hear it now was like a return to a loved and familiar place.

We stood in uncertainty some way from the Emperor. The last time the Englishmen and the interpreter, Aito Samuel, had seen the Emperor was in the treasury at Debra Tabor. The last time I had seen him was when he had tried to kill Herr Waldmeier. Now Aito Samuel gathered courage and went forward to announce us.

The Emperor came at once and seizing Mr Rassam's hand in his, pumped it up and down in pleased excitement saying, 'No bowing, my friend, today we shall all be very English and shake hands.' He looked searchingly into Mr Rassam's face and added quietly, 'They told me that since you were my prisoner you had become quite grey, but I do not see one grey hair on your head. Look at me and see how grey I have become since we parted.' And it was true, the three plaits of hair from his forehead to the nape of his neck were grey as ash. Also the sufferings that he had endured and caused to others had greatly marked his face. In so short a time I had forgotten how he had come to look, as I had forgotten the extreme beauty of his smile.

Now he graciously allowed the three Englishmen to sit down on a projecting rock where they might be the first to see the gun. Observing that they were tired he permitted them to put on their caps. Mr Rassam asked if he might also raise his umbrella. 'Yes, yes,' said the Emperor and

197

sent at once for one of his servants to fetch an umbrella for
the doctor. All these marks of favour were noted by the
crowd who whispered to one another that he did Mr
Rassam a great honour in allowing him to sit at his back
where by one motion of his arm Mr Rassam could have
hurled the Emperor over the cliff.

Aito Samuel stood bareheaded beside them, translating,
as the Emperor spoke in a pleasant formal style as if Mr
Rassam had only that morning arrived at his court. 'It
is a great pleasure to speak with you again, Mr Rassam,
after so long an absence. You perhaps find it strange that
I enjoy the conversation of Europeans but until my time
it was a very rare thing to see a European in this country,
indeed nearly all of the Emperors preceding me passed
out their lives without seeing one.'

Mr Rassam smiled and said in a pleasant voice, 'In
former times Abyssinia was only read about in books,
but now your Majesty's name has become so notorious
that every child in Europe knows who Tewodros is.'

'Why is that?' he asked gravely.

'Because Your Majesty put me in chains.'

Aito Samuel hesitated out of fear to translate this but
Tewodros nodded sharply at him and he repeated the
remark as best he could and all our eyes followed it to the
Emperor. We saw him raise his head and heard him
laugh. Then he drew his thin hands down over his face
and holding them up by his head, shaking them slowly in
the air, he laughed again delightedly, saying, 'Hear him.
Hear what he says. Oh, my friend Rassam, my friend.'
Then you could feel the fear slip away and the long-
forgotten laughter spread through the crowd like warmth.
Yet all the time we listened to the sound of the approaching gun; and when a crack rang out like a musket-shot
and echoed on the mountainside we knew that a rope had

snapped and that the great mortar was in danger. Then we stood stiff and silent, filled again with fear.

It was near enough now for us to hear the sound of the soldiers' voices break out in confused shouting. Tewodros sprang lightly to his feet and running to the edge of the rock raised his hand and called down in a clear low voice. Instantly the shouting ceased and in a moment the regular chanting began again to come closer and closer.

The Emperor turned back to Mr Rassam, his face smoothed with pleasure, and said, 'Ah, come now, my friend, and see Sebastapol.' Everyone moved cautiously forward, for the cliff was very steep, and saw behind the rows of bent and creeping backs the glittering mass of the great mortar.

All along the rocks above us, the women who had gathered to watch began to give their high trill of victory: *li-li-lil-li.* It rose like birds on every side and the joy rose in me and my tongue began to make soft licks along the roof of my mouth for I, too, can make that sound, although since I came to Gafat I know not to. Yet the wanting to was very strong at that moment for Sebastapol had come to Meqdela and I could still believe this to be all. Was it not the most powerful gun in all the world, and was not Meqdela an impregnable fortress? Now these two great things were come together. Tewodros had crushed the distance between them in his bare hand. What power is greater than this? This is all. Now we are safe. Such shrill cries permit no other thought.

Now the first men scrambled over the mouth of the road, bent double with the black leather thongs cut into their shoulders. The crowd backed to make room for more and more, straining up with the ropes. We could hear the grinding of the wheels that carry the mortar and then with a great jolt it was over the cliff, shining in

199

the road through the settling cloud of dust. More soldiers came behind, rushing to wedge stones under the wheels but when that was done the ropes fell to the ground and many of the men, too, panting and sobbing for breath, some clutching at their stomachs or rubbing their shoulders. Men were weeping. But some ran in among the crowd, embracing everyone they ran against, singing and laughing. The *lil-li-li-lil* fluttered like flags, as if the weight of the mortar fell from us all and the sound was free to rise in us and lift us.

In the bright haze of dust I can see Herr Waldmeier standing beside the gun. The sweat gleams on his face and his bare head. His yellow beard is dark with sweat. He, too, is smiling. He has seen me holding up Rosa to him ... he smiles at me. The sound goes on and on, so that all thoughts are made simple. He is still alive. He has come. This is all.

The Emperor is showing the Englishmen the mortar, putting his head inside its giant mouth, patting its thick sides. 'Waldmeier,' he calls out. 'Waldmeier, my son.' And when Herr Waldmeier stands beside him, he says, 'There have been but two happy days for me this past year: one when Waldmeier cast the cannon and one today.'

Then the sounds of rejoicing grew quieter and Herr Waldmeier was sent to order the dragging of Sebastapol further along the road to make room for the lesser guns, so we did not see him again that day.

Tewodros sat down again on the rock, beckoning Mr Rassam to sit close to him, for now that the great mortar was safely up there would be little difficulty in dragging the others and he was free to enjoy again the company of his friend.

'What do you think of my mortar, Mr Rassam?'

'Why, it is remarkable. A splendid piece of artillery, is it not?' And he looked to his two companions who nodded vigorously. 'I hope,' he went on, 'that soon the British will be looking at it with the same feelings of friendly admiration that fill my heart at this moment.'

Aito Samuel turned pale at this remark and shook his head beseechingly at Mr Rassam, but the Emperor had understood in part and he must translate.

'Yes,' Tewodros replied calmly, 'I hope so, too. And I hope, Mr Rassam, that when your people arrive they will not despise me because I am black. God has given us all the same faculties and heart.'

'It is quite impossible,' said Mr Rassam, 'that anyone would despise you.'

The Emperor was silent for a while as the next gun came onto the level ground. Then he turned again to Mr Rassam and began to tell him of the casting of Sebastapol and the long slow march, the building of the road, the hostility of his people and the reprisals he had felt forced to take against them. 'You see, my friend, I am like a woman large with child. I feel the first pains of labour come upon me and I wonder: will this child be a girl or a boy or will I perhaps miscarry and die?' Here he leant forward. 'I look to you, Mr Rassam, to assist me in the birth of a boy.'

'You know my only desire has always been for peace between our countries.'

'I hope that is so, Mr Rassam,' Tewodros said, looking at him sadly and intently. 'For all that is left to me out of all of Abyssinia is this rock.'

Mr Rassam said, 'This day is a day of rejoicing, Sire. You have, in the casting of Sebastapol and the building of the road, performed a feat of engineering of which any nation in Europe might be proud.'

'Yes, yes, I believe that is true. And I am glad that you are my friend.' The Emperor rose to his feet so that the others had to scramble awkwardly to their feet after him. Still he continued speaking to Mr Rassam alone. 'I know that my end will come and that the time is near at hand when you shall stand by the side of my dead body. Then you will think: Oh, Emperor Tewodros, how great was your sinfulness. But please do not judge me, because God will judge each one of us. I shall be judged as a king. You, my friend Rassam, will be judged as an ambassador, Waldmeier as a missionary and the poor beggars will be judged as beggars. Now,' he said, 'go back to Meqdela and I shall send for you soon again.' He turned, walked a few paces, and then, turning abruptly back, said to Mr Rassam, 'Tell me what is the correct charge of gunpowder for a very large mortar?'

Holy Wednesday

Today the Emperor sent for all the European prisoners to come down from the fortress to his camp on the Islamagee plain. Mr Cameron and Mr Stern were now freed of their chains, Mr Cameron so weak that the guards all but carried him down the path.

Ahead of us on the path crept long lines of the Emperor's native prisoners who had been kept until now at the farther end of the fortress in the common gaol. As we came up to them they were driven off the track to allow us to pass. Almost all these prisoners were still chained, some by the wrist, some by the ankles, some with one hand chained to their leg irons so that they must walk bent and twisted. Some had lived so for many years, convicted of crimes against the Emperor by themselves or members of their families – some crimes no more than misplaced laughter. Where their filthy rags did not extend, their skin was grey, and puckered with rashes like caked mud and broken with sores, so that a foul tired sweetish smell came from them like the beginnings of decay. Mr Rassam bunched his handkerchief over his face and murmured, 'How terrible, how terrible.' They were terrible beyond pity, too intent upon the effort to move and stay upright to call out to us, or even look at us as we overtook them.

'What could he possibly want with those poor creatures?' the doctor asked Mr Rassam. And the thought oppressed us all that the native prisoners being sent for at the same time as ourselves might in some way mean that our fates would be linked with theirs.

We were led through the camp to where a large crowd stood grouped before the Emperor's great red tent. The soldiers parted to let us through, leaning forward on their spears and muskets to stare at us. At the end of the path they had made we saw Tewodros hurrying towards Mr Rassam to greet him.

Usually he dresses as a common soldier with only the red silk border of his shamma to suggest that he might be a man of rank, but today he wore a tunic of great richness, made of many brilliant silks woven together, and over his head Walda Gabir held a great green silk umbrella flashing with sequins and gold fringe. He greeted Mr Rassam with courtesy and so with Dr Blanc and Lieutenant Prideaux. Then he turned to the consul and the two missionaries while everyone watched in anxiety, remembering how in the past the sight of these gentlemen had so often enraged him.

Mr Cameron stared about him, resting his pale eyes on nothing. Thin wisps of his hair rose in the wind. He shuffled his bare feet around in a circle to keep balance and swayed as he stood.

203

'What is the matter with him?' asked the Emperor without compassion.

'He is ill,' said Dr Blanc. 'With Your Majesty's permission, he would feel better if he might sit down.'

'Sit, sit,' said the Emperor and moved forward as if he would assist Dr Blanc in lowering the consul onto a rock, but he drew back before touching him and turning, looked shrewdly at the Reverend Mr Stern, and that gentleman returned his look with the same cringing arrogance that I remembered from childhood.

Tewodros spoke mildly enough. 'Oh Stern, why, if you are a priest, do you not shave your head? Instead you wear it plaited like a soldier. Do you, too, plan to take up arms against me?'

'Your Majesty,' said Aito Samuel quickly, 'it is not plaited but falls naturally to his shoulders.'

'Is that so?' said Tewodros, losing interest. 'Then it is of no significance.' He, too, selected a stone and when he was seated upon it he motioned the other Europeans to sit where they were. Then he said, 'I have sent for you as I desire to look after your safety. When your people come and fire upon me, I will put you in a safe place and should you, even there, be in danger I will remove you somewhere else. Have your tents been sent?'

'No, Sire,' said Mr Rassam.

'Then one of mine will be pitched for you.' He continued to talk, switching rapidly from one subject to another, and looking often over his shoulder as if his attention were distracted. Then, noticing a man had forced his way through the crowd and whispered something to Walda Gabir, he called out, 'What does he say? What does he say?'

Walda Gabir came forward, 'It is a rumour, Negus. He brings a tale from a village woman that the English

204

brought their horses and mules to water at the Bashilo last night.'

'So they are near,' he said softly and, raising his voice, he called out over the heads of the Europeans to his own soldiers, 'You hear of white men coming to fight me. It is no rumour but quite true.'

In the crowd a soldier raised his spear and shouted out, 'Never mind, Negus, we shall fight them for you.'

The Emperor turned his head slowly to where the man was elbowing his way to the front of the crowd. 'You are a fool,' he said looking coldly at him. 'You do not know what you say. These people have long cannons, elephants, guns that dazzle the sight, muskets without number that shoot and stab simultaneously. We cannot fight against them. You believe our muskets to be good, but I ask you this? Where did they come from? I did not have them made here. The English sold them to the Turks and the Turks sold them to me whom they hate. If they were good muskets they would not have done so. If they themselves had not procured better muskets they would not have sold these to me.' His head fell down to his chest. A few minutes later, ignoring even Mr Rassam, he rose abruptly from his rock and went to his tent.

I asked them where the missionaries were camped and being shown their tents nearby I took Rosa there. When she saw Madame she smiled, and for the first time said to me, 'Where is Papa?' But he was not there. He was clearing a road for the guns around the base of Salassie out on the western spur of the mountain which is called Fahla. 'He will come and eat with us at night,' said Madame. 'You will see him then. There is his tent but he never uses it. He sleeps always by the fire. So you and Rosa may have the tent if you continue here.' From the way that she spoke I sensed the effects of our absence. It was

205

a surprise to her to see us again, an effort to recall exactly how we had lived among them. She had come to think of Herr Waldmeier as a childless man who slept by the ashes out of some perversity.

In his tent was the little pile of torn German books. His carpenter's tools hung in a bag from the tent pole and in amongst them were the cows he had carved at Debra Tabor. Each of these things which were now all that he owned, I touched, so meeting him in advance, and showed to Rosa. She recognised them and looked pleased, settling at once to play on the dusty floor with her cows. I spread out his hide which was neatly rolled in the corner of the tent and lay on it, hoping to sleep out the time until he should come and find us there, and in a little while Rosa left her play and came and lay and slept against me.

It was not evening when we woke but late in the afternoon. Coming out of the tent we saw groups of people standing watching in the direction of the Emperor's tent. Sleep and drinking had changed his mood of the morning. Now he stood on a little hillock near his tent and in his gaudy tunic he shouted out his titles and his triumphs of the past to his assembled soldiers.

'I am Tewodros the creature of God. I am the lion that the other lions fear. I am the scourge of the perverse who will lead you to Jerusalem. I am the master of Sebastapol whose voice alone kills hundreds before he throws his ball. Saint Michael the horseman fights beside me. I am in league with Christ. Now men that fight for a woman march against me. They march to their death. They do not know the lion that awaits them in his lair. When the Turks attacked at Gedaref they were cowards and dared not fight like men but hid behind a wall. When the French sent soldiers to my country I led my army against them and they fled in terror at my name. If you fight with me you will wear clothes more splendid than these I wear now. The red coats of the English will make covers for your shields more thick and beautiful than hide. For I am Tewodros, the Chosen of God, the invincible. No men ruled by a woman can stand against me.'

His soldiers shouted with delight, and when he paused one by one their leaders danced before him, shouting out their own brave deeds and waving their sharp spears. There was no more looking through telescopes; everything was forgotten in the glory of the past. When the fire was lit and Herr Waldmeier returned, still his penetrating voice reached between the tents, hoarse now with the great number of his triumphs.

Some of the Europeans mocked him gently among themselves and some were afraid of his drunkenness and pride but I sat once again by the Gafat people's fire and carried Herr Waldmeier's food to him and held Rosa beside me until the warmth of the fire sent her to sleep, so that things had a semblance of returning to what they once had been.

Also much of what the Emperor said was known to me and at the sound of his voice I remembered how the earth had once moved with the number of his soldiers. It was easy to forget the battles he had yet to fight and remember only that he had never been defeated except once long ago by the cowardly Turks at Gedaref.

Maundy Thursday

This morning dark clouds rose from behind the surrounding mountains and lay heaped on their flat tops, ever piling higher so that the sun had no time to climb above them before being quite obscured. With no sun there could be no indication of the British army's advance, but early in the day a messenger came running into the camp

207

to report that their baggage train had been seen descending from Dalanta to the Bashilo. There were four elephants and only a few men, but many small white animals with black faces.

Then the Emperor sent a message to Mr Rassam and his party, and to all the Gafat people, saying, 'Let us go together and see what your friends and my enemies are doing.' We walked together behind him to the north side of Selassie, near to Fahla, where the guns would be positioned at a point where the Bashilo could be seen in that wide lower plain intricately patched with little fields. The Emperor raised his telescope in the direction the messenger indicated and stared through it for a long time at the slopes of the Dalanta Plateau. Then he let the arm holding the telescope drop to his side and his head fell forward abruptly as if the strings in him were cut, and he said to Herr Waldmeier, 'Take the telescope and see what I see.'

Herr Waldmeier took the telescope and pointed it in the direction that the Emperor had, and it came to me that he would see the English soldiers travelling towards us on the road he himself had built. I saw that he did not know what to say and kept the telescope to his eye to avoid looking at the Emperor, but his hand began to tremble violently.

The Emperor standing close, spoke in his ear. 'Do you not remember, my son, how we planned and worked together on that road? How we broke the hard rock with such difficulty? See now, how quickly those men and animals are marching towards me. Oh, I was a fool to have made that road. God blinded me for I thought I had made it to carry the guns to safety, but God intended it for my enemies. I brought them here and now I have smoothed a road before them.' And then as his mind
208

travelled farther along the road he added in a whisper, 'I have opened Meqdela to them. It is the will of God.' But his rage was not abated. He snatched the telescope from Herr Waldmeier, left us without a word and shut himself up in his tent.

Herr Waldmeier was sent back to clearing the road and the rest of us returned to the camp and waited there. It came to us in whispers that Tewodros slept. May he wake well.

Rosa slept, and I lay on the hide and watched light glow in the tent. I felt a great weariness but could not sleep. Time seemed gathered for some great movement forward but now it crouched and quivered and held its leap.

Even at noon the camp emits a humming sound of many people, and all sounds that are distinct must work their way up through that layer of common sound. So I heard a disturbance: a shout that rose and might have sunk again but others carried it on. A clanking and ringing of metal on metal. Voices that divided into words calling for God to have mercy upon them and some for food and some for water. The native prisoners were kept in tents near ours; it was they who cried out. Then the sounds died away and the humming rose up and covered them.

I lay and thought: shall I get up now? Shall I wake Rosa if I do? If I go outside this tent where shall I sit, to whom shall I speak, what shall I do? In accompaniment to these thoughts there came again the ring and whisper of chained feet moving past our tents. This sound went on and on, and where were they being taken? There were cries now that held great fear. Muskets fired singly one after the other at broken and irregular intervals. A man I had never seen thrust his head through the opening of the tent and said in a whisper, 'Do not come out or make a sound, for if you do he will surely kill you.' Before he could be questioned he had gone and I heard his hoarse whisper at the next tent.

Now the whole camp went silent and I continued to lie on the hide, praying that Rosa would not wake, listening for sounds that I might interpret. *He is with the guns,* I thought. Until the road is cleared to Fahla and the guns in position, the Emperor cannot do without him. Out of idleness, I began to make marks in the dust for every musket-shot, but it became tedious in time. It was difficult to distinguish the shots from their echoes and often in bursts they overlapped each other. My mind refused to offer any explanation for these shots, although afterwards, being told what had happened in the afternoon, it seemed that I knew well enough.

In the space of a few hours the Emperor, in drink or insanity, killed well over three hundred men, women and children: all but a few of the native prisoners. The first two he had cut down with his own sword, the third he came to was a child whom he found himself unable to kill and instead gave orders that he be thrown over the precipice behind the camp. Then he sat beside the cliff and one by one the prisoners were dragged before him and sentenced. Then one after another had their hands and feet struck from them and were thrown by the soldiers over the cliff. The Emperor's musketeers were lined along the edge and ordered to shoot at anything that moved on the rocks below. This work continued until the fall of darkness made it impossible to see, and the Emperor's need for blood was appeased.

I was told this as I tell it, in voices that shook at the things that had been seen, yet I myself saw nothing of this killing. Only at dusk, when the Emperor had retired to his tent and it was safe for us to move from ours, did I see the two ranks of musketeers with their shoulders hunched slightly over their downward-pointing muskets and heard the little careless sound of their firing. So a gun remains a thing that makes a noise, its consequences out of sight, beyond imagining.

Herr Waldmeier sits staring, sick and silent, into the fire for he has seen what I have not. There is a fire in Tewodros' tent. It can be seen to glow through the red fabric. It is said that since nightfall he has wept and prayed and said that he did not mean to do what he did, that he did it in a fit of drunkenness and therefore is not responsible.

Mr Rassam's fire is also visible. The bulging turbaned head of his Indian servant moves in front of it. There are little points of light where Mr Rassam and Dr Blanc and Lieutenant Prideaux sit on their folding chairs and smoke their cheroots. Beside the Gafat people's fire, Herr Flad reads rapidly and urgently from the German Bible.

Let not the martyrdom come upon you like some strange thing but think always that you are partaking in the Passion of Christ.

Good Friday

At dawn the priests in the church tent pitched beside the Emperor's began their lamentations for the death of Christ. At eight o'clock the Emperor left his tent and entered the church tent for absolution. His followers knelt in a great crowd on the ground outside.

It is overcast. The air is filled with a restless expectancy of rain. Aito Samuel has brought Mr Rassam an order that he is to return with his party to Meqdela. It is decided in conversation that I only understand in part, for the Arabic that Mr Rassam and Aito Samuel speak together is meaningless to me, that my fortunes and

Rosa's are from this time to be separate. She undoubtedly is her father's charge and must stay with him. I am under the Emperor's protection and must return to Meqdela and there stay, if I can, within the sphere of Mr Rassam's diminishing favour.

Rosa plays all unconcerned at my feet. When she notices that I am to go without her, she begins to cry, but Madame lifts her in her arms and jogs her up and down, chanting at her in French and calling to me, 'She will stop directly you are gone.'

I had not thought that I should ever do this. They say it is for the best. For whose best they do not say, for we loved one another and were a comfort each to the other when together and cannot be so apart. But nothing in me remains so strong that I can know better than they, and so I ride away from her as strange and unfeeling as when the Emperor had me taken from Herr Waldmeier: without a word because they have decided for me.

So I come to be outside Mr Rassam's Residency alone, hearing the priests sing in the church on Meqdela and smelling the rain approach the dry musty leaves of the tomato vine. I have been bidden here to the Reverend Mr Stern's Meditation on the death of Our Lord.

Mr Rassam, Dr Blanc and Lieutenant Prideaux, who are seated in their folding chairs, now rise. They do this because I am a woman. Mr Rassam comes smiling towards me. 'It occurred to me that you would be anxious, and missing little Rosa, and might care for some distraction. There is the matter of Mr Stern's Meditation to be got through and then would you care to see my photograph album? And apricot tarts? Can you smell them? Subhan is baking them especially.' He is a truly kind and sympathetic man.

The door of the hut has darkened behind me and the
212

Reverend Mr Stern enters in his black coat. He passes his Bible from hand to hand and says in a rich mournful voice, 'I regret that the consul is not sufficiently well to join us. The events of yesterday have caused him great agitation of spirit.'

'Shall I go to him?' says the doctor.

'No need, sir, no need. I have administered the Sacrament to him in private and prayed with him, so that now he seems somewhat calmer. Good day to you, Miss Bell,' he says when his dark eyes fix upon me. 'You may be unaware that it was I who gave Communion to your father shortly before his death. I pray that there is no melancholy coincidence in our meeting here today.' As the Bible passes from hand to hand he leaves upon it the shapes of his sweating palms. 'I would have you know that during my prayers for Holy Week I have found it in my heart to forgive Waldmeier the irregularities of his life here and his past callousness to our sufferings. He is a young man, far from home, a prey to the temptations of youth, and misguided, I suppose, by the promise of worldly position. But now, as I say, I forgive him and can honestly say I bear your family no ill will. It may comfort you, at the last, to know this. Let us pray.'

We kneel and the Reverend Mr Stern fills out his voice. 'My brothers in Christ, we are gathered together in a time of great stress, after many sufferings and tribulations, in hourly fear of death at the hands of a ruthless and blood-soaked tyrant, to meditate upon the death of Our Lord. Let us pray for our poor brethren of Gafat, who even now may stand face to face with their Creator ...'

I would gladly pray for Herr Waldmeier for I have been taken from him and do not know what may have befallen him. Also there is a feeling which no one expresses, that

213

there is no longer time for things to change and change again. But Mr Stern will not leave the mind to pray in peace other prayers than his.

'Bring us to the final temptation secure in the knowledge that we have held fast to Thy commandments. When Thine hour of vengeance is upon us, spare, Lord, Thy suffering and righteous servants.'

There is a movement sharper than the cautious shifting of knees. Lieutenant Prideaux has raised his head and, after turning it from one side to the other, inclines it to the doctor and whispers, 'What was that?' But the sound, which I heard too, is gone: a great sound far off, or a small sound near, I could not tell. Mr Rassam had heard it also. He, too, is turning towards the door of the hut. Only Mr Stern, with his hands clenched in front of his eyes, continues in his angry prayers.

'Cast into the eternal pit the tormentors of Thy children. Rain down Thy vengeance.' And as if at his behest the sky over Meqdela cracks with thunder. Rain batters at the thatch. From outside the servants struggle to fasten the reed door and shutters. The odour of the vine, released by rain, fills the room which is now quite dark.

It is a long time to kneel on the hard earth, subjected to these prayers. The hut shakes under the onslaught of the rain, and now, and again now, that fugitive sound breaks free from the din of the storm and the voice of Mr Stern. 'Amen,' he says at last.

He has scarcely drawn out the word to its final resonance before Lieutenant Prideaux bursts out, 'I'll swear I heard something.'

'Come now,' says the doctor. 'Don't raise our hopes. We must not count upon it. It may have been the storm.'

'No. It was gunfire. You heard it, Blanc. Whatever you say, you shan't make me believe otherwise.'

Mr Stern blinks slowly at them and, shaking each of us gravely by the hand, leaves the hut without a word.

'What a devilish depressing fellow he is,' says Dr Blanc. He cannot hide the excitement in his voice. 'Come, Prideaux, fetch your umbrella. You and I shall take our constitutional and see if we can find out what is going on below.'

And so that long afternoon passes in the Residency. I eat apricot tarts and, when I have washed my hands, turn the pages of Mr Rassam's album very carefully so as not to soil the brown and yellow photographs. Listening for the guns, I stare again and again at the variety of ladies, weighted to the grass with skirts like metal bells, who have paused in what they were doing to smile at him.

It is dusk. The rain has ceased. Evening sunlight lies in a straight band between the flat bottoms of the clouds and the flat tops of the mountains. And still we hear a booming like thunder and a rattling like small stones continuously falling.

'It is a battle. No question of that,' says Lieutenant Prideaux, happily shaking the rain from his umbrella.

'No question of that,' repeats the doctor. 'One way or another it will all be over soon.'

Easter Saturday

No one will tell us what has happened. At night we heard the sound of women lamenting on Islamagee. From earliest dawn the wounded have been brought up to the fortress and laid on the open ground outside the Emperor's house, where, as the sun has risen, their families have built straw bowers over them and squat beside those restless jerking limbs, waving away the flies. The doctor attends them there. The priests shuffle among them,

215

dabbing holy water from bottles onto pieces of cloth and pressing them to the soldiers' faces.

Through Aito Samuel the doctor questions those who are not too badly hurt.

'There were many killed,' they say.

'We did not return until dark and so we could not see who came with us and who remained.'

'There were great numbers killed. Blood ran on the rocks.'

'They said it was an easy thing to fight the English. The Negus said, "You must wait until they fire and then, while they reload their muskets, you jump up and run forward and kill them with your spear." But, Hakim, it was not so. As soon as their muskets fired one ball it fired another and another : balls so thick it was impossible to drive a spear between them.

'And from their guns they fired narrow balls as long as the distance between my thumb and my elbow and they were filled inside with powder and little balls so that when they hit the ground they burst and cast out their contents, killing many people all around.

'Some burst in mid air making a great sound. Some hit the thing they were thrown at and made no sound. Then they burst when no one expected it.'

'The Emperor's general, Fitawrari Gabrie, is dead.'

'I saw him. I saw his shirt all bloody on a man on the ground. I did not see his face.'

'He is dead.'

'And Tewodros?'

'May he sleep well.'

'Is he dead then?'

'No. No. He did not fight beside us. May he wake well.'

Herr Waldmeier has come to Meqdela. I smell the bruising of the vine. I look up, and he is standing at the doorway of the Residency. He holds his straw hat in his hands and twists the brim in his thick fingers this way and that so that the straw breaks and I want to tell him, do not do that, for he will need his hat.

'Waldmeier, for God's sake tell us what has happened,' says Mr Rassam.

There is heat across my eyes and pain in my throat. I am crying. My face is hot and cold with tears. I had not thought to see him again. And there is a kind of anger in all that wasted fear, now that he is alive and standing unchanged in the room, breaking the brim of his hat.

'It is all over,' he says. 'You are free.'

'What do you mean?' says Dr Blanc. It is too much for them, coming like that. 'What do you mean?'

'That he has lost everything. He wants you to go. He wants peace.'

'Are we to go free now?'

'Yes.'

'And you? And the others? Stern, Cameron, Rosanthal?'

'Yes. Yes.'

Then everyone is very quiet. And, staring at him, I see that he is worn and dirty and trembling as he stands.

'Well,' says Lieutenant Prideaux and because his voice sounds blurred he clears his throat. 'I'll smarten up a bit then.'

'Does Cameron know?' asks Mr Rassam.

'No, I came straight here.'

'Well, tell him, Prideaux, and the others, will you? Tell the servants. They'll want to pack.'

'You should have some brandy, Waldmeier,' says the doctor. 'You look quite done in.'

'We could all do with some,' says Mr Rassam. He hooks

217

with his thumb under his beard, and strokes with his finger up and down his bare cheek, and looks about the crowded room in perplexity. 'He wants us to go today?'

'Come, sit down,' says the doctor to Herr Waldmeier who shakes his head almost shyly and says, 'No. No.'

'Sit down,' orders the doctor and Herr Waldmeier looks from one chair to another and finally lowers himself into one of them while Dr Blanc pours out the brandy and hands the little metal cups around.

When Herr Waldmeier has thrown back his head and wiped his eyes the doctor says, 'What's that on your hands? Gunpowder?'

'He had Saalmuller and me weigh out a charge for each of the guns.'

'You fired them? Did they do any damage?'

Herr Waldmeier gives a shy proud smile at the ground. I see the little pulses in his thin cheeks. 'We weighed out a double measure of powder for each gun. They all over-shot their mark.'

'Oh, well done, well done,' says the doctor.

'Yes. Good fellow,' says Mr Rassam, who is putting the papers on his desk into a valise.

'Oh, I tell you, I was afraid.' He lifts his head and looks for me. 'As bad as Saalmuller. We did not know at all what the charge should be, only that we used too much. Every time they lit the match we shut our eyes and prayed. Believe me, I scarcely knew what I was doing. The gun Tewodros – you remember Tewodros, Louisa – exploded. It is completely ruined.'

'And Sebastapol?' I did not want Sebastapol to be ruined.

'When Tewodros exploded, he would not risk firing it. You see, he thought it was only a baggage-train coming out of the ravine and he sent every man that he had down with Fitawrari Gabrie, pouring down the mountain, hundreds of them. But it was no baggage-train. There were guns, all the time firing, firing, very rapidly so that the poor creatures were mown down like grass. But they did not understand. They kept coming back and back. On foot. With spears, good God. And cut down again, all cut down. Do you know what I thought?' In the earnestness of his talking he turns now to Dr Blanc. 'I thought: after all this, the gun is no heroic weapon. Even Saalmuller and I can fire a gun and stand there, way above the fighting, sweating with fear and weighing out gunpowder like a pair of grocers. But to run at a man with your spear, to mark out one single man and cast yourself against him ... Well, the spear was his true weapon, but he chose to stay with the guns. Always with the guns.'

The doctor leans forward. 'Have some more brandy.'

'No, no.'

But the doctor fills the little glass. 'What did Tewodros do?'

'Their shells began to reach us and he watched them like a child. There was wonder in his eyes, and I, too, Dr Blanc had seen nothing like this. You can see their shells coming through the air with smoke twisting behind them like a snake. One fell close to him and it killed a horse. He stood for a long time and stared at what it had done to the horse and then he sat down against the carriage of Sebastapol and hid his head under his shield, and there he stayed, not through fear – he feels no fear – but shamed, I think, at their power being greater than his. And yet, good God, his men were brave enough. They continued to charge against the rifles until nightfall. Then what was left of them came back. He got up, and as they passed he began to call out for Gabrie. No one answered, no one dared say he was dead, but of course the Emperor knew, and then he called out for all the chieftains, name after name, and there was no answer, no answer at all. They just went past him like the walking dead and left him to judge for himself the dead that lay below.'

'And how has he taken it?'

'He has tried to take his own life,' says Herr Waldmeier quietly, 'but the attempt failed.'

'The devil he has,' says the doctor.

'If only he had succeeded,' says Mr Rassam, 'it would have made everything so very much simpler.'

'Well he did not, Mr Rassam. He is still alive. He does not release you without conditions.'

'What does he want?' says Mr Rassam, looking over his shoulder in sudden alarm.

'He wants you to speak to the British commander on his behalf. He will not fight again. He wants peace. He believes that you can arrange that.'

'I am powerless.' Mr Rassam walks excitedly about the hut, lifting up his hands. He breaks off to say to his servant, 'No, no, pack the kitchen equipment first. I must do all this myself. I am utterly powerless,' he says again. 'Sir Robert Napier is in complete command. I can only receive orders from him. Now, what is it that the Emperor wants?'

'He does not know what they intend to do with him. They have promised him honourable treatment but he would not consider being held prisoner, for example, honourable. He wishes you to go to Sir Robert Napier with a gift and then return to him and tell him how the gift was received.'

'Return to this place?' says Mr Rassam with a harsh unhappy laugh. 'Then he is mad. We'll be damned lucky to get away in one piece. We're not out of this yet, you know.'

220

Herr Waldmeier says, 'He has saved your life in order that you may do this for him.'

'How is that?'

'When the people closest to him knew of the extent of the defeat, they wanted all the European prisoners massacred then and there for being the cause of all their misfortunes. They stood debating how to kill us. They would burn us, or mutilate us, or hang us all together on one tree, or cast us over the cliff onto the remains of those other wretches. Good God, I shook like a leaf. I felt each death enacted on me in turn and, just as they were at their most ferocious, he cut them short and said that we were all to be sent down to the British camp to ask for an honourable peace?'

'For peace? What does he mean by peace?'

'Well,' says Herr Waldmeier, and he continues to address himself to the doctor who has sat still and regards him attentively. 'I think his mind works in this way. He will die rather than face humiliation, but when he attempted death and the pistol failed he saw that as an act of Divine Intervention. God, he says, wishes me to live. And, to him, to live is to begin again. He is a man of infinite optimism. Now he says to himself, "The English have slighted me and ignored me but in the end I have managed to bring their army to my country to see me. Now that they have come, I will give them what they want and they will be my friends. With their superior weapons they will subdue the rebels and restore my country to me".'

Mr Rassam has turned fully around and now stands with his arms behind him gripping the edge of the table. He stares in astonishment at Herr Waldmeier and says in a high voice, 'He believes that?'

'I believe that is the way that he thinks at the moment.'

Mr Rassam stares for a moment longer at Herr Wald-

221

meier. Then he says, 'Ah well. Yes,' and comes towards him, holding out his hand and smiling. 'Waldmeier, I find the part you have played in all this entirely commendable and under the most trying circumstances. I shall take great pleasure in personally giving an account of all this to Sir Robert Napier and I am sure he will want to express his gratitude ...' Here his voice trails away in untold possibilities while Herr Waldmeier, who has now understood that he is being dismissed, rises to his feet and ducks his head and smiles too.

'One thing,' says Mr Rassam. 'Was any mention made of pack-mules? I shall need at least three, and the others one apiece, wouldn't you say, Blanc? I'd be most remarkably grateful, Waldmeier, if you could see to it. Miss Bell, you will want to make all manner of preparations. And Blanc, be a good chap and drop in on Cameron. There's no knowing how the shock of this may affect him. The strain has told on us all and we're not free of this damned place yet.'

'Then were we like unto they that dream'

At four o'clock we assembled at the upper gate of the fortress. Pack-mules and riding-mules had been provided and waited at the base of the steep path down to Islamagee. Mr Rassam, dressed in his blue political uniform, said his farewells to the governors of the fortress through Aito Samuel. The rest of us stood through these lengthy thanks and blessings: Mr Rosanthal and Mr Stern supporting the consul, Dr Blanc and Lieutenant Prideaux in their red military uniforms. Lieutenant Prideaux wore his monocle and swung a gold-topped cane.

'Do you think I will do?' he asked the doctor.

'Yes, yes. You are a splendid sight.'

'Oh, don't twit me, Blanc. You know it would never do to appear as if things had got one down in any way. My legs are so wretchedly thin that the trousers hang awkwardly but it will be dark when we get there. I dare say no one will notice. I say, I do wish he'd hurry up his salaams.'

'The waiting is intolerable now,' said the doctor. 'I wish to God we had all our goodbyes safely behind us.' For Herr Waldmeier had insisted that Mr Rassam see the Emperor one last time before he go.

The upper gate was opened. We climbed down to the lower gate and that, too, was opened. We mounted the mules and rode down Islamagee along the broad flat

223

road that led through the camp. The sun was in our faces, falling towards the mountains, drawing out their darker colours as it lost its brilliance. The great hum of the camp was subdued and at this hour, when fires are first lit, there seemed little life in it.

'It looks half deserted,' said the doctor.

Yet people called out blessings to us as we passed and more and more appeared from their huts and began silently to follow us, women with children and bundles, a few men, trotting to keep pace with the mules.

'What do you suppose they want?' Mr Rassam called back to the doctor. Then he spoke in Arabic to Aito Samuel, who in turn called out in Amharic to a woman with a little baby tied into her shamma, 'Why are you following us? What do you want?'

'I am going to look for my husband's body,' she said, instantly beginning to weep. 'Perhaps he is still alive. Perhaps I can recover him.'

'The vultures will have had him by now,' said Aito Samuel. Indeed we could see their heavy movements in the sky by the precipice where the prisoners had been thrown. They would be busy too over the battlefield where the dead were fresher. 'You lie. You are running away.'

'No, no,' she shouted at him, but she moved quickly back into the crowd where he could not see her.

Mr Rassam said anxiously to the doctor, 'They hope to get down off the mountain. I hope they will cause no trouble. Keep ahead of them if you can.' He squeezed the mule's flanks with his legs but it went at its own pace and the crowd continued to grow around us.

We had come now to the edge of the camp, where the road passes under the steep sides of Selassie. From below us on the mountainside rose the lowing of cattle and the particular clatter their long horns make against each other when they are herded close together. Passing a man on the track, Aito Samuel called out, 'Has Tewodros slept well?'

'Praise be to God, he wakes well,' and he turned and pointed along the road ahead of us where we knew the Emperor must be waiting.

'What is the sound of cows?' asked Aito Samuel.

'The Emperor has sent an Easter gift of peace to the English commander. Waldmeier has been sent ahead with them.'

'We shall catch up with him on the road,' said the doctor to me. 'We must be moving faster than he is.'

A few minutes later we came upon the Emperor sitting on a stone by the side of the road where we must pass close by him. Standing at a little distance behind him were a group of twenty musketeers and these, as we approached, ran down onto the road and formed a barrier across it.

'What now?' whispered the doctor under his breath, but it soon became apparent that the soldiers had orders to let the Europeans through. The people from the camp they shouted at and drove back with their muskets. We dismounted then, being near the Emperor's presence, and began to push our way forward as the crowd was pushed back.

It had been agreed that Mr Stern, the consul and Mr Rosanthal should pass the Emperor first, then the doctor, Lieutenant Prideaux and myself. Mr Rassam should remain until the last so that he might quickly intervene if the sight of those men whom Tewodros had hated should, at the last, enrage him again. Now, this order was confused by the press of people being driven back by the soldiers. Besides being on foot, now, and small of stature it was difficult for me to see who was ahead and who had fallen behind. I saw patches of the doctor's red uniform

225

before me. Then a soldier held his musket like a stick in both hands and forced me back with it.

I cried out to him, 'I am with the Europeans.'

'You are running away.'

I shouted, 'By the death of Tewodros I am with the Europeans. Do you not see that I have a mule? Would I have a mule if I were a camp woman?'

Then a hand caught my arm and I heard Aito Samuel's voice over my head, 'Let her pass. She is as she says. Do you not know me? Let her pass.'

It seemed to me to be a long time that he had kept me there. I thought: the others will be far ahead, and strained to hear the sound of the cattle and could not for all the shouting. Yet a moment later, with Aito Samuel still clutching my arm, we were at the front of the crowd and could see, only a little way ahead on the road, Mr Stern assisting the consul to mount his mule. Mr Rosanthal was mounted already and as Aito Samuel gestured urgently to them, they began to ride away towards the point where the road would take them out of sight.

Now Dr Blanc and Lieutenant Prideaux bowed before Tewodros and he inclined his head indifferently to them. Now, just ahead of me, Mr Rassam began to walk towards the Emperor and Aito Samuel, gripping my arm, whispered in my ear, 'Keep close to Aito Rassam. Try to pass them as they talk.'

But that was impossible for the Emperor had now come down onto the road extending his hands to Mr Rassam. At the same time he glanced up over his shoulder at the lowering sun and said abruptly without any greeting, 'Do you not think it is late for you to go this afternoon to your camp? Would you rather go at once, or spend the night with me? And in the morning I will send you straight to your people.'

226

There was a silence, until at last Mr Rassam answered in a voice unlike his own, 'Whatever plan would please Your Majesty would also be entirely pleasing to me.'

Tewodros looked at him sharply then. His face was very haggard and the shamma that covered his head was stained on one side with darkened blood from the wound he had inflicted upon himself in attempting to die. His voice was very sad, yet it was composed. 'Good,' he said to Mr Rassam. 'You had better go now.' Then he added quickly, 'But sit down now, only for a little while, and talk to me once more before you must go.' He signalled behind him and immediately a servant spread out a roll of carpet on the road and when Tewodros had settled himself upon it he motioned Mr Rassam to sit too.

The doctor and Lieutenant Prideaux waited uncertainly on their mules until Aito Samuel waved to them to go forward out of the Emperor's sight. He had taken the leading-rope of my mule now and dragging that and gripping my shoulder with his other hand, edged me closer and closer to the carpet where Tewodros now was saying, 'You know, Mr Rassam, that you and I have always been on good terms. God knows what is in your heart at this moment, but, so far as I am concerned, I have always had a sincere regard for you. It is true that I have ill-treated you, but what is past cannot be helped now. I can only say : God's will be done. But now it is necessary, Mr Rassam, that you befriend me and speak for me, as a friend, to your commander. Waldmeier, I have sent ahead with a letter and a gift of cows. This is the traditional gift for Easter. It signifies peace and I have given generously as befits a king. But your good word on my behalf is also needed, Mr Rassam. If you do not do this thing, I shall kill myself or become a monk.'

'Indeed, indeed, I shall do all that I can.'

The doctor and Lieutenant Prideaux had by this time ridden slowly out of sight. The light was perceptibly fainter and now the Emperor rose to his feet and said in the same sad and measured tone, 'Goodbye, my friend. It is getting late. Try to come and see me tomorrow if you can.'

Mr Rassam rose unsteadily to his feet and began to stammer out his thanks in a low indistinct voice. The Emperor caught hold of his hands and said again, 'Will you come tomorrow?'

'I will,' said Mr Rassam. Then he added, 'If I can, I will come.'

The Emperor said, 'Be quick it is getting late.' Tears were running down his cheeks, and he continued to keep Mr Rassam's hands held in his own until at last the thin brown fingers slipped away. He said again, 'You had better go,' and turned and hung his head as Mr Rassam began to walk towards his mule.

'Now,' whispered Aito Samuel in my ear. 'Now go past him.'

I was walking, running, weeping for what cause I did not know. I was lifted into the saddle and jolted, seeing nothing, down the track. Then, when the road had turned and it was no longer possible to see back, there were Mr Rassam and his party and the people from Gafat who had been waiting for us. I heard the doctor say, 'Here is Rosa,' and she was lifted into the saddle in front of me. Then I held her and wept onto her head, but she struggled to be free and jumped up and down to make the mule move on again.

I heard Frau Flad say, 'I received a most considerate message from Sir Robert Napier, asking if there were anything he might send us that would comfort us in our trials and I requested side-saddles for Mrs Rosanthal and myself,' and indeed now I looked and saw those two ladies were sitting sideways on their mules with their legs indivisible beneath their long skirts.

'Shall we go then?' said Mr Rassam and we began the long descent of the mountain. At that hour the light is sucked out of things. The distance shrinks and flattens. Sounds are very clear. We rode, without speaking, down Herr Waldmeier's road over the pitted dust and trampled dung left by the cows. At the steeper places we must dismount and follow the mules, which was hard on the men who had been chained so that they frequently stumbled, and panted in their throats like dogs, but when the road was less precipitous they rode again in silence with their faces lifted and without expression. So we rode for a long time.

It grew dark and the clanking and straining of the harness made a cold sound. We rode among the foothills and, coming to a rise, there suddenly was the British camp set out before us in a great square of white pointed tents all in rows of exact straightness, pricked out with camp fires.

Then everyone took heart and urged their mules forward. Mr Stern raised his voice in song: *When the Lord turned again the captivity of Zion then were we like unto they that dream. Then was our mouth filled with laughter and our tongue with singing.* When he was silent we heard above the sounds of the mules the murmur of that other camp and came shortly to an Indian soldier who stood across the road and shouted to us to halt and identify ourselves. This was answered in a small shaking voice, 'I am Hormuzd Rassam of Her Britannic Majesty's diplomatic mission to King Theodore of the Abyssinians. I wish to see Sir Robert Napier. These others are my party.'

The sentry stood back and let us pass and shouted over

our heads. We heard the shout repeated on and on. The hum of the camp intensified. The shouts grew distinct. Men came running, jumping up from their fires with cups and dishes in their hands and a young man, tall and thin as a stick, in bright clothing that clung tightly to him, came right up to us holding a lantern, staring, with food still moving in his cheek. Then he turned, running and shouting, 'Come quick, sir! I do believe it is the prisoners.'

Then all about us there was a great crowd, staring and shouting, with their caps snatched from their heads and waved wildly in the air. 'Hurrah, hurrah, hurrah!' they shouted continuously and now we rode through rows of such shouting faces, with men running behind us still cheering.

We were taken first to the tent of the British commander and there saw Herr Waldmeier, seated at a little table, translating the letter he had brought with him from the Emperor. When he had finished, he read it aloud in our presence to the leaders of the English soldiers: words that brought living into the tent that voice they had never heard, that seemed to come from a great distance off that darkened mountain.

In the name of the Father, of the Son, and of the Holy Ghost, One Lord: From the King of Kings, Theodorus. May it reach the beloved servant of the great Queen of England.

I am writing without being able to address you by name because our intercourse has arisen so unexpectedly. When I saw your manner of fighting and the discipline of your army and when my people failed to execute my orders then I was consumed with sorrow. Whilst the fire of jealousy burned within me, Satan came to me in the night and tempted me to kill myself with my own pistol. I cocked my pistol and putting it to my mouth, pulled the trigger.

230

Though I pulled and pulled. Yet it would not go off. But when my people rushed upon me and laid hold of the pistol it was discharged just as they had drawn it from my mouth. God having thus signified to me that I should not die but live, I have straightway sent to you Mr Rassam.

Today is Easter; be pleased to let me send a few cows to you.

You require from me all the Europeans, even to my best friend Waldmeier. Well, be it so. They shall go. But now that we are friends, you must not leave me without artisans, as I am a lover of the mechanical arts.

We heard too that the Emperor's peace gift of cows had not been accepted but remained picketed outside the camp while it was decided whether the water could be spared to keep them alive.

On Easter Sunday there were many services of thanksgiving and much praying for peace. On Easter Monday the British soldiers began to climb at dawn with their guns to Meqdela. From the camp they could be seen, marching in regular patterns of red, blue, and green up Herr Waldmeier's broad road. As they moved upwards a brown mass moved down the mountain on either side of them and it was clear that great numbers of his people were deserting the Emperor.

At three in the afternoon the firing commenced. We could see rockets rush burning through the air like stars of great power to burst within the fortress, throwing up dark specks of earth and stone among their brightness, but the sounds were confused and distorted by the echoing mountain.

At length the sounds and flashes came to an end, and some hours later the shout went through the camp,

231

'Tewodros is dead! The monster is dead!' accompanied by much cheering.

That evening Dr Blanc found his way to the tent in which I had been put with Rosa. He sat on Rosa's bed and took her on his knee and said, 'Waldmeier is well. I have not spoken with him, but I saw him this afternoon on Meqdela and he was unhurt.'

'On Meqdela?'

'Did you not know? He went as scout for the expedition, for he knows all the tracks up there – but no,' he said quickly, 'no one will have thought to tell you and he will have had no time, poor fellow, to visit you. Has he seen Rosa?'

'Not since we came. '

'Oh don't be downcast. It is always like this at these times: everyone preoccupied and bustling about. He will come when he can. He is to stay up there for a day or two, sorting out the booty and the Queens and so forth. You knew about the Emperor's death?'

'I heard them say that he was dead.'

'But not how? Well, he shot himself.'

'You are sure?' For it was far better that he should have had the choice in this.

'Oh, no doubt about it. That is why I went up there this afternoon. To make quite sure. He had put the pistol in his mouth again, but no Divine Intervention this time. It was all shot out. Powder burns. All quite as it should be. They say he rode out at the end with his spear and gave a challenge of single combat. But no one would have it, of course, and he was driven back into the fortress. He tried to drag the smaller guns in with him but there was no time. They defended the first gate but our lads got over the wall easily enough, and when he saw them he went inside the fortress and shot himself. Ras Ingada was dead

232

a little way from him. There weren't many others that had stayed. All dead, of course.'

'How did his face look?'

'It is strange that you ask that, Miss Louisa. We have watched his face so closely – have we not? – for every change of mood. It seemed to me that all his power lay there and, though he was so dead, I was still watching him, trying to read some mood that had gone. It was extraordinary to see his face and not to see it alter. He looked peaceful enough; he was smiling in a way. But empty, you know, quite gone. Rassam was most affected, after what he'd said about their both being judged. But still, there it is. They've made him a sort of grave up there.' He sighed and set Rosa down. 'I'll come again. This must be a strange place for you to find yourself in. Once they decide what to do with you, you will feel better, you know. Whatever the decision may be.'

But no decision is made concerning me, or if it has I have not been told of it. They have cleared Meqdela of every living soul. The entire camp has moved away on Herr Waldmeier's road carrying its possessions and the wounded men on litters. Now they camp on Dalanta, protected by the British from the rebels. From there, they must make their own way back along the long road to Begemeder and thence to their villages. They have journeyed past the British camp and I have heard them chant this song:

> *The king who ruled the land from end to end,*
> *Is made so wretched that he swallows metal balls.*
> *From the heart of Meqdela comes a lament*
> *For he is dead that had nothing in him of the woman.*
> *In the heart of Meqdela have you seen the lion die?*
> *Death were a dishonour at any hand but his.'*

233

I think that I should be with them yet I have continued to wait these few days with Rosa.

Now the British too are to leave this camp. They have made explosions in the gates and the walls of the fortress and the whole surface of Meqdela is covered in flame and smoke. They have exploded, too, the guns that Tewodros had collected and had cast for him at Gafat. But when they came to Sebastapol, although they put as large a charge as they dared into it, they were unable to destroy it and they have left it there on the empty mountain for they think it is unlikely now to do anyone any good or any harm.

And the tents are packed and we are waiting on our mules in readiness to go. A patient and sweating young officer is reading names from a list: *'Herr Flad, German. One wife, German. Two children. Three pack mules. Three servants.* All over here if you please.'

There is much waiting and great noise and confusion for in the days following the fall of Meqdela, the Flads and Herr Saalmuller and Monsieur Bourgaud have greatly increased the number of their possessions from the storehouses there, until they exceed anything they owned at the height of their prosperity at Gafat.

'Herr Moritz, Polish. One wife, Abyssinian. One child.' For Herr Moritz's wife has within the week given birth to a baby girl whom she has called Theodora and in consequence there are more mules and more servants to cause delay. There is also the continuing problem which is being debated now in whispers by the doctor and Lieutenant Prideaux as to whether Consul Cameron or Mr Rassam should head the procession of the former prisoners when we finally do move.

A bearded gentleman sits on a little stool and draws sketches of us as we wait, which he will send to an English

234

newspaper. Near him stands another European gentleman who glances down onto the sketch and then raises his head and stares at me, and, looking now at him, I see that he is Herr Waldmeier. A tall hat hides his bare head and his beard is neatly trimmed. The tight European clothes seem to have shrunk him for although they do nothing to cover his thinness they have taken away all suggestion of his strength. Rosa who sits restlessly in the saddle with me has not recognised him.

'Herr Waldmeier, Swiss. One child.' He raises his hand, calls out that he is present, and comes towards us for Rosa should be with him. But before he can speak to us another British officer comes up to him. 'Herr Waldmeier? Colonel Milward says you haven't had time yet to have a good look at the Schneider rifles – the breech-loader, you know, that did all the damage. If you'll come along now he'd like to put on a little demonstration for you, before you all move off.'

Herr Waldmeier lifts his tall hat and smiles politely. 'There has been some mistake I think. He must have meant some other person. I am a missionary and know nothing of guns.' And before the young man can protest he pushes past him.

'Miss Louisa Bell, English,' calls the officer and looks about him in confusion. I answer. He looks at me. He looks at his list. And I must answer a second time before he connects me with that name and shrugs and marks the paper.

'With whose party do you travel?' he asks, speaking very slow and clear and patient.

'She goes with me,' says Herr Waldmeier. And to me, with his hand on the mule's bridle, he repeats this in the other languages we speak.

Author's Note

Abyssinia is now called Ethiopia, and the events leading up to the march on Emperor Theodore in his mountain fortress of Magdala (Tewodros and Meqdela are approximations of the Amharic pronunciation) by the British forces under Sir Robert Napier, are a part of history. This book, however, does not set out to be an accurate historical account. The story is based throughout on incidents recorded in the various accounts written by the European prisoners after their release, but, in being made into a narrative, events have constantly been simplified, the action has been concentrated in as few places as possible, and the number of people involved greatly reduced.

Theodore himself was a most remarkable man. Many of the issues that would be necessary to create a full portrait of him have not been mentioned, and he is seen here only in his decline from a position won by his outstanding military talents and by personal qualities that inspired men to follow him. He greatly impressed everyone who ever met him. He had also, in earlier days, a reputation for mercy and moderation in dealing with his enemies. Wherever possible in this story he speaks in his own words, or, more accurately, contemporary accounts of his own words, for his conversation was recorded from memory after it took place and has often passed through two or more translations.

In simplifying the involved negotiations over the final release of the prisoners I have done less than justice to their courage, particularly Lieutenant Prideaux'. He readily agreed to return to Magdala after being given his own freedom, to urge Theodore to free the other Europeans.

Above all I have taken great liberties with the history of the Bell and Waldmeier families. John Bell is said to have had four children by an Abyssinian wife. There are various references to three of these children: Susan who married Theophilus Waldmeier two years before her father's death, Mary who married Carl Saalmuller, and a son, Aligas. The real Susan Waldmeier survived the cholera epidemic and after the Emperor's death went with her husband to a new mission station in the Lebanon.

The only reference I have found to a possible fourth child was the name *Louisa Bell* on the list of the released prisoners recorded by the Royal Geographical Society's observer, C. R. Markham. It is possible to surmise that, as she was unmarried, she was the youngest, and that as she was at Magdala she may have been living with the Waldmeiers at Gafat. In all probability she would have returned to her mother's family at Mount Guna after the destruction of Magdala, but there is no foundation that I know of for any of this. Louisa as she appears in this story is a fiction based on nothing more than a name.

It is possible now to travel by road to within a half a day's mule-ride of the summit of Magdala. Nothing remains there of Theodore's stronghold except the ruined walls destroyed in 1866. A rough grave piled with stones is said to be his. Across Islamagee it is just possible to see the wide track of the road built for his guns, and towards the farther end of that high plateau Sebastapol still lies where it was abandoned, cracked, corroded, forgotten, but in one piece. It has resisted more than one attempt to move it down from the mountain top.